THE RANKINS OF PRATT COUNTY

ROBERT L. BINGHAM

ISBN: 978-1-09833-843-5 (print)
ISBN: 978-1-09833-844-2 (eBook)

Cover painting: "Blue Ridge Mountains in Fall" by Julie Riffey

Robert L. Bingham, 7650 Brookview Lane
Indianapolis, IN 46250, E-mail: RLBing48@gmail.com

For Minnie with love and gratitude

PART I

1

FEBRUARY 5, 1982
LANCASTER, IL

———

THE escalating conflict between Russell Rankin and his mother's latest live-in boyfriend gnawed at Russell throughout the school day. Last night's argument with Dominic proved to be the most heated exchange to date. Dominic had made it clear that he was not open to compromise. As long as Dominic paid the rent, Russell was to do what he was told from a man that he had come to loathe.

To compound the situation, Dominic had boasted, in full presence of Russell's mother, Loretta, that he knew how to handle Russell, whatever that meant.

Dominic's taunting of Russell resumed as soon as the two made eye contact Friday morning. The previous night's unresolved issues had spilled over to the morning as Russell readied for school and ate breakfast. At one point, Dominic sneered in Russell's face and said, "Why don't you leave some frosted flakes for the rest of us? Ever think of that?" Russell left for school earlier than usual in order to avoid additional badgering.

The high school day dragged from the onset. Russell was relieved that no quizzes or tests were scheduled on this wintry Friday. He was desperate and felt helpless. He was certain that additional conflict was in store upon his return home later that day. This time, he feared that conflict might turn physical.

What further jumbled his thoughts and emotions was the recent stance taken by his mother. As Dominic stoked the discord, Loretta seemed powerless, even unwilling to intervene. She chose to retreat and withdraw even though her oldest child was at risk.

Russell didn't want to go home. No way did he want to spend additional time with Dominic. He needed to steer clear of him as much as possible. By design, Russell had stayed after school to complete his homework in the school library. But with homework completed, he ran out of reasons to avoid returning home.

When he stepped outside, he saw that three inches of additional snow had fallen since earlier in the day. He shivered from the cold. No gloves or boots in this chilly weather, just a hooded sweatshirt. Russell began the dreaded half-mile walk home.

In less than twenty minutes, Russell stomped off the caked snow from his wet Nikes in the depressing, tired foyer of the Albemarle Arms apartments. Russell had lost count. This was either the sixth or seventh apartment building he had lived in with his mother and younger sister Rachel since his parents divorced almost seven years ago.

These apartment buildings all seemed the same to him: four-story brown brick buildings that catered to low-income tenants. They were shabby and tired structures with worn stairs, flaking plaster, dim lighting, and a musty smell encouraged by poor maintenance. As a rule, apartments were small and sparsely furnished. Utilities were substandard and often inconsistent.

Russell reluctantly took the stairs to the fourth floor and quietly entered apartment 404. He was greeted by Rachel who shushed him to be quiet. She then tapped her head and pointed to Loretta's bedroom. Russell understood instantly that Loretta was suffering from a migraine.

After Russell removed his wet sweatshirt and shoes, Dominic appeared from the kitchen and gruffly instructed, "I want no shit from you. Understand? Your mother's got one of those bad headaches and she's out of her pain pills."

Russell nodded.

"Where the fuck have you been, anyway?"

"Doing homework in the school library."

"Yea, I'll bet. That's A good one."

Russell and Rachel understood the protocol. Light and noise were Loretta's principal enemies during her migraine episodes when she required complete bed rest, a darkened bedroom, and most of all, peace and quiet.

After checking on his mother, Russell retreated to the bedroom that he shared with Rachel. For the next half-hour, brother and sister whispered their conversation so as not to cause any disturbance. Much of their talk centered upon transportation should Loretta require a trip to the emergency room at Prairie State Medical Center.

It was 4:55 p.m., and Dominic was in the kitchen preparing a spaghetti dinner. Russell stood silently at the entryway that separated the living room from the kitchen as Dominic continued to cook.

Dominic was four years older than Loretta. This most recent boyfriend stood about five feet nine inches and was of medium stature. He was physically solid due to his interest in weightlifting. Not a devotee to hygiene, Dominic was often in need of a shower and shave. His thinning black hair was slicked with Vitalis. His breath stank of unfiltered cigarettes.

Russell knew little of his background save for the fact that Dominic was born and raised in Milwaukee.

In noticing Russell's presence, Dominic glared and barked, "Whata you lookin' at?"

"Nothin."

"You need to understand something real quick ... real quick, boy." Dominic reinforced his message by pointed wooden spoon. "As long as I'm payin' the fuckin' bills around this place, I'm due respect. I don't want to hear no more bullshit, that you don't have to listen and I'm not your real dad, either."

Hard as it was, Russell remained calm and diverted attention to Loretta. It was clear that Dominic was itching for conflict.

"When these migraines get really bad, she goes to the emergency room at Prairie State."

Continuing his sarcastic tone, Dominic bellowed, "Jesus fuckin' Christ, Russell, I think I can handle it if she needs to go to the emergency room. You just do as you're told. I do have a truck, you know." Again, motioning with the wooden spoon, he snapped, "Get your sister 'cause the spaghetti's ready."

The sharing of the meal at the small kitchen table was awkward and tense.

Conversation was infrequent. Silence dominated the group. At Dominic's direction, Rachel and Russell cleaned up afterward as Dominic tended to Loretta. Upon exiting the bedroom, Dominic said, "Your mother just threw up all over the bathroom. She didn't make it in time. Russell, clean it up. Bucket's in the kitchen closet."

Although disgusted by the duty, Russell complied as it gave him a chance to reconnect with his mother, who had collapsed in pain on the bed. After cleaning the bathroom, Russell relayed Loretta's request to be transported to Prairie State.

Upon hearing the news, Dominic flew into a rage.

"You just don't stop, do you? Who the fuck are you to tell me what to do? I'm a fuckin' grown man. Isn't that between your mother and me about Prairie State?

Emphasizing with his fingers, "What is fuckin' with you, anyway?"

Russell was torn. He longed to respond, but he also knew that a verbal battle with Dominic was the last thing that his mother needed as her pain was now excruciating. As if to referee, Loretta dragged herself from the bedroom to the living room. Out of fear and mounting worry, Rachel joined her mother's side.

Loretta pleaded, "Please, Dom, he didn't mean nothin' by it. Please. No fightin'… no more. I'm beggin' you. I can't take it, the yellin', the noise, my head's about to come off. Please, please, no more!"

Shaken by Loretta's directness, Dominic regained his composure, consoled Loretta, and escorted her back to the bedroom where she changed clothes. Russell and Rachel retreated to the privacy of their bedroom. In Russell's and Rachel's absence, Dominic phoned the Lancaster Police.

At 6:05 p.m., a knock on the door revealed that LPD officer Benjamin Skinner had been called to the apartment. Russell was sure that this had been Dominic's doing. He grew angry and confused when the officer told him that assistance had been requested on a domestic disturbance. *I've done nothing wrong* Russell thought, but as usual with Dominic, the situation had escalated and grown threatening.

Officer Skinner inquired, "So what's goin' on here? Oh, sorry about the wet boots and all."

Before Russell could respond, Dominic wrested control of the discussion.

His voice was aggressive and loud. "I'm tired of his mouth. I'm tired of his disrespectin' me all the time. I'm the one who pays the rent, not his mom. I'm the one that puts food on the table. And all I get is his smartass attitude. Money's missing from my wallet, too."

Russell erupted, responding directly to Dominic, "What? Money missing? What are you talkin' about?"

Russell turned to Officer Skinner. "It's not like that. I don't know what his problem is anyway. He's always on me, always tryin' to pick a fight."

Due to the commotion, Rachel appeared at her bedroom door. Wide-eyed, she gnawed at her fingernails as the disagreement between Dominic and Russell mounted.

Dominic moved closer to Officer Skinner. "See, see, see? That's what I'm talkin' about. He thinks he' so slick tryin' to blame me ... so typical, and if it weren't for me, his ass would be on out the street, his sister, too." Dominic screamed, "God damn it! I put up with his shit every day ... not any more. I want that little bastard out of here! Now!"

Neither Dominic nor Russell was backing down despite Officer Skinner's attempts to reason and deescalate. Officer Skinner resembled a boxing referee positioning himself between two combatants as he demanded that they keep their distance and lower their voices. As a safety precaution,

Officer Skinner instructed Dominic to stay in the kitchen while Russell occupied a seat on the living room sofa.

The verbal sparring continued with Dominic and Russell becoming more anchored to their positions. Dominic again requested that Russell be removed from the home, with Russell countering that he had done nothing wrong.

In exasperation, Officer Skinner cautioned, "That's enough. I said that's enough from both of you. For now, I want nothin' more from either one of you. I need to speak with Russell's mom about all of this to get her side of things."

Dominic interrupted, "She can't help with nothin," as he motioned to Loretta's bedroom. "She's in there with a migraine. I gotta get her to Prairie State for a shot. She'd agree with me anyway."

Russell bristled with rage to Dominic's claim. "That's a lie, that's nothin' but a fuckin' lie," as Officer Skinner blocked Russell's approach to Dominic.

Shocked, Rachel said in alarm, "Momma would never say that, never!"

Officer Skinner demanded that Dominic and Russell retake their seats as he continued his questioning.

"Son, do you have a place you could stay tonight, other family, a friend's house or somethin' until things simmer down?"

In a sad, yet respectful, voice, Russell answered, "No, sir."

Officer Skinner then suggested that it be best for Russell to spend a night or two at St. Olaf's youth shelter for a cooling-off period.

Russell grew more tense, even fearful at the suggestion since St. Olaf was viewed by some teens as a gateway to juvenile court. His feet nervously tapped the floor. His hands were clasped in a tight grip. His stomach turned on the lousy spaghetti dinner. Showing marked anguish, he said, "I don't get it. This is so unfair. Why do I have to go to St. Olaf's when I'm not the problem?"

Knowing that Russell's claim would get an instant reaction from Dominic, Officer Skinner motioned for Dominic to remain seated and quiet. His attention became focused on Russell.

"Son, right now, I'm concerned that this situation's just going to get worse. Both of you are really locked in. I don't want to see anyone getting hurt or arrested, and unless we do something now, right now, I think that's real likely to happen."

Officer Skinner continued. "Son, St. Olaf's would only be temporary over the weekend. They have counselors there, good ones, that can help sort out everything. You'll be back here after a night or two. They're good people. We need to do something here for sure because if we don't, this situation's only gonna get worse."

Russell's anxiety increased. His whole body tightened and his face flushed.

"Now, I'm going to find this out anyway, but are either one of you active with the courts or the Department of Corrections?"

Dominic's head sank. He quietly answered, "Yea, I'm on probation." Russell sensed a minor victory.

"What was your charge?"

"Theft."

"Any history with DOC?"

"Nope."

"Russell, how about you?"

"No. I've never been in any trouble."

"No arrests?"

"None."

During the confrontation, Rachel had slipped unnoticed into her mother's bedroom. Breaking the tension, she opened the bedroom door to escort her unsteady mother from the bedroom. Loretta Rankin pleaded, "Dominic, we gotta go. I can't take it anymore. We gotta go now!"

As if to be helpful, Rachel said, "She just threw up again all over the bed." Weary, teary-eyed Loretta turned to her son uttering words that shook Russell to his core. "Go to St. Olaf's, Russell. It's only for a night or two. It's not like anyone's gonna forget about you. Dominic, we gotta go."

This is when Russell ran. This is when Officer Skinner fell, breaking his elbow. Russell knew then and there that Dominic had scored the perfect ambush.

2

FEBRUARY 5–6, 1982

———

RUSSELL had panicked, pure and simple. Dominic's accusations toward him were outrageous enough; however, the prospect of staying at St. Olaf's tipped the scale, proving overwhelming. Upon running from the scene, Russell recognized that he had made a bad decision, a faulty choice that played perfectly into Dominic's hands.

On today's walk home from school, Russell had considered Litchfield Gardens as a temporary overnight place to stay should relations with Dominic continue to worsen. When he had lived there previous to Albemarle Arms, he remembered that the latch to the basement's storage locker never fully locked.

This was his hope this February evening as he ran the one-mile route of snowy alleys and icy streets to reach his former apartment building. During the run, he cursed that he had failed to grab hat and gloves as he raced out of his apartment. His weathered brown corduroy jacket was too small, plus the front zipper was broken. He was poorly prepared for northern Illinois streets in early February.

Fortunately in reaching the building's main entrance, Russell intercepted an elderly man entering the building so he followed the man's lead to gain entry.

Russell took worn tiled steps to the basement, and to his good fortune, the storage locker door latch remained unlocked. After a quick inspection, he found a folded lounge chair that would serve as his cot for the night.

An undistinguished lounge area was located in the basement, and to Russell's surprise, it contained a dusty and dated black and white RCA console television set that actually worked. The set provided needed entertainment for the rest of the evening.

On one occasion, a building resident questioned, "Can I help you, son?" Russell responded convincingly, "No thanks, just waitin' on my mom."

Somewhat to his surprise, Russell slept well that Friday evening. He awoke covered in sweat, with his blond hair matted to his forehead. His Chicago Bears T-shirt clung to his body.

Despite the cold, wintry temperature outside, Russell nearly roasted that Friday evening. The storage locker was adjacent to the building's furnace, which caused the basement to be extremely warm, if not hot. Fortunately, his coat and worn Nikes had completely dried during the night.

In need of a bathroom, Russell rose, quickly dressed, and returned the lounge chair to its original location. He then left the building and proceeded to the twenty-four-hour Rainbow Laundromat across the street where he used the unlocked bathroom.

The plan for Saturday morning was to return to the Old Market section of Lancaster to work some hours at the Stavros Brothers' Family Restaurant, a popular eatery located on the edge of downtown Lancaster. Through his mother, Russell knew the Stavros family who managed the business, a fixture in Lancaster's small, rejuvenated Old Market commercial district.

No questions would be asked; Russell would bus tables and wash dishes during the Saturday morning breakfast rush in order to earn a meal and some pocket money. The plan also kept Russell indoors, another plus considering the weather.

The walk to Stavros Brothers' was less than a mile, but it involved snow-packed sidewalks and slick streets. Russell's route crossed over the icy, slow moving Kishcasaw River that divided Lancaster, north and south, the city that had been Russell's only home for over fifteen years.

As the skies lightened, Russell viewed the modest skyline of downtown Lancaster, population 120,000, and some of its major buildings and landmarks: the federal courthouse, The Lancaster Public Library, the county courthouse and justice complex, The Mueller pretzel factory, Grande's Opera House, the YMCA, and the restored Benzinger Theater.

One business had remained solvent and prosperous in Old Market over the years, the beloved Scandia Bakery, a Lancaster institution since 1922. Russell had the warmest recollections of this store. Overtaken by nostalgia, he paused as he looked in the large storefront window, observing not a single change within the spotless interior. Pies, cakes, cookies, doughnuts, strudels, and other pastries decorated the store's display window, tempting all passersby.

Loretta had brought Russell and Rachel here on occasion. She would purchase a thirty-five-cent bag of assorted day-old doughnuts, "remnants" as she called them that included multiple varieties. Russell could smell and taste those morsels now, and their memory conjured a bittersweet smile.

The rusted blue-and-white neon sign, which announced the restaurant's presence from its second-floor rooftop, was now in sight. Russell increased his pace to a slow jog. In less than three minutes, and upon entering the restaurant's side entrance, he received immediate instruction from the youngest Stavros brother, Nick, to strap on an apron and begin bussing tables.

"Russell! Am I glad to see you. I was hoping you'd show up. It's very, very busy this morning, and we can sure use you. Can you work through the lunch crowd too?' Nick asked.

"Sure," Russell said.

Nick was right. The restaurant was as busy as Russell had ever known for a Saturday morning. Upon filling his first cart with dishes, he entered the kitchen and was relieved to see his two favorite cooks, Otis and Sonny. Russell had known Otis Barnes since his mother had worked at Stavros' as a greeter and cashier. Like so many others, Otis was attracted to Loretta, and while the two had never been a couple, Otis had developed a fondness for Russell, that was ongoing.

"My main man, Russell," Otis boasted loudly. "Nick was hopin' you'd show up.

That 4-H crowd got us hoppin'."

"4-H?" Russell asked as he began loading the dishwasher.

"You know they got some big 4-H competition or show or somethin' goin' on at the Events Center. Got a lot of out-of-town folks joinin' us for breakfast this mornin'. That's why we be so busy."

Otis was a character, a burly, animated black man in his late forties. He sweated so profusely in the kitchen that he wore layers of paper towels on his forehead, held in place by a thick rubber band, to catch his perspiration. His white T-shirt hugged his thick torso from body sweat.

Otis handled his kitchen demands with ease. "Shit, if I can feed thousands of sailors on an aircraft carrier, I sure as hell can handle a family restaurant."

The other cook, Sonny Pham, had migrated to Lancaster with his wife and daughter via Seattle, after Saigon fell to the Communists in 1975.

In broken and unsteady English, Sonny acknowledged, "Good to see you, Russell. Sure need your help today. Here a bacon sandwich before you start work."

Russell worked hard that Saturday without a break, until 2:00 p.m. The arrangement, struck over a year ago year with Nick and his older brother, George, was for Russell to be paid in cash upon finishing his shift. Usually, Nick and George paid Russell from a roll of bills that they each carried in their trousers. Such was the case today.

Russell was actually relieved that he had thought little about his current dilemma during his shift. He and another boy, a new employee with whom he had never worked, bussed all the tables while another hire, Enrique, primarily operated the dishwasher and stacked dishes and silverware.

It was now 1:30 p.m. Nick motioned for Russell to take a break. Russell gathered a chicken potpie, a piece of Dutch apple pie, and a tall glass of milk. He ate his meal alone at a dinette table reserved in the kitchen for employees. Otis, who had recently finished his shift, soon joined him.

Not surprisingly, Otis inquired, "How's your momma? Haven't seen her since I don't know when. She seein' anyone regular right now?"

Based on Russell's dejected delay, Otis sensed he had raised a sensitive topic.

Russell reestablished eye contact with Otis. 'She's been seein' some guy since around Christmas. He moved in last month. He sells cars."

Otis had been sweet on Loretta since 1979 when they both worked at Stavros'. He had been attracted to her, as was the common reaction from most men. Loretta was pretty, seductively figured, personable, and flirtatious, adroitly straddling the fence between sexy and slutty.

On his second marriage and five kids, Otis often strayed, developing brief affairs outside his marriage. His second wife, Vivian, a heavy stay-at-home woman addicted to soap operas, tolerated Otis' wanderings as long as he remained financially attentive to her and the couple's three children.

"Could you tell your momma that Otis be asking for her?"

"Sure, I can tell her, but I don't think it will matter any 'cause of Dominic."

"They be serious?"

"Dominic pays the bills, Otis. I don't think she would want to do anything to piss him off, that's all."

"Russell, answer me straight. How you get along with this Dominic?"

Surprised by the boldness of Otis' question, Russell stared at the saltshaker that he cradled in his hands. "Not good, Otis, not good."

"I knew somethin' be eatin' you boy. Well, situations be changin' all the time. Just remind her that Otis think she be one fine lady."

Russell smiled warmly and nodded, "I'll do that, Otis." Otis left the table and gathered his coat and Chicago Bulls hat from a coat closet.

"My ride most likely be waitin' for me outside. You workin' tomorrow?"

"Maybe breakfast."

Otis exited through the restaurant's back door, then returned to the coat closet to retrieve a shiny blue Detroit Tigers jacket accented by orange and white ticking.

"Here. Take this. Some customer left it in a booth months ago. No one be comin' back for it. May be a little big, but based on that sad thing you be wearin' this mornin', you could use it." He tossed the oversized coat at Russell.

Otis gave him a wide smile that evolved into a gentle, reassuring chuckle.

Russell readily accepted the gift. "Thanks, Otis, thanks a lot."

Otis paused at the back door still smiling, pointing at Russell, "Be sure to remember me to your momma, now."

The clamor of the lunch trade had died down, and restaurant employees assumed a slower pace. Russell continued to sit alone at the dinette table. He returned to cradling the saltshaker in his hands as if it contained some magical answer to his problem. He knew, sooner or later, he'd have to return home and face any consequences developed by last night's incident. Shaking his head, he also felt sorry for his mother and hoped that her migraine had subsided. Minutes passed.

An unfamiliar voice questioned from behind, "Are you Russell Rankin?"

Russell turned to view two Lancaster uniformed police officers standing before him.

"Yes, sir. That's me."

"Is your date of birth August 8, 1966?"

"Yes, sir."

"Stand up, son. You have an outstanding delinquent warrant. We need to take you downtown."

In shock and disbelief, Russell asked, "A warrant for what?"

"Assault and battery on a police officer. Seems like you caused Officer Skinner to break his elbow."

* * *

Russell was officially admitted to the Lancaster County Juvenile Detention Center at 4:09 p.m. on February 6.

After a brief interview and a completion of a questionnaire, he was allowed to call home. The phone call went unanswered, a development that further discouraged him. Prior to taking a shower, Russell asked the middle-aged detention attendant, "Does Brad Terrell still work here?"

"Sure does … he's the deputy superintendent. How you know Mr. Terrell?"

Russell was relieved at the news. "He was my coach in youth football a few years ago. Is he workin' today?"

"No, he's off until Monday. Will he remember you when he checks the admissions list Monday morning?"

"Monday morning? I need to talk with him before Monday morning."

"Are you sure he's gonna remember you?"

"Yes, sir. He'll remember me."

"Well, son, I think you're just gonna have to wait. He's not going to be able to do nothin' for you anyway cause you'll be scheduled for court on Monday. He could be out of town anyway. He didn't work Thursday or Friday, and I'll bet that he's taken a long weekend visitin' family down in Mississippi."

Showing increased anxiety, Russell asked, "So what happens if I can't get a hold of my mom?

"Son, we're trying too. If we can't reach her by phone, either one of our staff or a Sheriff's deputy will visit your house later this evening to let her know of your whereabouts or leave a note."

Russell was assigned a single room located next to the detention center's control center on the boys' unit. The room included a steel-framed bed, a small desk, and chair all bolted to the tiled floor. The room had no window. A single ceiling light illuminated the room.

Russell's jacket, clothes, shoes, and $9 in cash were stashed in a padlocked security basket in the hall property closet. His detention uniform included a loose-fitting pullover khaki top and elastic-banded trousers. Footwear was now a pair of plastic slippers.

Russell's first exposure to the other residents took place at dinner. Russell sat at the end of the metal dining table as he ate a plate of roast turkey and mashed potatoes. He recognized one boy from his grade school days at Danforth Elementary.

After dinner and as fellow residents watched TV and played Ping-Pong in the activity room, Russell called home a second time, still no answer.

Room confinement was scheduled for 8:30 p.m. It could not come soon enough. Russell yearned for solitude to review what had happened since being taken into custody.

All that was familiar to him was collapsing around him. The more he thought and tried to analyze his plight, the more anxious and depressed he became.

Russell hoped that Brad Terrell would have needed answers for him Monday morning. He figured that tonight's attempt at sleep would be unproductive in his strange, new surroundings. He also knew Sunday would be a boring and lost day, but perhaps Loretta would visit him once she knew of his whereabouts. There was that one prospect to look forward to in the midst of Russell's uncertainty.

One issue lingered and haunted him above all others. Even though the question had a logical answer, Russell did not recognize it. In a monotonous manner, he questioned as to how the police knew of his presence at Stavros Brothers' Saturday afternoon.

He would learn that troubling connection early next week.

3

FEBRUARY 6, 1982

———

INGRID Bohars' ride to work was proving more challenging than anticipated. During the night, a mid-winter storm had smothered Lancaster with six-plus inches of fresh snow.

Much had changed for Ingrid during the past year: a promotion at work, a new car, living on her own in a new apartment, but most importantly, the traumatic ending of a two-year relationship with a Lancaster firefighter. At twenty-nine, willowy and attractive Ingrid Bohars was definitely on her own.

Despite a challenging fall and winter, her workplace of seven years had proven to be a welcome haven where she could shut out the pain and disappointment of a failed romance.

Between work and her final semester of evening graduate school, Ingrid had remained busy and focused to the extent that she gave herself little time to grieve. For now, work and grad school demanded her complete attention.

On her way to work, Ingrid encountered poorly plowed streets and a thin veil of ice under much of the snowy surface. She saw effects of two minor accidents, and traffic lights were out at a key intersection. The storm had been accompanied by strong winds, which would impact school bussing operations in the rural sections of the county.

17

After grabbing a large coffee and a Danish from a convenience store, she remembered that today marked the beginning of a new parking arrangement at work. Probation department employee parking had been moved from a convenient lot servicing the Courthouse and county justice complex to a not-so-convenient lot located two blocks south.

Ingrid parked and then sloshed her way to the probation office, joining office mate, Julie Van Allen, who was already engrossed in Intake Unit paperwork received over the weekend.

"Fun commute, huh?" Julie said.

"Don't get me started. Great job getting the plows out, highway department. Sidewalks weren't clear from Luther Street, plus the damn gate was stuck at the parking garage for ten minutes so a line of us just sat there until someone from courthouse maintenance showed up. Yea, wonderful way to start the workweek. And more snow on the way this afternoon. Yuck."

After ridding herself of her belongings in the cramped office, Ingrid disappeared for her start of the workday cigarette in the break room away from Julie and her tobacco allergy. When Ingrid returned, Julie said, "Brad's already been down to see you. Seems that he knows one of the kids admitted over the weekend. He wants you to call him first thing. Get ready because he's really worked up about this one."

"What's the kid's name?"

"Ah, a Russell Rankin." Julie handed Ingrid the police report and intake paperwork.

"Assault and battery on a police officer. Read the reports; it doesn't add up."

Deputy detention superintendent, Brad Terrell, entered the office. "Ingrid, we need to talk about this Rankin boy admitted Saturday morning. I know this boy from football. I coached him for two years. I know his mother and father too. He's a good kid, just in a shitty home situation."

"OK. Give me ten minutes, and I'll be up to see you. Julie's covering the other admissions so I have the time. Your office?"

"Let's do a visitation room, not as noisy, less interruptions."

"OK, sure thing. Ten Minutes."

During the interim, Ingrid reread the police report in detail and checked whether Russell had any previous contacts with law enforcement ... this was his first offense. She also reviewed child welfare records. During a span of seven years, Russell's family had been referred three times to the Illinois Department of Children and Family Services. These referrals were all rated "unfounded."

After being buzzed in by security to the building's detention wing, Ingrid walked to the visitation room where she met Brad Terrell. Terrell had worked his way up the ladder from detention officer to Juvenile Detention's assistant superintendent during a nine-year career. He was approachable, respected, well-liked, and especially adept in working with wayward teenagers and their families. In his spare time, he was passionate about coaching youth football and baseball.

When not used for its designed purpose, Visitation Room #1 was often the site for conferences between detained youth and their probation officers, detention staff, attorneys, and law enforcement. The windowless room was long and rectangular, furnished with four small, round tables and plastic chairs.

At the far end of the room stood three, coin-operated vending machines, which staff and visitors frequented. Baskets of toys and books were available to entertain smaller children who might accompany a parent during a visit. Assorted motivational posters decorated the walls as well as artwork created by the center's residents.

"So, Brad, tell me what you know?"

"You remember Jerry Tompkins from LPD, right.?"

"Sure."

"Well, Jerry and I coached Russell in youth football for two years back in '79 and '80. He's a good kid, just stuck with two loser parents." Shaking his head in disgust, Brad continued, "I was shocked to see him on the admits list this morning, really shocked. Parents had already divorced when I coached

Russell, but there was still a lot of friction between them, especially over child support, Loretta's lifestyle, lack of supervision at home."

"Whoa, whoa, whoa. Loretta's *lifestyle*? What's that mean?"

"Loretta has a reputation of going man to man. Russell can give you a better feel for what's happenin' now, but I doubt it's any different than when Jerry and I were coaching him. Shit, she was even on my tail at one point. I talked with Russell this morning, and it seems like the same old pattern of one boyfriend after the other, no money, his mom's inability to hold a job, and poor supervision at home. And then there's the drinking and drugs."

Ingrid checked her intake paperwork. "What do you know about the father, a Peter Rankin?"

"I got this from Russell. He's in rehab right now at Holcomb Valley. His main problem from what I can tell is alcohol, but he's held onto his post office job over the years so he must have somethin' goin' for him. I wouldn't rule out a minor arrest record … just a hunch"

"Mother have any arrests?"

"I don't know. I didn't check."

Ingrid inspected the police report again. "This all started as a domestic call with the live-in boyfriend, a Dominic DiNardo, arguing with Russell. Things just got worse when police arrived. Says here that Russell ran when the LPD officer suggested that he go to St. Olaf's. The charges must apply to the officer being injured and breaking his elbow. He had to have surgery."

Brad sighed in recognition of the need for surgery and countered, "Yea, I know. Russell said he didn't hit anyone. He was emphatic about that. He just brushed by the officer as he ran from the apartment. Shit, the surgery changes everything. Damn it, Ingrid," In exasperation, Brad slammed the table with his hand. "I know this boy. He's a good kid, Ingrid, just a shitty home life, that's all."

Ingrid grew more concerned for the boy. She had worked with Brad Terrell her entire seven years with Probation. She valued his analysis, which was always level and on target.

Brad continued, "To help out at home, the kid's worked part-time since the fifth grade, bussing tables and washing dishes. He gets paid with a meal and some cash under the table."

Brad referenced that these earnings served as emergency funds for Russell's mother on occasion, but Russell used them at times to buy clothes or shoes for his sister and himself at the Salvation Army and a Presbyterian thrift shop. "Hard to believe that through all of the turmoil at home, Russell's remained a very good student who's proud of his grades and attendance."

The detention hearing was already scheduled for 1:30 p.m., so Ingrid had the entire morning, barring any emergencies, to devote to the Russell's case in preparation for the afternoon hearing. The meeting now shifted to Russell's input.

Brad escorted Russell into the room. Ingrid was struck by Russell's size. At fifteen and a half years of age, he was a lanky six feet one or two inches.

"Russell, this is Ms. Bohars from Probation. She's goin' to talk to you about your detention hearing. She knows her stuff. She's good. She'll do her best to answer your questions and tell you what's next." Brad then left the room after a warm nod and pat on the shoulder to Russell.

Ingrid shook Russell's hand, which was her custom. "Good morning, Russell. Nice to meet you, but I know you'd prefer meeting elsewhere." He responded with a soft shake and weak smile.

"You go by Russell, is that right? Not Russ or Rusty?"

"Russell."

"Russell it is."

Once they were seated, Ingrid proceeded in general terms to explain the purpose of the meeting. During her years of working probation, she had developed a skill set, which quickly cut through the common issues and typical facades displayed by arrested juveniles. Her initial impressions were usually accurate; her graduate course work in counseling had helped sharpen her interview and diagnostic skills.

Alert and tense, Russell sat with his hands folded on the table. He was attentive and respectful, and unlike most other detained youth, he maintained eye contact in Ingrid's presence.

"Russell, you've been charged with aggravated assault and battery of a police officer."

Russell interrupted, "It wasn't like that. It really wasn't. You need to know what really happened."

"Hold on, Russell, hold on. I've already spoken with Mr. Terrell, and I know you have strong feelings about the charges, and we'll get to that. We really will. But for now, you need to understand the process and what happens next."

Ingrid leaned forward in her seat. "Russell, I need you to listen right now, focus, and really listen. I know you're upset, I do. But, I need your help. I am responsible for writing a report to the court about your arrest and status here in detention. This report includes a recommendation from me about your remaining in detention or going back home, to emergency foster care, or some other place. Understand?"

"Yes, ma'am." Russell remained alert yet anxious.

"Again, we'll get to the charges, I promise. Trust me. We want to hear what you have to say."

Russell nodded his assurance to listen and follow Ingrid's lead.

"There's really two parts to the detention hearing. One is called probable cause."

"Hold on, hold on. Why do we need a hearing?" Russell was already pleading his case. "Why can't I just go home?" Why do I need a hearing at all? I keep telling people that I didn't do anything."

"That's a fair question. Russell. I'll do my best to explain. You were held Saturday afternoon because of what is called an automatic hold. The juvenile court in Lancaster County has a policy where youth arrested on certain charges are held automatically in detention when police bring them to intake. These are most always serious charges like aggravated battery, armed robbery, burglary, and so on. But the court has also ordered that a juvenile is to be held in detention if the arresting police officer is physically injured to any degree during the police contact. That's why you were held."

Showing ongoing frustration, Russell shifted his gaze from Ingrid to his folded, restless hands. "So, I can't get out of here without a hearing, right?"

"That's right."

"So that hearing will be sometime today?"

"Correct. Your hearing is scheduled before Judge Brandt at one-thirty today.

The first part of the detention hearing deals with probable cause. That means it has to be established in court with known facts that a delinquent act has been committed."

"What's that called again?"

"You mean probable cause?"

"Yea, that's it."

Russell hesitated, attempting to allow Ingrid's explanation to sink in. His hands had become sweaty during the initial minutes of the interview, and out of embarrassment, he shifted them to rest on his thighs under the table.

"But there wasn't any crime. I didn't hit anyone. I keep tryin' to tell everybody that." Russell's feet tapped nervously on the floor.

Leaning forward again with unwavering eye contact, Ingrid explained, "OK, Russell, this is where you and I have something in common. Neither one of us is a lawyer. Sure, I work with lawyers every day, but I'm not an attorney. And as a probation officer, I am not allowed to provide legal advice. I don't have their training or knowledge. That's why you will have a public defender assigned to you. He will be representing you in court this afternoon. He'll meet with you sometime today before your hearing. I'll talk with him as well before we go to court.

"This is what we do know. Police were called to your apartment because of a domestic disturbance last Friday night. Upon investigating the situation, it was the judgment of the police officer for you to go to St. Olaf's for a night or two to allow things to calm down. You didn't want to go. For whatever reason, you ran, and in the process to stop you, the police officer fell and broke his elbow."

Ingrid continued. "Maybe you didn't mean to harm the officer, and my guess is that you didn't, but the end result was a police officer was injured to the point where surgery was needed to fix his elbow. If you had done what the officer requested, you wouldn't be here as best as I can tell. Then you and I wouldn't be having this conversation. I know, believe me, this news is not what you wanted to hear, but I owe it to you to be upfront about where this is all going."

Russell continued paying strict attention to Ingrid's explanation.

"So, if this possible"

"Probable cause," Ingrid said.

"Yea, if this probable cause is, what'd you call it?"

"Found, established."

"OK, then what?"

"The detention hearing then shifts to a phase called urgent and immediate necessity."

"What's that all mean?"

Russell stiffened his body. Small beads of sweat were now evident on his forehead.

"In simple terms, it means you will stay in detention if the judge believes you are a danger to the community or yourself, or you are unlikely to appear for the next scheduled court hearing."

Pausing, Russell considered his next question. "OK. I still don't see where this involves me."

Recognizing Russell's inability to grasp his situation, Ingrid said in sterner tone, "Russell, I need to be as clear as possible with you because you are not recognizing the seriousness of what happened Friday night. A Lancaster police officer was injured on the job due to your actions. He's undergone emergency surgery already, and he will not be able to return to full duty for several months. The State's Attorney will likely view you as a risk to community safety because of Officer Skinner's injury."

"Well, why can't I go home? This was all an accident. I didn't mean to hurt anyone. Just put me on probation or home detention or somethin' like that."

Ingrid changed course. "There are other options. Maybe right now, going home may not be the best plan considering all that's happened. If you have any ideas about where you could stay for a few days, I need to know them now. This would be temporary until things at home can be worked out. We need to come up with a plan that both your lawyer and probation can back you on. Do you have other family in town or Lancaster County?"

"No, ma'am."

"OK. Well, that doesn't help. Anyone else you might be able to stay with that the court could consider? Maybe a family friend or neighbor?"

Russell shook his head. "Nope."

Ingrid paused briefly. "You need to be prepared that the State's Attorney is sure to recommend that you remain in detention. That's just how the system works."

Saddened by the news, Russell dropped his head and stared at the floor's worn gray carpeting.

Brad Terrell appeared at the door and interrupted, "Ms. Bohars, Russell's mom is on the phone."

"OK, thanks, Mr. Terrell. Transfer the call to my office if you would, please, and I'll take it there. Russell, I'll see you later this morning or early afternoon after I speak with your mom. Mr. Terrell, can I see you for a second outside? Russell you wait here."

In a private space down the hallway, Ingrid whispered to Brad, "This kid's screwed. You know what the State's going to recommend. This is slam-dunk, Brad. We both know it. The problem is that Judge Brandt's subbing for Judge Shields this afternoon. You know what that means; he won't consider any alternatives."

A few minutes later, Ingrid was in her office, speaking on the phone with thirty-eight-year-old Loretta Rankin. After learning of Russell's current circumstances, Ms. Rankin agreed to attend the 1:30 p.m. detention hearing. She appeared tentative about Russell's return home.

Ingrid ended the call and took a short smoke break. After placing a brief phone call from her office, she returned to detention to continue her discussion with Russell. She found Russell and Brad Terrell in deep conversation in the visitation room.

"Ms. Bohars, Russell asked me to stay and sit in for your meeting. That OK with you?"

"That's fine as long as you have the time."

"I've got the time."

"Russell, I promised you time to explain what happened in your apartment last Friday night. All we have right now is a police report. Now is your chance to tell us what happened in your own words. So, what exactly did happen?"

"Dominic was all over me since I'd gotten home from school. He's always on my case, but this time he kept bringing up respect, that I didn't respect him like I should."

"Dominic is your mother's boyfriend?"

"Yes, ma'am."

"So, what was your response?"

"I tried keepin' quiet. I didn't want to do anything to piss him off."

"How'd that go over?"

Russell dropped his head to avoid eye contact and took a lengthy pause before answering, "Not good. That's when he really started yellin'."

"And?"

"I thought he was actually going to fight me, but then he backed down and just called the police behind my back. He also accused me of takin' money from his wallet?"

"Any truth to that?"

Russell shook his head in disgust and said, "No way. That's the first time he ever accused me of stealin' from him. I want nothin' from him, nothin' at all."

"Where was your mother in all of this? What was she doing?"

"She was in bed cause of her migraine"

After a short pause, Russell remained subdued but volunteered, "You gotta understand somethin'. My mother hasn't worked since before Christmas. Dominic's her meal ticket. He pays the rent and the bills. My mother has no money."

Brad sighed and shook his head.

Ingrid continued, "Was your sister there?"

"Oh, sure. She was there, too, hidin' in the bedroom, but she's never the problem. Plus, Rachel is scared of Dominic. She would never challenge him, never."

"OK, but tell me now about what happened when Officer Skinner arrived."

Brad hunched forward from his chair in anticipation of important details to come. Ingrid remained attentive as well.

Russell contemplated his response over several seconds. "It got worse. Dominic kept sayin' that I had to leave and get out, that he wanted me out, right away."

"Russell, where was your mother during all of this?"

"She stayed in the bedroom."

"Did Officer Skinner ask your mom what she thought was best?"

"Yeah, as she was gettin' ready to leave for the Prairie State, she said I should go to St. Olaf's. She just shook her head and said she couldn't take the yellin' and fightin' anymore."

"So, you decided to run when it looked like you'd be going to St. Olaf's? Is that right?"

"Yeah, but I didn't hit him, I swear. I brushed by him and that's when I heard him fall 'cause he must have slipped on the floor from the snow. I heard him scream when I ran to the door."

Russell's eyes begged for understanding. "I never meant to hurt anyone, honest."

After Ingrid summarized Russell's interpretation of the incident, she went on to explain that the usual juvenile court judge, Judge Shields, was at state training and that the hearing would be conducted by newly appointed associate judge, Judge Calvin Brandt.

"Russell, a public defender, either a Mr. Franz or a Mr. Holland, will be your attorney and will represent you during the detention hearing."

"So what's going to happen? Am I getting out of here or not?"

"Russell, I'm not the judge. One of the first things you learn as a probation officer is not to make predictions or any promises. Probation doesn't make the call here; that's the judge's job. I need to speak with your public defender about a release plan for you should the court consider letting you out later today. There's a possibility that you might not be going home right away. Temporary foster care may be an option recommended to the judge, until your home situation can be ironed out."

"Foster care?"

"Again, this would be temporary until we get you back home. The probation department has emergency foster care homes that could be used, but the court has to approve. Your mom will have an important say here too. In light of the conflict between you and Dominic, where is she going to stand with all of this?"

Russell bowed and shook his head. "I don't know. I really don't anymore."

"And just to be clear, Russell, we can't consider your dad as a possibility because of him being at Holcomb Valley."

* * *

The detention hearing lasted all of fourteen minutes. Judge Calvin Brandt found both probable cause and urgent and immediate necessity for Russell's continued detention. Despite this arrest being Russell's first, the court rejected a foster care recommendation out of concern for community safety.

Russell did not take the news well. At his own choosing and with detention staff support, he remained isolated in his single room until Tuesday morning, passing on dinner and scheduled evening recreation.

4

FEBRUARY 8, 1982

JUDGE Brandt's decision came as no shock to anyone in the courtroom except Russell. Ms. Bohars and Deputy Terrell knew it was coming. The assistant public defender, Jack Franz, knew it was coming, as did the bailiff and the court clerk. Russell had naively thought his unique circumstances would produce a different outcome.

Russell's extended stay in Juvenile Detention was directly tied to the absence of Judge Carol Shields. She was the first and only female on the county's bench of fifteen judges and had served for three years.

The appointment of Judge Shields was deliberate to replace seventy-year-old Judge Johnson M. Hilliard who had served twenty-two years as the county's sole juvenile court judge.

Judge Shields, at age forty, brought twelve years of legal experience to the bench as an assistant prosecutor and public defender. She was no stranger to juvenile court either. After she passed the Illinois bar exam in 1970, she began her legal career as an assistant public defender assigned to the Lancaster County Juvenile Court.

In many respects, Judge Shields was the refreshing and needed successor to Judge Hilliard who had grown irascible during his final years on the bench. He had also abdicated much of his supervisory responsibility of the juvenile probation department as he neared retirement, allowing the twenty-person office to languish in accountability and professionalism.

Ms. Bohars and Deputy Terrell knew Russell would have received a different response from Judge Shields had she presided at his detention hearing. In all likelihood, temporary foster care would have been Judge Shields' order, allowing Russell and his mother some time to regroup and resolve differences at home.

Judge Shields was not a proponent of juvenile detention because she recognized the harm that could be caused by secure confinement and removal from family. In most instances, she favored use of less restrictive, less costly options.

Regardless of the circumstances and personalities influencing Russell's arrest and detainment, he was the one who had lost his freedom. Russell reluctantly entered a world he had intentionally chosen to avoid during his adolescence.

He had experienced firsthand the devastating effects of alcohol and drugs on his parents. He had known nothing but family discord and uncertainty. Life became even more unpredictable for Russell and his sister when his parents divorced. When it was finalized, eleven-year-old age Russell had foolishly thought life at home might stabilize since at least the violent arguments between his parents, which occasionally turned physical, would cease.

But Loretta Rankin was overwhelmed as a single parent, unable to financially or emotionally care for her two children. Peter Rankin's inconsistent compliance with court-ordered child support payments worsened as he further withdrew from his ex-wife and children.

Food became scarce. Meals were inadequate. Housing was always temporary and substandard, with abrupt relocations the rule. Clothing was secondhand. Medical and dental care was unavailable except for dire emergencies.

Loretta chose the only vocation she knew, working in restaurants as a hostess, waitress, or cashier. She routinely established a pattern of unreliable attendance and spotty work performance that shortcut any steady pattern of employment. It was through Loretta's employment that Russell started "unofficially" working restaurants as a relief busboy and dishwasher when times were especially rough.

Not your typical teenager, Russell was mindful of his whereabouts, his circumstances, and his associates at all times. His primary goal had been to avoid all forms of delinquent behavior, including associating with youth who were prone to challenge authority and test societal limits. Above anything, he had wished to avoid conflict with police and the Lancaster County Juvenile Court.

Even as a young teenager, Russell had yearned for a better life, a stable life with purpose. That goal was now in serious jeopardy.

5

FEB 12:

Coach Brad said that I should keep a journal. He thought it would help me get some of the anger out. Maybe it will help. This is my first try. I owe him a lot. He always repeats, *Take it, day by day—one day at a time.* I know what he's saying. He checks in with me every day that he's on duty. He says he has to be careful so it doesn't look like I'm his favorite. School is easy. My teacher is Mrs. Blasingame. She told me today that she doesn't get many students like me who are not behind in school. She asked me if I would help her as a student teacher because so many kids are behind and need help. I said yes, but I can only help her after I get my own work done. I go to court on February 22, ten days from now. Ten days is like forever. There's a chance I can go home then, but Miss Bohars said not to get my hopes up. Miss Bohars is really nice. She has a very hard job, but she takes time to see me when she can even though she has a lot to do. I made Honors Room today. That's because I have no write-ups or demerits since I was admitted and also because I am doing so good in school. Now, I get a single room unless the center gets filled up.

I know two kids here. One kid—Ellis Gravely was in my third-grade class at Register Bluff with Mrs. Gray. He and I figured it out yesterday in the day room as we were playing ping-pong. He's here for burglary. The other kid I know from middle school. His last name is Bonner. I remember him from school being a bully, a real trouble-maker, always getting suspended.

33

They called him "T-Bone" back then. All he talks about is gangbanging and messing with anyone who gets in the way. He's called me out twice already. I just ignore him. All he can mean to me is trouble. Momma is supposed to visit tomorrow.

FEB 13:

Momma visited me this afternoon with a bunch of quarters. We hit those vending machines hard. It was real nice because she got here when all other visitors had left. We had the visiting room all to ourselves. I can tell that things aren't right. Momma is very quiet. She seems nervous and unhappy. She doesn't look at me direct much, but when she does, her eyes are sad and empty. She looks tired. She cries a lot, too, saying that she blames herself for me being locked up. She tells me over and over about how sorry she is that she wants to make things right with me. She says Rachel cries every night with me being gone. Momma looks at the clock a lot. I worry about her and what's happening with Dominic. You would think that I would feel better with Momma visiting but I don't. I just wish I could walk out the door with her and go back home but when she leaves I feel even worse. When I feel like this I just go to my room and hit my bunk. And I start the whole stupid movie all over again.

I also told her that I figured that Dominic was the one who tracked me down at Stavros Brothers'. She didn't know what to say. She looks lost and lonely.

FEB 15:

Detention filled up a lot over the weekend. We cannot watch news on TV so we don't know what happened, but a couple kids overheard staff talking about a 7-11 store shooting where three juveniles were arrested. Staff here is real nervous so it must be serious. So these three kids were admitted Sunday morning. I haven't gotten a good look at them, but I don't think I know any of them. Their supposed to be from the "R.V.G" or

Reservoir Gang from the north side. They are crazy loud and just want to cause trouble.

Miss Bohars and my public defender Mr. Holland stopped by after school. I have one week to go until my trial. I'm halfway there—halfway home.

FEB 16:

I couldn't concentrate very well in school today. Mrs. Blasingame knew it right away. I couldn't focus on any work. I kept going back to that Friday night and the fight with Dominic. That's all I could think about. When school was over, I went to my room instead of going to gym for rec. That's one of the good things about being in Honor's Room. I can stay in my room during rec or free time. I need to write today. I can never accept why I'm here. It is so unfair, so fucking unfair. I never meant to hurt that officer—NEVER! And I did not hit that officer. Yea, we bumped into each other, but I didn't push him or fight back. I don't care what anyone says. My whole time here is unnecessary. They can't say it, but I know Coach Brad and Miss Bohars and Mrs. Blasingame and others know it too. But no one says anything or does anything to stop it. Then, why am I fucking here? Fuck this Goddamn place—fuck it! I can be angry with police and the judge, but Dominic made that phone call. It all started with him. Momma could have stopped it, or at least tried, but she just sat there and sobbed about her migraine. Momma just sat there like she was paralised or something. I shouldn't have run then. Maybe I should have gone to St. Olaf's but I didn't do anything wrong. This is why Momma doesn't like visiting, why she isn't herself, why she doesn't look me in the eye, why she's always looking at the clock because she could have stopped it all, but didn't. So who am I angry with? Answer: Dominic, Momma, the police, detention, the states attorney – try the whole fucking city. But especially Dominic—that son of a bitch!

FEB 17:

Momma was late for visiting. Weekday visiting runs from 3:30 to 5:00 p.m. She got here at 4:30, plus she brought only $1.00 worth of quarters. Not a good visit.

Something is happening. I know that but I can't figure it out.

The three kids brought in over the weekend were all detained on Monday and they are causing a lot of trouble, threatening people, talking about jumping staff, breaking out, and talk of are you in or out. Momma told me that the 20 year old girl clerk who was shot is in intensive care at Prairie State.

FEB 19:

The three kids charged with the 7-11 store shooting were moved from here this afternoon to some special juvenile section at the jail because the 20 year old girl died last night. It all happened real quickly with a lot of police deputies moving them. Staff say that all three are being charged with murder in adult court. Coach Brad and other detention staff seem relieved that they are gone. I'm glad they're gone too.

FEB 20:

Momma visited for a full hour this afternoon. She looked better and not as tired. She said the D and L cafeteria had called and wanted her to work some hours as a hostess. She had worked a total of twenty hours the last three days. Momma looked happy and was more herself. She had talked with Miss Bohars who seemed to think that there was a chance that I could be released back home on Monday.

FEB 22:

Miss Bohars and Brad met with me for an hour after today's hearing. They knew how upset I was. Who wouldn't be? Momma has always been full of surprises, but if she had said "yes," I'd be back home today. But from out of nowhere she says that she is no longer sure she can handle me at home! I can't believe it. This is Dominic doing the fucking talking. Where the fuck did this come from? I hate that mother fucker!!!

Now, I have to wait another fucking week to find out whether I'm ever getting out of this shithole or not!!! No more fucking writing ... no more!!! What good does it do anyway?

FEB 23:

Miss Bohars came to see me late this afternoon to tell me that Momma, Dominic, and Rachel had moved out of the apartment. I could tell that she was worried about how I would handle the news. She also learned that they were late with the rent. They must have left last night. I can't believe any of this. I can't believe any of this shit. It just gets worse and worse. The last thing I need is more fucking surprises. She asked me if I had any idea where they were going. I said I thought they might be going to Chicago to visit Momma's family. I gave her my grandmother's name and the name of the street in Chicago where she lives. I can't believe I remembered it. Miss Bohars has always been real nice and straight with me, but, I could tell, she was real upset by all of this. She couldn't hide it. She left detention to make some phone calls from her office and then said that she would see me before she went home.

FEB 24:

I was right about Chicago. Miss Bohars found out that Dominic and Momma dropped Rachel off with Grandma Packer for the day. They said they were getting married and would it be OK for Rachel to stay there while they got married. They said they would return to pick Rachel up the next day. Miss Bohars stayed late to help talk with me about all of this. She understands how angry and confused I am about this. She's a really good listener who just lets me talk. She said she could read the disappointment on my face. I shouldn't have cried but I did. I didn't care who saw it. Miss Bohars left for a minute and came back with a box of Kleenex. She just sat there real quiet while I cried. I'm pretty certain this hurt will never go away. I can't see it ever going away. I wonder how I'm going to handle all of this now and later on. The shit just keeps piling on. I'll never understand how I deserved any of this. I'm tired of being confused. I'm tired of being shit on. I'm tired of people with no answers. I'm tired of being let down. What about ME? WHAT ABOUT ME!!! Who's really looking after ME? Who's in my fucking corner? Who? NO ONE!!!

FEB 25:

I decided to stop writing journal notes earlier this week because of Momma disappearing. I didn't see where writing any more would do any good. Sometimes writing stuff down just makes me feel worse. I'm giving up on journal writing. But today I finally got some good news, I think. Miss Bohars helped me come up with a place to live. I talked with my grandmother in North Carolina on the phone. It looks like she may be willing to take me in for some time until everything here settles down. I don't remember her much 'cause I only visited down there twice. She seems like a real kind lady, and if she is OK with, I'll make it work. It will be a big change.

I've never lived anywhere but Lancaster but it may be for only a few weeks or maybe until school is out. Still no word from Momma—big surprise. The hardest part of this is her just taking off without Rachel and me knowing what's next. This is all Dominic's doing.

FEB 26:

A lot happened this morning. It's good news for a change. I spoke with my grandmother again on the phone, and she's willing to take me in. She and my Aunt Helen are driving up from North Carolina this weekend so they can be at the court hearing on Monday. Coach Brad and Miss Bohars seem good about how Judge Shields is going to handle it all. Mr. Holland also stopped by to tell me that he is OK with the plan for me to stay in North Carolina to live with my grandmother. He also said the states atorney is OK with the plan too.

I think this will be my last journal note.

6

LANCASTER COUNTY JUVENILE COURT

200 North Plymouth Street Lancaster, Illinois

The Honorable Carol W. Shields

State's Attorney: Joyce Ryan-Duckett

Defense Attorney: Timothy Holland

SOCIAL HISTORY

In the matter of: Russell Owen Rankin (J# 11816), alleged to be a delinquent child.

JUVENILE INFORMATION

Legal Name: Russell Owen Rankin

Alias(es): N/A

Address: 1840 North St. Ives Street, Apt. 404
Lancaster, IL

Home Phone: 1-916-623-2754 (disconnected)

Personal:

Age: 15.8

DOB: 8-8-66

Birthplace: Lancaster, IL

Race: White

Sex: Male

SS# xxx-xx-xxxx

Height 6 '2"

Weight: 155

Hair: Blond

Eyes: Hazel

Parents: Peter W. Rankin (Father)

Loretta Packer Rankin (Mother)

Sibling: Rachel Lynn Rankln, DOB: 8-19-69

INSTANT OFFENSE

Probable Cause:

"On 2-5-82 at 1805, LPD Officer Benjamin Skinner, Badge #330, responded to a complaint of juvenile beyond parental control at 1840 South St. Ives Street, Apt. 404, Lancaster, IL. Prior to the officer's arriving at the apartment door, shouts were heard coming from the apartment's interior.

Upon entering the apartment, an argument was underway between juvenile, Russell Rankin, W/M, DOB: 8-8-66, and Dominic DiNardo, W/M, DOB: 12-20-39, the boyfriend of Russell Rankin's mother, Loretta Rankin, who was also present.

Several minutes were spent listening to the accusations between Mr. DiNardo and the juvenile. Mr. DiNardo stated that he deserved respect since he was paying the apartment's rent. The juvenile claimed that he did not have to listen to him since DiNardo was not his real father.

The threats and accusations became so heated that it was clear that a time-out was required for all parties to calm down.

When a suggestion was made for the minor to spend a night or two at St. Olaf's, the minor refused to leave since he stated he was not the problem. As Officer Skinner approached the minor to escort him to his patrol car, the minor bolted past the officer, causing Officer Skinner to slip on the wet floor, falling backward injuring his arm as he hit the floor. The minor then grabbed his coat and ran from the apartment.

Backup was called, but the juvenile was not apprehended. Due to the severity of the injury, Officer Skinner was transported to St. Benedict's Hospital Emergency Room for medical treatment that resulted in surgery for a broken elbow.

Minor is charged with aggravated assault and battery of a police officer.

Juvenile's version:

The minor willingly admits to fleeing his apartment on 2-5-82 to avoid removal by police to St. Olaf's Shelter, however, he denies any intentional battery of Officer Skinner.

HISTORY OF DELINQUENCY

Save for the instant offense, no formal history of delinquency exists.

FAMILY INFORMATION

The biological father is Peter W. Rankin, W/M, DOB: 10-2-42, born in Colby, NC, to Lester and Esther Rankin. He is a 1960 graduate of Pratt County High School in Colby, NC. Mr. Rankin is an honorably discharged U.S. Navy veteran having served from 1960-1963 with the final two years of that service deployed to South Vietnam.

Mr. Rankin is currently on medical leave from the U.S. Post Office in Lancaster for which he has been employed as a letter carrier since 1964. Presently, Mr. Rankin is being treated for alcoholism at the Holcomb Valley Hope Center, a 4-6 month residential treatment facility for alcohol and drug abusers. Upon discharge, from treatment, Mr. Rankin is scheduled to return to his full-time position with the Lancaster Post Office. Presently, Mr. Rankin does not have a permanent residence to which to return upon discharge from Holcomb Valley.

Loretta Packer Rankin, W/F, was born in Chicago, IL, on 12-12-43. She is a 1961 graduate of Archer Technical High School in Chicago. She was last employed this winter as a hostess/cashier at the Birchwood Family Restaurant in Lancaster. Ms. Rankin's whereabouts are currently unknown. The last contact between Mrs. Rankin and Juvenile Probation took place on 2-22-82.

Peter Rankin and Loretta Parker met in Chicago upon Mr. Rankin's discharge from the U.S. Navy in 1963. They married on 2-20-64, in Chicago. Two children were born of this union, Russell Owen Rankin and Rachel Lynn Rankin, DOB: 8-19-69. The minor's sister has no recorded history of delinquency and is currently in the temporary care of maternal relatives in Chicago.

Both parents have recorded minor criminal histories with the Lancaster County Courts. On 1-7-75, 3-28-76, and 4-2-80, Peter Rankin was arrested and charged with public intoxication. Loretta Rankin was arrested on 10-24-76 and charged with drunk and disorderly. These arrests all resulted in fines, stayed jail commitments, and court-ordered educational programming.

A check with the Illinois Department of Children and Family Services indicates three referrals from1975-1980 with these referrals all concluded as "unfounded."

As reported by both parents and the minor, the Rankin marriage was unstable and chaotic during the minor's early school years. The couple divorced in April 1977, with Loretta Rankin assuming custody of the minor and his sister. According to parents, verbal confrontations, physical violence, excessive drinking, accusations of infidelity, and poor money management were common elements during the eleven-year marriage.

Since the divorce in 1975, Loretta Rankin has relocated with the minor and the minor's sister on "six to eight" occasions, claiming that inconsistent child support payments from Mr. Rankin forced the moves.

NOTE: Mr. Rankin is presently $1,875 in arrears on child support payments.

Mrs. Rankin last lived with her two children and live-in boyfriend, Dominic DiNardo, at 1840 South St. Ives Street, Apt. 404, Lancaster, IL. Prior to entering substance abuse treatment, Mr. Rankin resided in the Meridian Island Trailer Court in Aubrey, IL.

Interviews suggest that the relationship between the minor and the mother's current live-in boyfriend, Dominic DiNardo, is extremely strained. This conflict was the cause of police being summoned on the evening of 2-5-82 when the instant offense occurred.

NOTE: Mr. DiNardo, W/M, DOB: 12-20-39, is employed as a used-car salesman at Sam Dunkle Ford in Lancaster. He is currently serving a two-year period of probation for theft and receiving stolen property (gambling equipment). His criminal history includes six adult arrests dating back to 1959. He has served no commitments to the Illinois Department of Corrections.

JUVENILE INFORMATION

SCHOOL

The minor attended two elementary schools in Lancaster and Lucille Mott Middle School. Currently, the minor is a 10th grade student at Simon Brewster High School. The minor has a positive school history from kindergarten to his current grade.

Attendance has always been good. No disciplinary infractions are on record. Grades are consistently honor roll level. The minor is involved in interscholastic football and baseball.

EMPLOYMENT

The minor has worked as a bus boy and dishwasher on an "as needed basis" on weekends and holidays at the Stavros Brothers' Family

Restaurant in Lancaster for the past three years. He averages less than eight hours a week and is paid minimum scale in cash.

MEDICAL/DENTAL

The minor received a physical exam from Phyllis Collins, RN, on 2-9-82 (report attached). The minor is a healthy 15.8 years old adolescent who stands 6'2" and weighs 155 pounds. All vital markers were normal on the date of exam. Blood and urine samples were unremarkable. No allergies were reported. The minor takes no daily medications. The minor did undergo an emergency appendectomy at age twelve at Prairie State Medical Center in Lancaster.

Dental cleaning/examination was completed by dental hygienist Judy Peterson and senior year dental student Dennis Grant (report attached). Minor admitted not seeing a dentist since age 7-8. Examination indicated six cavities including a cracked tooth, which requires immediate attention. Recommendation was made for all wisdom teeth to be extracted prior to the minor's 18th birthday.

PSYCHOLOGICAL/PSYCHIATRIC

No indications of psychological/psychiatric disturbance were noted in school records, detention report, or subsequent interviews with minor and parents. A psychological screening was not ordered at time of detention authorization.

DRUGS/ALCOHOL

The minor admitted limited alcohol and marijuana use since age twelve. This statement was not corroborated by either parent. The minor does not use tobacco in any form.

HOBBIES/INTERESTS

The minor enjoys playing football and baseball at Simon Brewster High School where he co-captained the 1981 junior varsity football team. He enjoys music and reading history and science fiction. The minor also occasionally attends school-related functions such as athletic events, dances, etc.

EVALUATION

The instant offense is the minor's only recorded delinquency. The minor's family history has been disruptive with biological parents divorcing in 1977 when the minor was eleven years old. Home life for the minor and his younger sister has been chaotic due to alcohol abuse of both parents and the frequent relocations caused by parental inability to meet monthly rent. Both biological parents have minor criminal histories, and their personal relationship remains volatile.

The minor regrets the physical harm caused to Officer Skinner, and from all accounts, the resulting injury was unintentional. On his own, the minor wrote a formal apology letter to the arresting officer.

Since the minor's arrest and adjudication, the minor's mother has disappeared and vacated her apartment on North St. Ives Street in Lancaster. Currently, Loretta Rankin's whereabouts are unknown. However, it is speculated that she may have left town during the week of February 22nd with her current live-in boyfriend, Dominic DiNardo, after relocating the minor's younger sister, Rachel, to maternal relatives in Chicago. Due to the biological mother's abrupt disappearance and Peter Rankin's ongoing residential treatment for alcoholism, no viable caretaking option was immediately available for the minor.

Through the efforts of the Juvenile Probation Department, the minor's paternal grandmother, Esther Rankin, was contacted in Colby, NC, and she has agreed to assume temporary custody of the minor until a long-term residence can be established.

Esther Rankin's background is stable and positive. She is a sixty-year-old widow who has worked as office manager/bookkeeper for almost twenty years at Hamilton Brothers Hardware and Lumber located in Colby, NC. Mrs. Rankin is also very active with the Colby Methodist Church, serving as church's musical director for fourteen years. She has agreed to travel to Illinois to attend the 3-1-82 dispositional hearing.

RECOMMENDATIONS

Upon adjudication of delinquency on 2-22-82, the following recommendations are submitted in the interest of Russell Owen Rankin, DOB: 8-8-66:

1) A one-year period of probation be ordered with courtesy supervision transferred to and provided by the North Carolina Division of Juvenile Services;

2) Temporary guardianship be awarded to James T. Drury, Chief Juvenile Probation Officer, Lancaster County Probation Department;

3) Temporary custody be awarded to paternal grandmother, Esther Rankin, of Colby, NC;

4) Minor to regularly attend Pratt County High School in Colby, NC;

5) 20 hours of public service work be completed at the direction of the North Carolina Division of Juvenile Services;

6) Minor to abstain from the use of alcohol and all illegal drugs;

7) Medical and dental expenses be assumed by the Lancaster County Probation Department;

8) 60-day progress reports be submitted by the North Carolina Division of Youth Services to the Lancaster County Probation Department via Interstate Compact.

I, Ingrid A. Bohars, of the Lancaster County Probation Department, affirm under the penalties for perjury, that the above and foregoing representations are true.

RECOMMENDED AND APPROVED BY:

Ingrid A. Bohars   Lori M. Seymour
Juvenile Probation Officer II   Juvenile Probation Supervisor

7

MARCH 1, 1982

————

THE courtroom is small and rectangular with recently installed beige carpet with brown flecks. The smell of carpet glue hovers in the air. The courtroom's walls are covered in dark-brown wood paneling. The judge's bench is moderately raised, with a brown and gold seal of the Illinois courts mounted front and center of the bench. A simple black-and-white placard mounted above the court seal identifies the presiding judicial officer as The Honorable Carol W. Shields. A standing Illinois flag and a U.S. flag flank the judge's entry door immediately behind the bench.

The furniture is a handsome mix of dark brown tables and wheeled chairs cushioned in black, shiny fabric. Lighting is subdued, but brighter over the bench and the well of the courtroom. Permanent reserved stations for the clerk and court reporter are attached in front and below the judge's bench. A witness stand is attached to the right of the bench.

A rolling podium is centered before the bench with defendant's table and prosecutor's table slightly behind to the left and right. Thin, flexible, silver microphones are mounted on the bench, witness stand, podium, and counsel tables. There is no jury box.

The only wall mountings are a large framed photograph of Juvenile Court Judge, The Honorable Johnson M. Hilliard, and a large paper calendar hanging on a nearby wall to one side of the bench, which the judge and clerk consult for scheduling purposes.

Public access to the courtroom is through two wooden doors that lead to a narrow walkway that divides two rows of gallery seating reserved for visitors. A round black-and-white clock hangs over the entry doors. A low wooden railing and swinging door separate the gallery from the well of the courtroom.

(The clock reads 1:34 p.m. The date is March 1, 1982.)

BAILIFF

Good afternoon. The Lancaster County Juvenile Court is now in session, the Honorable Carol W. Shields, presiding. All rise.

(The judge enters through her chamber door.)

JUDGE CAROL W. SHIELDS

Good afternoon, everyone. Please be seated.

(There is a thirty-second pause as the judge takes her seat and briefly examines documents before her.)

Ms. Ryan-Duckett, please identify the cause presently before the Court.

JOYCE RYAN-DUCKETT (ASSISTANT STATE'S ATTORNEY)

Your Honor, we are present today in the interest of Russell Owen Rankin, white male, DOB: 8-8-66, Juvenile #11816.

On 2-22-82, a plea agreement was accepted by the Court wherein the juvenile was adjudicated a delinquent minor on the charge of battery. Today, this cause is scheduled for disposition.

JUDGE SHIELDS

Thank you. Before we proceed any further, would the parties present in the gallery please stand and identify themselves by name and interest in this case?

(Ms. Ryan-Duckett motions to the visitors to stand.)

ESTHER RANKIN

Your Honor, my name's Esther Rankin, Russell's grandmother, from Colby, North Carolina.

JUDGE SHIELDS

Thank you, Mrs. Rankin, very much for your presence here today.

HELEN WHITLOCK

Your Honor, I'm Helen Whitlock, I'm Russell's aunt, also from North Carolina.

JUDGE SHIELDS

Ms. Whitlock, I'm assuming that you traveled to Lancaster with your mother for today's hearing?"

HELEN WHITLOCK

That's correct, Your Honor.

JUDGE SHIELDS

Thanks very much for doing that. You ladies may be seated.

OFFICER BENJAMIN SKINNER

Officer Benjamin Skinner, Lancaster Police Department, Badge #330.

JUDGE SHIELDS

Officer Skinner, you were the injured officer in this case, were you not?

OFFICER BENJAMIN SKINNER

I was, Your Honor.

JUDGE SHIELDS

How is your recovery coming along?

OFFICER BENJAMIN SKINNER

Really good, Your Honor. Thanks for asking. HR says I can return to desk duty later this month.

JUDGE SHIELDS

Wonderful. That is excellent news for sure. Thank you, Officer Skinner, for your appearance here today. Please be seated.

Mrs. Rankin, Ms. Whitlock ... by the way, I forgot to ask. How far a drive is it from your home to Lancaster?

HELEN WHITLOCK

(Helen Whitlock stands after consulting with her mother.) Seven hundred and forty-five miles one-way, Your Honor.

JUDGE SHIELDS

Oh, my. That really is a drive, isn't it? Did you folks drive through or stop for the night?

HELEN WHITLOCK

We got as far as Bloomington yesterday. We drove the remaining distance earlier today so that we could meet with Russell and Ms. Bohars before today's hearing.

JUDGE SHIELDS

Well, thank you again for the time, effort, and expense in travelling here to Lancaster. You may be seated. All right, Ms. Ryan-Duckett, please proceed.

JOYCE RYAN-DUCKETT

As stated previously, Your Honor, a plea agreement was reached and accepted by the Court on 2-22-82, at which time a social history report was ordered. That report was completed by Ingrid Bohars of the Lancaster County Probation Department and is included in the court file.

Mr. Holland and I have conferred, and the State is in agreement with Probation's recommendations contained in the social history. At this time, I wish to call Ms. Bohars to the stand to present and support Probation's recommendations.

JUDGE SHIELDS

Very good. Ms. Bohars, please take the stand and be sworn in.

BAILIFF

Raises your right hand and identify yourself for the court record.

INGRID BOHARS

Ingrid A. Bohars.

BAILIFF

Do you solemnly swear to tell the whole truth and nothing but the truth in this case so help you God?

INGRID BOHARS

I do.

BAILIFF

Please take the stand.

JOYCE RYAN-DUCKETT

Please state your name, start date with Lancaster County Probation, and your currently assigned duties.

INGRID BOHARS

Ingrid A. Bohars. My start date with Juvenile Probation is 8-20-77. At present, I am the Juvenile Division's senior social history writer.

JOYCE RYAN-DUCKETT

Ms. Bohars, would you please summarize the key issues in this case and the Probation Department's recommendations?

INGRID BOHARS

Your Honor, may I consult my notes, please?

JUDGE SHIELDS

Certainly.

INGRID BOHARS

Thank you, Your Honor. The cause before the Court is the minor's only police contact. The minor has no prior arrests. Russell was born in Lancaster on 8-8-66 and has lived here his entire life.

Russell's parents married in 1964 and divorced in 1975. Loretta Rankin, the minor's mother currently has custody. Relations between father and mother are very strained. Peter Rankin, the minor's father, is in arrears for child support payments, and he only sees Russell and sister, Rachel, on holidays and special occasions.

Peter Rankin is presently a patient at Holcomb Valley and not scheduled to be released until summer.

The family has lived in several Lancaster locations in recent years.

Russell has always maintained excellent grades and attendance within Lancaster Public Schools. Right now, Russell is a sophomore at Simon Brewster High School.

Normally, the probation department would be recommending a return home, but events over the past week have forced a new plan. Since the February 22nd hearing, the minor's mother, Loretta Rankin, and live-in boyfriend, Dominic DiNardo, have moved out of the Albemarle Arms apartments without any notice or forwarding address. Russell's mother, Loretta Rankin, left Russell's younger sister, Rachel, temporarily with maternal relatives in Chicago. Supposedly, the couple planned to wed later that day in Chicago to be followed by a brief honeymoon to Wisconsin.

My last contact with Loretta Rankin was during a February 24th phone call. Her current whereabouts and Mr. DiNardo's are unknown.

JUDGE SHIELDS

Ms. Bohars, when you last spoke with the minor's mother, was there any indication that she was unwilling to have Russell return home?

INGRID BOHARS

She appeared torn about the minor returning home.

JUDGE SHIELDS

And what do you believe was the source of her indecision?

INGRID BOHARS

I believe the conflict between her boyfriend and Russell.

JUDGE SHIELDS

I see. Do you recall who called whom?

INGRID BOHARS

I believe she called me, Your Honor.

JUDGE SHIELDS

Please continue.

INGRID BOHARS

Thank you, Your Honor.

Considering the minor's limited juvenile record, Probation began to investigate residential options with relatives. Russell's maternal grandmother, Vivian Packer, rejected Russell joining his sister with relatives in Chicago due to lack of space caused by a recent house fire. Also, Mrs. Packer feels betrayed by her daughter for her leaving her granddaughter with her. She rejected any plan to care for Russell.

Russell, himself, suggested his paternal grandmother in North Carolina as an option. After some consideration, Mrs. Rankin was open to Russell temporarily staying with her under the circumstances. Again, Russell's living with his father, Peter Rankin, is not a workable option due to Mr. Rankin's ongoing residential treatment for alcoholism.

Oh, Your Honor, I need to add that through a contact this morning with the clerk's office in Cook County, a check was run on Dominic DiNardo and Loretta Russell, with no marriage application for the couple being on file with that department. Also, there is no record of any civil marriage ceremony occurring on that date in Cook County.

JUDGE SHIELDS

Thank you for all due diligence on this case. I understand that this matter has been eventful and time-consuming.

Ms. Ryan-Duckett, anything you wish to add prior to Ms. Bohars providing Probation's recommendations?

JOYCE RYAN-DUCKETT

Judge, no, nothing at all.

JUDGE SHIELDS

Mr. Holland, anything you wish to add as defense counsel?

TIMOTHY HOLLAND, ASSISTANT PUBLIC DEFENDER

Nothing to add, Your Honor, at this time. Ms. Bohars testimony coupled with the social history well present events.

JUDGE SHIELDS

All right. Ms. Bohars, please proceed with your recommendations.

INGRID BOHARS

Thank you, Your Honor. The Probation Department recommends a one-year period of probation to be provided as courtesy supervision by the North Carolina Division of Youth Services; Temporary guardianship to be assumed by the Lancaster County Probation Department, James T. Drury, Chief Juvenile Probation Officer; Temporary custody to be awarded to the minor's grandmother, Esther Rankin of Colby, NC; Minor is to cooperate with all directions and instructions of his grandmother; Minor is to regularly attend Pratt County High School in Colby, NC; Twenty hours of community service work is recommended to be completed at the direction of the North Carolina Division of Juvenile Services; Minor is to abstain from the use of alcohol and any illegal drugs;

60-day progress reports are to be submitted by the North Carolina Division of Juvenile Services via Interstate Compact.

These are Probation's recommendations.

JUDGE SHIELDS

Very good, Ms. Bohars. One question, however. You mention the Division of Youth Services in North Carolina being the agency to supervise the minor's probation.

INGRID BOHARS

That's correct. In North Carolina, a state agency supervises juvenile probationers, not the county.

Your Honor, I apologize that the background report on Mrs. Rankin is not nearly as complete as is expected by the Court.

JUDGE SHIELDS

The court understands the unusual circumstances at play here. Ms. Bohars, you may take your seat. Mr. Holland, as Russell's counsel, what are your thoughts and recommendations in this matter?

TIMOTHY HOLLAND

Thank you, Your Honor. I've interviewed the minor on three occasions in Juvenile Detention and received frequent updates from Ms. Bohars as to developments.

Events are most unusual. The suggested plan that has been developed by Ms. Bohars seems workable. My client would prefer to remain in Lancaster but is willing to give the temporary stay in North Carolina a chance. My office is accepting of the recommendations as contained within the social history.

Your Honor, I wish to bring to the Court's attention that Ms. Bohars and I visited Peter Rankin, Russell's father, last week at Holcomb Valley, and the court file now includes his notarized letter stating his agreement with the proposed temporary custody and housing arrangement for Russell in North Carolina.

JUDGE SHIELDS

Thank you, Mr. Holland, for that update. Mrs. Rankin, the plan that has been recommended to the court by the Probation Department revolves so much around you that I am compelled to ask you some questions.

ESTHER RANKIN

(Esther Rankin stands) Your Honor, I don't mind.

JUDGE SHIELDS

Thank you. Counsel, are you accepting of Mrs. Rankin testifying from her seat as opposed to the witness stand?

JOYCE RYAN-DUCKETT

No objection, Your Honor.

TIMOTHY HOLLAND

No objection from my office.

JUDGE SHIELDS

Thank you, Counsel. Mr. Jackson, please swear in the witness.

BAILIFF

Ma'am, please raise your right hand. Do you solemnly swear to tell the whole truth and nothing but the truth in this case so help you God?

ESTHER RANKIN

I do.

BAILIFF

Please state your name and home address for the Court.

ESTHER RANKIN

Esther Owens Rankin. 415 Grouse Hollow Road in Colby, NC.

JUDGE SHIELDS

Mrs. Rankin, I have a few questions that shouldn't take too long. What is usual practice here is for the receiving state's probation department to complete what we call a home study. A probation officer from the receiving state makes a visit to inspect the house as to its size and suitability. The probation officer also asks a series of questions primarily about finances. The court needs reassurance that the home is big enough for the child and that the receiving family is able to absorb expenses such as food, clothing, school supplies, etc.

Because of time constraints, the home study could not be completed in time for today's hearing.

Probation has completed a criminal records check, and you have no criminal record of any kind, correct?

ESTHER RANKIN

(Esther Rankin smiles.) That's correct, Ma'am.

JUDGE SHIELDS

And your employment is full-time with Hamilton Brothers Hardware and Lumber in Colby?

ESTHER RANKIN

Yes, ma'am.

JUDGE SHIELDS

What are your current work hours, if I might ask?

ESTHER RANKIN

I generally work 7:30 a.m. to 4:00 p.m., Monday through Friday."

JUDGE SHIELDS

I see. And how long have you worked at Hamilton Brothers?

ESTHER RANKIN

Since 1963, Your Honor.

JUDGE SHIELDS

And what are your specific duties there?

ESTHER RANKIN

I manage the office, handle the books, accounts receivable, do purchasing, do payroll.

JUDGE SHIELDS

Sounds like you're a busy lady.

ESTHER RANKIN

Yes, ma'am.

JUDGE SHIELDS

Mrs. Rankin, do you believe that Russell's living with you would cause you any excessive financial burden, any undue hardship?

ESTHER RANKIN

(Esther Rankin smiles)

Well, I do believe I'll have to make more runs to the market with Russell in the house. But, no. My house and car are both paid for. I don't believe in credit cards. I pay everything in cash or by check. I have no significant debt of any kind. I have adequate savings as well.

JUDGE SHIELDS

Very commendable, Mrs. Rankin, on your part. Will Russell have his own bedroom?"

ESTHER RANKIN

Yes, ma'am. Russell will have his pick of three bedrooms.

JUDGE SHIELDS

The court recognizes that this is an unexpected responsibility that you are assuming. What are your thoughts about taking this on?

ESTHER RANKIN

Your Honor, I was certainly surprised last week when I got the call from Miss Bohars. My oldest son and I are not close, at his choosing, and I hadn't seen Russell in close to five years till this morning. I told Miss Bohars when she first suggested the idea for Russell to move in that I needed to sleep on it and pray on it. I did just that.

I also had a long talk about Russell moving in with my sister who lives near Charlotte. My sister, Libbie, is a surgical nurse down there, and I've always trusted her opinion, her understanding of things and such.

Miss Bohars was kind enough to arrange some phone calls between Russell and me that were helpful in understanding all that has happened. Helen and I had a good talk with Russell this morning, close to an hour's worth, and I feel even better about him coming to stay with me for as long as needed.

I think the plan will be good for both Russell and me. I'm all for it as is my daughter here, who lives just a few miles down the road. My other two children, Daniel and Andrew, are on board too. They live nearby as well. I plan to keep the boy busy. My son, Daniel, manages a local market, and he hires teenagers as part-time help all the time. Russell will also go to church with me every Sunday at Colby Methodist.

JUDGE SHIELDS

Thank you, Mrs. Rankin. One point struck me just now. You commented that Russell's coming to stay with you would be good for you as well. What did you mean by that, if you don't mind me asking?

ESTHER RANKIN

Your Honor, I don't mind at all. It's real simple. My husband, Lester, died three years ago from a cerebral hemorrhage, and I have a big old house all to myself. I certainly have the room. Russell being there will give me a new responsibility, an additional purpose that I'm actually looking forward to.

JUDGE SHIELDS

The court is obliged of your candor, Mrs. Rankin. If you would please, what was your sister's opinion about all of this?

ESTHER RANKIN

Libbie simply said I should go with my heart. And that's what I'm doing with God's help.

JUDGE SHIELDS

Thank you. You may take your seat. Ms. Whitlock, anything you wish to add?

HELEN WHITLOCK

(Mrs. Whitlock stands)

Just that we'll make this work as a family. Your Honor, the plan has my full support.

JUDGE SHIELDS

That's good to hear. Ms. Whitlock. The court certainly appreciates your presence here today. You may take your seat.

Counsel, I'd like to ask Officer Skinner a few questions. Mr. Jennings, please swear in the officer.

(Officer Skinner remains in the gallery and stands to be sworn in by the bailiff.)

JUDGE SHIELDS

Officer Skinner, you were the injured officer in this case. Please share your thoughts and opinions, sir."

OFFICER BENJAMIN SKINNER

Your Honor, I have been a Lancaster police officer going on four years now, and this incident is the first time I was ever injured on duty. This situation was an accident. The minor just panicked at the thought of going to St. Olaf's and made a bad decision when he ran from the apartment. He brushed by me, and I fell on the wet floor. I never felt that Russell meant to hurt me. This is also the first time that I ever got an apology letter (holding the letter in the air) from a juvenile or an adult, for that matter, who was arrested.

I support the plan developed by the Probation Department.

JUDGE SHIELDS

In light of your injury, thank you, Officer Skinner, very much for your service and presence here today. The court wishes you a speedy and full recovery. Please be seated.

Russell, you most likely think I had forgotten about you, but I haven't. Far from it. You are the key player here. Your opinions about your situation and the court's recommendation are very important. If this court orders you to move temporarily to North Carolina to live with your grandmother, what will you do to make this plan work?

RUSSELL RANKIN

Well, I need to listen to my grandma, go to school, and stay out of trouble and do what my probation officer tells me to do.

JUDGE SHIELDS

All right, that's a start. This is a big transition for you. We hope that it is temporary. It's unfortunate that neither one of your parents is available to care for you right now, but you need to do your best to make this all work in North Carolina. That's the best we can hope for now. And again, this is temporary until a residence, here in Illinois, can be worked out within your family. Can the court count on your cooperation, on your playing your part?

RUSSELL RANKIN

Yes, Your Honor.

JUDGE SHIELDS

Very good, Russell. Anything further, Mr. Holland?

TIMOTHY HOLLAND

No, Your Honor. I believe Russell understands and accepts the conditions of probation as proposed.

JUDGE SHIELDS

Ms. Ryan-Duckett, anything further?

JOYCE RYAN-DUCKETT

No, Your Honor.

JUDGE SHIELDS

All right, with all said and heard, oh, wait just a minute. I do have one more question for Ms. Bohars. Ms. Bohars, the social history does not make mention of a referral to the Department of Children and Family Services in relation to Russell and his sister. Has that referral in fact been made?

INGRID BOHARS

Your Honor, I apologize for that omission in the social history. Yes, I personally made the referral to DCFS intake. Just a minute, the date is somewhere here in my notes. Here it is, the referral was made to DCFS central intake on both minors on February 26th.

JUDGE SHIELDS

That would be a Friday. By the way, Ms. Bohars, do you recall the name of the DCFS worker who took your referral?

INGRID BOHARS

Yes, Your Honor. It was actually supervisor Geraldine Proesser.

JUDGE SHIELDS

Very good, Ms. Bohars. Thank you for that.

All right, with all said and heard and the minor having been adjudicated a delinquent minor on 2-22-82, the following dispositional order is entered:

A one-year period of probation is ordered with courtesy supervision to be provided by the North Carolina Division of Juvenile Services. Transfer of supervision is to be administered through Interstate Compact with the Lancaster County Probation Department remaining active in monitoring the minor's progress;

Temporary guardianship is awarded to Chief Probation Officer James T. Drury, Lancaster County Probation Department, Lancaster, Illinois;

Temporary custody is awarded to paternal grandmother Esther O. Rankin, 415 Grouse Hollow Road, Colby, NC;

Minor is to enroll and regularly attend Pratt County High School in Colby, North Carolina;

Twenty hours of public service work is ordered to be completed at the direction of the North Carolina Division of Juvenile Services;

Minor is to abstain from the use of alcohol and all illicit drugs;

Sixty-day progress reports are to be submitted by the North Carolina Division of Youth Services to the Lancaster County Probation Department via Interstate Compact;

A $200 clothing voucher is awarded to Esther Rankin as applied to the minor's care;

Medical and dental expenses for the minor are assumed by the Lancaster County Probation Department.

Mrs. Rankin, I did not include part-time employment and church attendance as conditions of probation; however, I certainly believe they are good additions. Curfew will also apply to North Carolina law. Also, Ms. Bohars indicates in the social history that Russell is in need of some dental work. Can you take care of that upon your return to North Carolina?

ESTHER RANKIN

Your Honor, I'll call Dr. Bower, he's my dentist, to set an appointment as soon as we get back home.

JUDGE SHIELDS

I appreciate that. And again, this court has assumed Russell's medical and dental expenses, as long as guardianship remains with the Probation Department. Should you have any questions about this, please check with Ms. Bohars. She'll have some papers you'll need to sign and take with you.

Russell, the court understands that a lot has happened to you in recent weeks. What has happened here isn't fair, with your mother's disappearance and your father's current inability to take care of you. I can't change any of that for you; I wish I could but none of us can change things as they are.

I need you to honor that commitment that you will work hard, as hard as you can, with your grandmother, school, and probation to make your stay in North Carolina successful. Again, this is a temporary arrangement until either your mother or father is capable of caring for you. Understand?"

RUSSELL RANKIN

Yes, ma'am.

JUDGE SHIELDS

Any additional questions, anyone? All right, being none, all order of business in this cause is completed. Mrs. Rankin, allow Ms. Bohars here a few minutes to get Russell discharged from detention. You can meet Russell in the Probation Department's lobby, let's say in about fifteen minutes. You drive carefully back to North Carolina.

Thank you again to everyone for your attendance here today. Russell, you make us proud and do right, understand? Make good decisions down there. Court is adjourned.

(The clock reads 1:59 p.m.)

8

MARCH 1, 1982
LANCASTER, SHELLSBURG,
AND DANVILLE, ILLINOIS

―――――――

WITH Russell's hearing concluded, Brad Terrell escorted him to Probation's lobby. Here, Brad met Esther and Helen for the first time. The meeting was brief but genuine as Brad thanked them for stepping forward on Russell's behalf.

"It's a wonderful thing that y'all are doing for Russell. This was a weird, weird situation. Never seen one like it before." Brad turned his attention to Russell, "This is a good kid, here. I know because I coached him for two years. He's one heck of a football player too, got real potential. Hey, Russell, did you say good-bye to Ms. Bohars?"

"Yes, sir, right after court."

"Thank her too?"

"Yes, sir."

Esther added, "We met her too. Nice, nice lady."

"That's good because she sure put in the hours for you. She went way above and beyond."

Brad shook Russell's hand and gave him a strong hug as he whispered, "Remember, Russell, let the town come to you. Write me when you can, hear? Promise?"

"Yes, sir. Thanks for everything, Coach." Russell said with a grateful smile.

Esther and Helen expressed their gratitude as well with soft hugs. The Probation lobby door opened, and Russell took in his first gulp of real-world air in twenty-three days. Most snow and ice had disappeared during his detention stay. Today's temperature was approaching an unseasonable fifty degrees.

Aunt Helen asked, "Russell, how far is it to your old apartment?"

"A couple miles."

Can you direct us there?"

"Sure."

"Helen, what's this all about? We don't have any extra time. We need to get on to see Peter before we leave town."

"Just trust me, Momma. Trust me. This is important."

After walking a short block to the public parking garage, Aunt Helen took command of Esther's Malibu. Esther rode in the backseat while Russell provided directions from up front.

In less than ten minutes, Helen stood in the rental office of the Albemarle Arms apartments speaking with the apartment manager. In an additional fifteen minutes, Aunt Helen and Russell were stuffing seven large plastic bags of clothing and personal items into the crowded trunk and backseat of Esther's car.

"Daughter, how'd you negotiate this?"

"I relied on some experience learned from my graduate school days in Boston. That apartment manager was madder than a wet hen about them skipping town, but twenty dollars changed her mind about retrieving leftover clothing in a basement locker. Russell and Rachel's clothing were bound for charity; bags were still sitting in the basement."

Russell was ecstatic, not so much for the clothing but for some books, photos, and a treasured Glenn Beckert baseball glove.

"Thank you, Aunt Helen, for doing this. It means a lot. It really does," he said as they drove on to visit his father.

* * *

By previous agreement, Esther, Helen, and Russell were scheduled to visit Peter at Holcomb Valley Hope Center before beginning the return trip to North Carolina. The meeting would be brief because of time constraints.

Holcomb Valley was located a dozen miles west of Lancaster outside the tiny farming community of Shellsburg. In the very cramped sedan, Helen drove the short distance having no difficulty finding the facility off a county blacktop.

Approaching the fifty-five-acre site, they saw a plain white farmhouse and six residential cottages flanking the farmhouse to the left and right. A renovated barn, now an Activities Center, was situated behind the farmhouse. A new-looking building, Horizon Hall, was linked to the Activities Center by an enclosed walkway.

The grounds included picnic tables, horseshoe pits, a volleyball net, a basketball court, a softball field, and a large pond complete with fishing dock and canoes.

Rita Birch, Director of Treatment, met the group on the front porch of the farmhouse, which served as Holcomb Valley's administration building. An unavoidable placard greeted all who entered the building. Neat, green lettering on a cream background read: "Your new life begins today."

In short order, Ms. Birch explained, "I'm going to give you a brief tour of our campus, fifteen to twenty minutes or so, while Peter and Russell get together. Peter said he wanted private time with Russell first. Then you can all meet as a group.

Work for you folks?"

Esther and Helen agreed despite the unexpected delay in meeting Peter.

Ms. Birch excused herself and walked Russell to a vacant multipurpose room that was used for visitation.

A pale and tired Peter Rankin, thirty-nine years of age, sat on a worn olive-green couch as Russell entered the room. Peter smiled while struggling to stand. Russell failed to hide his distress at his father's physical appearance; he was taken aback by Peter's weight loss and frailty.

Peter had been five feet ten inches when he had enlisted in the navy, but he seemed shorter now; his shoulders were hunched forward as if by some invisible burden. His hair was thinning, now more gray than blond. His color was dull, almost lifeless.

"Hey, Daddy."

Father and son embraced.

Peter's eyes welled with tears as he mumbled some indiscernible words to his oldest child. The hug grew tighter.

Taking a step back for inspection, Peter said, "You're looking good, son, and where'd you get this height from? What are you now? Six one, six two?"

As soon as they were both seated on the couch, Peter began exploring his son's arrest and involvement in the juvenile justice system.

"Russell, I have some sense as to what's happened to you, but are you all right?" Peter's voice elevated. "What the hell happened? This doesn't sound like you."

Embarrassed, Russell began a rehearsed summary of recent events.

"Daddy, I never hit anyone. I didn't mean for the police officer to fall and break his elbow, but that's what happened. Yeah, I brushed by him, but I never tried to hurt him. Honest."

"I believe you, son. I do. It just seems that the situation got the best of you to where you panicked and flipped out. What's important here is that you learn from this. That's somethin' my daddy, your grandfather, always used to say. This is a tough experience for you, an unfair lesson, but you just gotta deal with it as best you can. Court hearin' go as expected?"

"Yes, sir."

"That's good, real good. And while I know you're probably not happy about movin' to North Carolina, remember that's all temporary. Once I finish treatment and earn my discharge, you and Rachel can move in with me. I should be out of here by May or June and back with the post office."

During their talk together, not once did Peter cast blame or criticism toward others. "You know, son, I kind of liken my life up 'til now to some littered mountain road back home, all hilly and twisted with a lot of wrecked dreams, wasted plans, and wounded people along the way, too many potholes and dips in the road, not enough road signs and guardrails."

Peter offered fatherly advice. "Maybe this is a good thing for once, you're going to Colby. I'm done with excuses and blamin' everyone includin' your momma. It's one thing to near ruin my own life, but you've got to rise above the spot you're in. Listen to me, son. Colby's goin' to be good for you, good for you," as Peter tapped Russell's' shoulder for reassurance.

Russell slowly nodded in agreement as a tranquil lull took over them both. Peter abruptly shifted gears. "I talked to Rachel on the phone yesterday. She's not doin' so good in Chicago. Pretty clear to me that she's just a bother to them. I think that's Rach's feelin' too." They have this service here where volunteers provide rides for residents, and a man is drivin' me all the way to Chicago and back on Saturday to see Rachel. I'll get a better feel about her situation this weekend."

Impressed, Russell said, "That's good, Daddy, real good that you're doin' that. Tell her that I miss her, and that I'll be OK down in North Carolina. Tell her not to worry. Let her know that I'll call as soon as I get settled in with Grandma."

"I need to ask about your momma. She's done some crazy shit before, but I didn't see this comin'. Her leaving Rachel and you like this is surprisin', even to me. All I can figure is that this new boyfriend really has got a hold on her and is usin' her for selfish reasons. What's he like? Why'd she take up with him anyway?"

"He's a total creep, Daddy. Rachel and I didn't like him from the start.

Before we knew it, he'd moved in. He only cares about himself. Momma doesn't see any of this because he knows how to play her. Rachel and I have been in the way from the start. Oh, yeah, he's on probation, too. I overheard them talkin' one night at the kitchen table, somethin' about him stealin' slot machines. All they ever seemed to talk about the past few months was movin' and startin' over."

"It looks to me like your time in detention gave them the opening they were lookin' for. I am surprised, though, really surprised at your mother. I never thought she'd stoop to something this low, to go runnin' off like this. Hard for even me to see her doin' this." Peter forlornly shook his head.

"Son, I know you have little memory of your grandmother, but you will be in the best of hands down there with her. Life will be very different for you goin' from Lancaster to a small town like Colby, but your grandmother is a rock. Believe me, she will do whatever is best for you, and you'll get to know Aunt Helen, Uncle Daniel, Uncle Andrew, and your cousins. Again, this is temporary until I get back on my feet.

"Russell I should have asked you sooner. Are you OK with movin' down there?"

"Yes, sir."

Peter smiled and softly patted Russell on his cheek. "Proud of you son. You're going to do just fine."

Peter grew reflective. "I know I haven't been a good father to you or Rachel. I haven't been much of a father at all. I can finally admit that now, which is somethin' that's always needed to happen. I ran from bein' a father for years. I want to become the father you and Rachel deserve.

"Look at me, son. This isn't bullshit. I mean this as sure as I'm sittin' here." Peter gripped his son's arm for emphasis.

"There's still time. I know how to reach you now. I lost touch last fall. I know it's a bullshit excuse, but I didn't know where you'd moved to. I'm going to write you; that's a promise. I'd like you to write back. Would you do that? I mean write me now and then telling me how you're doin'?"

"Sure, Daddy, I'll do that."

"This is important to *us* as a father and as a son."

A soft knock was heard on the room's door as Mrs. Birch accompanied Esther and Helen for their reunion with Peter. It had been three years since Lester's funeral, the last time Esther, Helen, and Peter had been together.

With some physical difficulty, Peter rose from the couch to hug his mother. The hug was long and lasting as tears flowed freely. Eventually Peter stepped back and smiled in warm appreciation.

"Let me just look at you. You're lookin' so wonderful, Momma, just wonderful. You haven't aged a bit. This is a dream come true seein' you here." He dabbed his face with an already damp Kleenex.

Eventually Peter broke the embrace to greet and hug his only sister. "Helen, it's so good seein' you even if it's here. You look prettier than ever."

Helen, overtaken by emotion, said, "Oh, Peter, I've missed you more than you know. It's so grand seeing you, so grand."

Peter placed his hands on Helen's shoulders, tilting his head backwards. "You know, sis, you're the only human I know on the planet who calls anything grand." He smiled lovingly. "But I accept the compliment."

Esther joined Peter on the couch as Helen and Russell sat across from them on wooden chairs.

"Peter, it's been way too long, way too long, son. We've both got to be better at this, and now Russell is such a concern and Rachel."

"How'd the court hearing' go, Momma?"

"Well, Russell was released from detention, placed on probation, and he's gonna be livin' with me in Colby, at least for a while."

Peter was elated. "That's good news, real good news, Momma." Peter smiled and winked at his son. "Russell gave me a clue earlier of what happened in court."

"How's your treatment goin', son?"

"Better this time around, Momma. It's got to be. This is my third go at it. I gotta make this work. I'm runnin' out of chances. It's that simple. You know that sign out front, did you see it on the front porch? That sign has everythin' to do with me. I think of it every day, every single day. It reads 'Your new life begins today.' That sign's talkin' to me, Momma. I gotta get it right this time. I just gotta."

A short silence followed.

"How long have you been here, son?"

"I just finished my fourth month. I'm better than halfway through completin' the program. A lot of it has to do with my counselor, Eric, who I really like and respect. He's a lot like me 'cause we have a lot in common. You know, Vietnam and all. He's been alcohol and drug-free for eight years now."

"Peter, how's your health, son? You look so thin."

"That's part of it too. My doctor says my medical problems are linked to wear and tear from the alcohol. I have liver disease. I got heart problems, too. I just got to turn everything around, no booze or drugs, ongoin' treatment, better diet, medicine, exercise."

Peter looked at her sadly as he grabbed his mother's hand. "And it has to stick this time, Momma. That clock is tickin.'"

Peter shifted the conversation. "Are you still workin' at Hamilton Brothers, still payin' the bills, and doin' payroll?"

Esther nodded, "I reach my twenty-year anniversary come December. I figure I still have a few good years left."

"Good for you, Momma, good for you. That store's been lucky to have you for all those years."

"And son, how about your job with the post office? Hard to believe that you've held on to it considerin' all you've been through."

"My boss has been unbelievable. I owe him a lot. He could have given up on me a long time ago. He and I go back as far as my early years in Lancaster. We sort of started together. He's had some tough times too, but he always knew I was a good worker, got the job done despite my problems *outside of work.* One strange thing about my drinkin', I never drank on the job. Never, not once."

For the next thirty minutes, Esther and Helen recounted family news involving Peter's three siblings and their families. Helen mentioned developments in Pratt County. "It's changing, Peter. We're not as sleepy and undiscovered anymore. Colby got its third traffic light last year. When we were growin' up, we had one blinkin' light downtown at the crossroads. Remember, one blinkin' light."

"That's the price of progress, I suppose, if that's what you call it. I'm comin' back home to visit as soon as I can earn some time for days off at the post office. You can count on that."

Pleased with Peter's announcement, Esther said, "I hate to say this, but we've got a long drive ahead of us, and ought to get on the road. Been a long day already."

Peter checked his watch to realize that the return drive to North Carolina was behind schedule. "C'mon, we gotta get you three on the highway. I figure Helen will be doin' most of the drivin' because Momma is so averse to night drivin.'"

The family returned to Ms. Birch's office and thanked her for her time and hospitality. During the brief walk down the hallway, the visitors grew more alarmed of Peter's slow and labored movement.

Goodbyes were long and heartfelt; tears returned.

"Helen, we didn't get to talk much, but I sure do appreciate your drivin' up here and back with Momma. Thanks for doing' that. We're goin' to have more time down the road to catch up. Just you wait. You look just fabulous, still the sweetest, best-lookin' girl in Pratt County," Peter said.

"I so look forward to that, Peter. We'll make up for all the lost time. You take good care of yourself now; I'm going to write and call," as Helen flashed a Holcomb Valley Hope Center business card.

"That would be fabulous, sis."

"Love you brother."

"Love you too, sis."

Brother and sister shared a final hug that was followed by Helen whispering in her brother's ear, "Come back home to us, Peter, come back home." He was touched by the unexpected encouragement.

Helen turned to Russell. "Why don't we head to the parking lot and warm the car up for your grandmother."

Russell hugged his father long and hard. Peter broke the embrace to cradle Russell's face with his hands. Peter spoke eye to eye. "You're in the very best of hands, son, down there in Colby. I have every confidence that you're goin' to do well. I love you, son, now more than ever."

"I love you too, Daddy."

Russell and Helen departed for the parking lot, leaving mother and son alone.

"Momma, I can't thank you enough. I am so grateful for your takin' in Russell for a while. Hopefully, it will only be for a few months, maybe into the summer, and then he can move back here to live with Rachel and me."

"Peter, as I told the judge earlier today, I'm lookin' forward to it. I've got a better purpose now takin' care of Russell. I have your address now. I'll be writin' you, son, and callin' now and then to check on you. The best thing you can do for Russell, Rachel, me and, yourself is to finish this program. Mrs. Birch says you're a model resident right now, that you've made tremendous progress. That's how you can thank me, take full advantage and finish this program. This has got to be permanent, you hear me now, son?"

"I definitely hear you, Momma. Nothing has ever been clearer to me than right now. I know you gotta run, but I've thought long and hard about somethin'."

Peter then hesitated.

"You can tell me, son … what is it?"

"I've been thinkin' for a while about transferrin' to North Carolina, to Colby or someplace close. The post office allows employees with years of service to transfer. It wouldn't be right away, but maybe in six months or a year. Plus, there's got to be an openin' in Colby or some other branch nearby. I have to first get settled back in the job in Lancaster. Whaddya think?"

Esther hugged Peter in a strong embrace. "That would be the greatest gift of all; it would be the answer to my prayers."

Esther gazed lovingly on his eldest son, "I love you, Peter Wallace Rankin." "I love you, too, Momma."

Kisses and a final hug followed as Esther hurried off to the parking lot.

Peter's eyes glistened as he viewed the departure from the wooden front porch of the administration building. All too quickly he lost site of the car with the North Carolina license plates as it retreated from view toward the Lancaster County blacktop. A long, exhausting return drive to Pratt County awaited the three passengers.

Peter turned to leave and glanced for the umpteenth time at the front porch greeting that had given him so much hope - "Your new life begins today."

9

MARCH 1–2, 1982, DANVILLE, IL TO COLBY, NC

As anticipated, Helen was the sole driver that late Monday afternoon. The plan was to drive as far as Danville, IL, where the threesome would spend the night.

Esther was not a fan of fast food restaurants. She had not eaten fast food for several years. But due to the late hour, she acquiesced when Helen went through the drive-thru window at an Arby's outside Lancaster.

Esther was sitting next to Helen in the front seat, separated by a plastic bag stuffed with clothing. Russell had jammed his long body into the backseat among additional bags of clothing. The trio pretty much ate in silence. When they'd finished, Esther said, "Russell, whaddya call that place again?"

"Arby's, Grandma. Arby's."

"We'll, it's pretty good. Helen, how come we don't have any Arby's back home?"

"We do, but they're closer to Winston and Charlotte. Remember, Hardee's has roast beef sandwiches too."

"That's right, come to think of it, you're right. Well, you learn somethin' new every day. That sure was a good sandwich, tasty French fries, too. Hit the spot."

After a few minutes of silence, Esther asked, "Helen, how long's the drive to where we're stayin'?"

"I figure at least three more hours."

Russell, how you doin' back there? You look awful cramped competin' for space with all those bags. We can switch around some 'cause I'll fit back there better than you do."

"I'm fine, just tired."

Esther interjected, "That's understandable, Grandson. You've had a long day. We've all had a long day. Try to put the past few weeks behind you. The worst is over."

"I'll try. I'm just glad to be out of juvie."

"Oh, Grandson, I've been meaning to ask you somethin'. Have you been around dogs and cats much?"

"No, ma'am. Momma wouldn't have it. She always said that dogs and cats were an extra expense that we didn't need."

Esther wasn't surprised with Russell's response. "I reckoned that might be the case. I've got a dog and a cat that you'll soon get to know. Maddie's the fat beagle. She's a little standoffish at first, and she can get ornery at times. Just let her be, and she'll come around. Gus is the orange tabby. He's real affectionate, probably will be sleepin' on your bed in no time."

Helen interjected, "Gus has a particularly bad habit of patrolling the counter tops in the kitchen. When you see him up there, just gather him up and redirect him elsewhere."

Esther continued, "Maddie likes to roam. Gus stays close to the property. They both like to be outside except at night. They both need to be in at night because of coyotes."

Russell questioned with a raised eye, "Coyotes?"

Esther added, "Oh, sure. Sometimes at night you can hear them howlin' down in the holler. That's enough of that."

Despite his tiredness, Russell could not sleep; he only rested with eyes shut. His mind continued to race. Upon his release from detention, he had hoped that his ongoing review of his arrest and his mother's abandonment would cease. Any mental respite was short-lived. With frustrating regularity, the same doubts and nagging questions replayed as he rode down this stretch of lightly traveled state highway.

Russell had spent many hours in detention agonizing about his mother and the controlling impact that Dominic held on her. Loretta had never been a pillar of strength or consistency. She was weak and lacked confidence in managing her life and the lives of her two children. All too frequently and especially when a man was not active in her life, she leaned on Russell to make even the most basic of decisions.

However, when a man was on the scene, the inappropriate reliance on Russell, even during his pre-adolescent years, shifted from son to boyfriend. Loretta appeared to gain strength, even a fleeting degree of confidence, from the unhealthy romantic relationships she established.

Loretta did a poor job of balancing her male relationships with responsibilities of motherhood. She depended upon financial support from boyfriends since her restaurant earnings were meager and inconsistent. She spent much of her pay on alcohol, cigarettes, lottery tickets, and junk food at overpriced neighborhood convenience stores.

The family was forced to travel by city bus or an occasional cab since Loretta did not own a car or even have a driver's license.

Dominic DiNardo's influence on Loretta was powerful and more disabling than previous suitors. Unlike his predecessors, he made little attempt to join with Russell or Rachel. His focus was strictly on Loretta, and that was where the rub developed between Russell and Dominic. As in the past, Russell believed that Loretta's relationship with Dominic would fade in the expected frame of two to three months.

However, the February 5th incident had broken the pattern.

While in detention, Russell had come to the painful understanding that on that February evening, Loretta had made a deliberate choice between children and Dominic. At that time, Russell had failed to grasp the long-term impact of Loretta's betrayal. Russell, nor anyone else, could have possibly predicted what lay ahead.

During Russell's twenty-three day stay in detention, Loretta had visited on three occasions. Those visits were unproductive as were the three to four phone calls between them. Loretta did state that she was not worried about Russell's physical safety while in detention saying that, "You've always been able to take care of yourself. Your size helps, plus your mouth isn't going to start problems either. You'll do OK. You're a survivor like me."

As nighttime more fully settled, Russell's thoughts were interrupted as Helen slowed to stop at a railroad crossing for a passing train.

"Aunt Helen, how much longer are we gonna be drivin' tonight?"

"I reckon at least an hour, maybe hour and a half. This train isn't helping."

Esther and Helen had previously agreed to keep the conversation light and comfortable during the drive to North Carolina. This was not the time for interrogation, Russell having been through enough of that recently. They were more fixed upon Russell's adjustment to Colby and Pratt County than what had transpired in Lancaster.

As the train moved on and the drive continued, Grandma Esther slept soundly. Aunt Helen asked, "So Russell, what do you know of your family in North Carolina?

"Not much," said Russell.

Aunt Helen was not surprised by Russell's ignorance of family history. "Well, both your grandparents were born and raised in North Carolina. Your grandmother was born on a dining room table in Pratt County near the small town of Grappler.

Your granddaddy was born two years earlier in Wheeler County, which is right next door. They both graduated from Colby High School, which is now Pratt County High School where you'll be attending."

Russell's interest was stirred. "How'd they meet?"

"Well, that's a sweet story. They both said they didn't know each other in high school. Your grandma was working at the Chevrolet dealership right out of high school. Your Grandpa Lester came in wanting to buy a car. They met when he signed the papers on his new car. They started dating, sparks flew early, and in seven months, daddy proposed to momma on Christmas Eve. In June, the next year, they were married by your great-grandfather."

"So, my great-grandfather was a minister?"

"Yep, a Methodist preacher. He was sort of part-time. His main job was surveying for the state highway department. Your great-grandmother taught grade school for thirty-eight years."

Russell asked, "How many kids did they have besides Grandma?"

"Only one, Libbie. You'll meet her soon. She's two years younger. She's a surgical nurse and works and lives near Charlotte. She's a lot like your Grandma 'cept she's never married."

Helen slowed the car as they entered a small town. Shifting subjects, she mentioned that she would be present Wednesday morning for Russell's admission to his new school. In an effort to jump-start Russell's likely enrollment, Helen had contacted the guidance department at Pratt County High School the previous Friday as to events.

Esther continued to sleep. Russell rested as evening fell, leaving Helen alone to navigate unfamiliar stretches of straight and flat two-lane highway. Traffic was light that wintry evening; the roads were clear of any snow and ice. For the next half hour, Helen speculated about how Russell would adjust to his new way of life in Pratt County. She agreed with her mother that Russell's presence would be good for Esther, that it would provide her added purpose.

Helen's thoughts were drawn back to the haunting image of her brother.

She'd always had a soft spot for her oldest younger brother and had hoped for some meaningful private time with him during the Holcomb Valley visit. She had so many questions to ask, but time was limited. Helen accepted that her questions could be posed at a later date over the phone or in letters.

Helen had overestimated the mileage to Danville. Only sixty miles remained on the first leg of the return drive home. In less than an hour, Helen turned into a Holiday Inn parking lot. Esther and Russell stirred from their slumber as the car ground to a halt in a near empty parking lot. The clock read 9:20 p.m.

"Wait here, Momma, while I get us registered. I'll try to get us something on the first floor."

In less than ten minutes, Room 110 was secured and occupied. There was little small talk as all quickly readied for bed. Russell took the bed closest to the door while Esther and Helen shared the other. Esther set a portable, windup alarm clock for their agreed wake-up time of 6:00 a.m.

* * *

As the alarm clock rudely introduced the morning, Esther encouraged Russell to sleep while she and Helen took quick showers and dressed. He eventually did the same, grateful that he had a change of clean underwear and a collared shirt and jeans.

When Russell exited the steaming bathroom, Esther said, "We need a good sit-down breakfast before we leave. Everybody on board?"

Helen smiled. "I knew you'd want a good breakfast, Momma, so I asked the front-desk staff last night if she could recommend any restaurants. She said Hillerman's is close and where the locals eat."

Hillerman's Family Restaurant was yet to be busy. Grandma Esther, Aunt Helen, and Russell sat in a window booth. A middle-aged waitress offered coffee, much to Esther's delight.

"Thank you, Miss. Does this ever smell wonderful."

"Be careful now, Ma'am. Coffee's very hot."

Helen requested a cup, and to the surprise of his relatives, Russell did too. "Grandson, when did you start drinking coffee?"

"Probably when I was twelve or thirteen. Helps me wake up, but I use cream and sugar."

"Mercy, I did not see that comin', oh, but this is wonderful coffee, just wonderful." Esther said with an appreciative smile.

"Russell, you've just learned one very important trait of your grandmother.

She adores good morning coffee, but, and this is important, it has to be freshly brewed and good, *really* good to earn your grandmother's stamp of approval. And don't even waste her time with instant."

In prompt fashion, breakfast orders were taken and delivered to the table.

Eating was more intentional and driven than social since all anticipated a demanding drive to Pratt County. Long hours in the car lay ahead for conversation.

Russell was the last to finish, nearly licking clean his plate of linked sausages and blueberry pancakes, not a crumb wasted. Helen and Esther observed in amazement. I-74 awaited and soon, the group was on their way.

Russell was happy to see that Helen was an excellent driver. She was both responsible and capable behind the wheel.

As Helen accelerated to the speed limit, she spoke to Russell. "You know, this was my first trip by car to the Midwest. I've been to Chicago, but I flew there for a library conference. I can't imagine driving around that big city with all that traffic and congestion. Not as bad down here, but it's so flat. Certainly not going to be like where we're headin'. Pratt County is definitely not flat. Do you remember the last time you visited?"

"Yes, ma'am. I think that's the only time we were all here together. I remember Grandma's house 'cause that's where we stayed. I remember Colby a little bit, a picnic that we had at a park on some river - that was a lot of fun. Oh, yeah, I remember the mountains and lots of creeks."

"Not much like Lancaster, is it?"

He shook his head. "No, that's for sure."

"Are you anxious about school?"

"I haven't thought about it that much. It'll be OK because it's just a couple of months before summer vacation."

Russell then recalled a small white envelope he had found after showering. It had been included in the clothing bag provided by detention staff. Due to the hurry to vacate the motel room, he had not opened it but stashed it instead in his back pocket. As the conversation eased, he withdrew the envelope, opened it, and began reading:

Russell,

You've been a wonderful student, perhaps the very best during my five years teaching at Detention. You have a bright and curious mind and are a hard worker. I know you're moving to North Carolina to live with your grandmother. I wish you well down there as you adjust.

I have no doubts that you will be a success in life. Thank you for being such an exceptional student and such a big help.

Sincerely,
Valerie Blasingame

"Whatcha reading?" asked Helen.

"It's a note from the teacher in detention."

"Oh, that certainly was nice of her."

"Yeah, it was. It really was." Russell folded the message back into the envelope, returning it to his back pocket for safekeeping.

After a fifteen-minute gap in conversation, Russell said, "Grandma sure does sleep a lot in the car."

"Like a rock, something to do with the motion of the car, but only when she's a passenger. It doesn't affect her when she's driving. She must have slept more than half the time driving up here. A wonderful talent, Russell. I wish I had it."

Russell grew serious and appreciative. "Thank you for doin' all of this for me, Aunt Helen."

"Russell, this is all about family. You are very welcome."

As Esther continued to doze, Helen and Russell became better acquainted, covering multiple topics, with the time passing quickly.

In less than two hours, Esther stirred in the cramped backseat. "Where are we now?"

"We just passed through Indianapolis. You still want to drive some, Momma?"

"Sure, I don't want all of that burden on you, whenever you want to change."

"I'll keep driving past Cincinnati, and we'll switch around there. I want to take a different road through Kentucky to West Virginia, get off the interstate for a while, kind of a shortcut that may save us some miles."

"Daughter, this new route doesn't have anythin' to do with antiques, does it? You know we both need to be at work first thing tomorrow mornin'. And Lord knows, we don't have room for anythin' anyway."

Helen smiled. "No, Momma, it has nothing to do with antiques."

* * *

It was now early afternoon, and after a lunchtime stop at a Cincinnati-area Arby's, as insisted by the senior passenger, Esther took control of the driving on a Kentucky two-lane highway, which headed east toward Huntington, West Virginia. Helen shared the front seat while Russell sat in the back.

"How long are we on this road, Helen?"

"About a hundred miles. The only disadvantage is the speed limit, which they've cut to fifty miles an hour. That makes no sense to me, so Momma, watch your speed. The last thing you need is a speeding ticket."

After about thirty minutes of driving, Esther broke the silence. "This was a good call, daughter, a good call. Charming country and hardly any traffic."

The rolling highway only passed through three small towns. Small white churches dotted the landscape every few miles, as did vacant tobacco barns and distant houses set off from the highway. The route was isolated as Russell slept nestled in the back seat among bags of clothing. Esther was so captivated by the beauty and simplicity of the drive that her speed raced, causing a Kentucky state policeman to pull her over.

"Mercy, goodness gracious. Helen get me the vehicle registration from the glove box if you would. I'll grab my license. I haven't had a ticket in thirty-two years. Mercy. This is awful, just awful."

Aunt Helen offered advice that was ignored. "Momma, settle down. This isn't the end of the world. Maybe you'll just a warning. Try to relax."

Russell was awakened by the flurried activity in the front seat.

The patrolman delayed his visit to Esther's car for several minutes, but when he appeared, Esther had already rolled down the window and had both driver's license and registration in hand.

Greeting Esther was a tall handsome officer, who smiled but then politely requested her documents. The placard on his jacket identified the officer as Earl Carothers.

After inspection, Officer Carothers said, "Ma'am, you're obviously not from around here, that right? Ever travel this road before?"

"No, Officer. This is my first time. We're drivin' back from Illinois. We just wanted to get off the interstate and drive somethin' different."

"I see. The problem is this road almost invites cars to race since it is so wide open. Did you have a sense as to how fast you were goin'?"

"No, officer, I really didn't. The country just got the best of me. It reminds me some of back home. I'm so sorry. I haven't had a ticket in thirty-two years."

"Ma'am, I know what you're sayin'. I've been patrolling this road for close to three years now, and many people have trouble regulatin' their speed especially after they've been drivin' the interstates. You're not the first one"

Returning the documents, he said, "Ma'am, I'm only givin' you a warnin' this time. Just better check your speed in the future. You have a safe drive back to North Carolina, now, hear? Where exactly are you headin' down there?"

"Colby, North Carolina, northwestern part of the state. Thank you, Officer, thank you very much. I'm so sorry once again."

As Officer Carothers began the return to his patrol car, Esther asked through the open window, "Excuse me, Officer, one more thing. How fast was I goin'?"

"Pushing seventy, ma'am. Enjoy your day now."

* * *

After having reached Princeton, West Virginia, they agreed to stop for dinner. The threesome had made good time with sunny skies, limited road construction, and highways clear of accidents. Esther made it clear during the drive that there was to be no lull in Russell's schooling once he arrived in North Carolina. She had even volunteered for an additional turn at the wheel on the West Virginia Turnpike, knowing that Helen would be driving after dinner. As evening approached, the temperature dropped and a light rain began to fall.

Dinner was at a local restaurant that had attracted Esther's attention from billboard advertising adjacent to the West Virginia Turnpike. The meal was better than anticipated. Esther paraphrased one of Lester's philosophies: you hardly ever go wrong in ordering a hot roast beef sandwich and mashed potatoes when traveling. This time, Lester was right on the money. Helen figured a little more than three hours to go before they would arrive at Esther's home. The "Welcome to North Carolina" sign on I77 felt good to everyone, even Russell, as the exhausting trip neared its conclusion.

The final thirty-seven miles were traveled on winding, but familiar, North Carolina state roads. Just short of 10:30 p.m., Esther's Malibu arrived in her driveway. Total return distance covered from Lancaster, IL, seven hundred and fifty-three miles.

PART II

10

MARCH 3, 1982
COLBY, NC

———

As was her practice, Esther rose at 5:00 a.m. and immediately completed her morning regimen. While listening to her favorite Kenny Rogers song on the country music station, she prepared hot oatmeal for Russell complete with toppings of raisins and brown sugar. She prepared a sack lunch as well.

Prior to breakfast, Russell showered, brushed his teeth, and combed his unkempt blond hair. While detained, Russell had missed a haircut opportunity that was scheduled within the facility. In the past, Loretta had home cut Russell's hair.

On yesterday's drive, Esther had announced that a haircut was on the weekend calendar. "Russell, it isn't so much the length, but it sure needs cleanin' up, too scraggly, needs some thinnin' out, too." An upcoming trip to Kelso's, a Colby institution, would be Russell's first trip to an actual barber in over five years.

Several bags of teenage boys clothing had been delivered over the weekend to Esther's home by Aunt Helen's husband, George. The items had been collected from a variety of sources, but Russell opted this morning to wear his own clothes. From the collected wardrobe in Lancaster, Russell chose a safe combination of shirt and pants. His Detroit Tigers jacket would suffice as outerwear. His worn Nike's completed the ensemble.

"How'd you sleep in your new bed, Grandson?"

"Real good. The cat joined me at the foot of the bed sometime durin' the night."

Esther smiled. "That doesn't surprise me much at all. Russell, I hope the C&O station clock didn't bother you none."

"I heard it this mornin'. I got a close look at it just now before breakfast."

Russell had paid little attention to his new home the previous evening as he had gone straight to bed upon arrival. He would learn that the house included a dated kitchen, a living room complete with stone fireplace, a dining room, two first-floor bedrooms and a bath, and two upstairs bedrooms with bath. With the exception of the living room, rooms were small but adequate.

The home's interior was warm and welcoming with comfortable furnishings.

A framed needlepoint sampler over the living room entry greeted visitors with the message:

Count your age by friends not years...
Count your life by smiles not tears.

Esther motioned for her grandson to sit down at the kitchen table. "Oatmeal's all ready, just the way you like it. 'Bout that clock, your grand-daddy bought that clock at a farm auction a few months before Pearl Harbor. Been in the family ever since. It's like a member of the family."

After a brief ride from her home, Aunt Helen had joined her mother and nephew as Russell was finishing his breakfast. Like her mother, Helen was an attractive woman, but thinner and taller. Her brunette hair was cut short and simple. Even though Russell was no critic of fashion, he surmised that his Aunt Helen dressed older than her years would suggest.

Aunt Helen had volunteered to drive Russell to his new high school and serve as his representative through the enrollment process. Grandma

Esther would need to sign papers as custodian. Eventually, it would be brought to the school's attention that Russell's guardianship status was active with an out-of-state juvenile court.

As soon as Aunt Helen and Russell left for school, Esther was on the phone to her sister, Libbie, providing a detailed recap of the Illinois trip's events.

In less than ten minutes on a cool, overcast morning, Helen wheeled into the high school parking lot where she parked in the visitors' space.

Russell's first impression of his new high school was not a good one. The drab two-story main building of faded brown brick seemed to sag and almost moan from age. Six portable classrooms were scattered to the left and right of the main building. From his experiences in Lancaster, Russell surmised his new school would be crowded and likely antiquated. As he and his aunt walked to the front door, he realized that the school served both senior high and middle school populations.

Aunt Helen had timed their arrival during first period. With school underway, the school's hallways were empty, giving Russell a good opportunity to observe the interior of his new school. As he entered the building, he was greeted by the smell of musty, uncirculated air.

Like the high school's outside, the inside was unremarkable. Administrative offices flanked the main entrance to the left and right, with a large glass showcase displaying Pratt County High School artifacts, sports trophies, and miscellaneous memorabilia to all who entered through the main entrance. The walls were composed of glazed tan cinder block. Floors consisted of wood or tile. Lighting was poor, as dusty, original globe fixtures lit the foyer and main hallway.

A large bulletin board provided the only contrast, colorfully promoting Pratt County High School's spring dance billed as "Spring Fling, '82." All in all, the school was similar in many ways to Russell's former high school in Lancaster.

In entering the counseling office, Aunt Helen and Russell were greeted by the freshman/sophomore guidance counselor, Rob Cornelius, a thin, prematurely bald man in his late thirties who led aunt and nephew to his small cramped office.

Mr. Cornelius was well prepared for the meeting, and with minimum small talk and an awkward attempt at humor, he presented Russell with an assigned list of classes:

HR		NH 112	Abernethy
1	English	NH 106	McGraw
2	Algebra II	NH 210	Hufnal
3	Biology	NH 101	Gooch
4	Am. History	NH 115	Sullivan
	B Lunch		
5	Spanish	NH 200	Gibbs
6	Health/Gym	SH 120	Murphy/Gilroy
7	Home Mtn.	SH 116	Wilkes

Russell examined the list without response, and then shared it with Aunt Helen for her inspection.

"Any questions? 'Bout what you expected?" Mr. Cornelius asked.

"A lot like what I was taking back in Lancaster except for that one course," as Russell stalled for the title.

"Probably home maintenance, right?"

"Yes, sir. That's it."

Mr. Cornelius smiled. "Yep, that's the course that surprises people not familiar with the district. It's unique to PCHS. The course covers home maintenance and automotive repair. It's designed to give students a basic understanding of such trades as electrical, plumbing, carpentry, automotive maintenance, etc. The course is very popular with students and is taught by Mr. Wilkes, the head football coach. He's going to be glad to see you." Russell's eyebrows arched in surprise.

Mindful of the clock, Mr. Cornelius provided general orientation materials for Helen's review plus multiple forms that required Helen or Esther's signature. "We've got less than ten minutes before the period two bell. I want to give Russell a quick tour of the school during first period. Fortunately, many of his classes are in North Hall, first and second floors. Mrs. Whitlock, you're free to accompany us, although I know you're familiar with the school."

"Russell, with your OK, I think I'll head on to work. You know how to meet your grandmother when school's let out, right?"

"Yes, ma'am. Thanks for driving me."

"Oh, Russell, by the way. Here's your lock, combination, and locker number. Since you came in second half, you won't have a locker mate. Locker 89 is located on North Hall, first floor."

The threesome emptied out into the counseling office waiting room.

Cornelius announced to the administrative assistant, "Gail, I'm going to take our newest student here, Mr. Rankin, on a quick tour of the school before period one ends. I'll be back shortly."

After hugging and giving Russell a kiss on the cheek, Aunt Helen left the building through the school's main entrance while carrying a folder of documents intended for Esther's attention. Russell carried his lunch, several spiral notebooks, pens, and pencils to his first class, algebra two.

Cornelius accompanied Russell down the main hallway past the administration offices and the nurse's office to North Hall. He led the way, walking swiftly without conversing. He was on a mission and a tight time frame to complete his enrollment responsibility and connect Russell with his second period instructor. In methodical fashion and while often checking his watch, Cornelius pointed out several classrooms associated with Russell's schedule.

As the end of first period approached, they hugged the wall next to Room 106 and waited for the passing bell to sound. At 9:20 a.m., a loud, irritating horn signaled the end of period one. Noisy, self-absorbed students tumbled out of Betty Hufnal's algebra class, with some students offering bland greetings to Mr. Cornelius while being more attentive to the new student. Mr. Cornelius responded with a toothless smile and mild wave. When Mrs. Hufnal's classroom fully emptied, Russell was ushered into the classroom.

"Mrs. Hufnal, I have a new student for you here. This here is Russell Rankin."

With a genuine smile, Mrs. Hufnal extended her hand. "Russell, welcome to algebra two. If I might ask, where'd you move from, son?"

"Lancaster, Illinois."

"My, my. This will be quite the change for you. OK, take a seat in the front row next to the window since that one is unoccupied for second period. Hold on, let me check my seating chart to make sure."

"Mrs. Hufnal, time for me to get out of the way. Russell is all set with his schedule, locker, etc. He is in Mrs. Gooch's biology class following yours. Russell, if you have any issues today, I want you to see me when school ends."

Russell smiled and nodded his appreciation.

As Cornelius exited and students started to flow into NH 210, classmate attention was instantly drawn to the new student being oriented by Mrs. Hufnal.

Most girls were attracted; boys appeared disinterested or standoffish.

"Russell, here is your textbook. We're wrapping up chapter nineteen today, starting on page two seventeen."

Russell anticipated the curious stares and whispers from his new classmates.

He had been through this process several times before, but switching schools in Lancaster had been less drastic, less eventful because he remained rooted in his hometown.

On this occasion, he felt like a true outsider, an alien whose every action was being scrutinized by students and teachers alike. The inspection continued throughout the day in his new classes, in the hallways, and at lunch where he ate alone at an empty table.

Russell was comfortable with his algebra curriculum and confident that he would make a good transition. Biology seemed more challenging with the instructor, Jan Gooch, immediately demonstrating demanding expectations. Russell's American history section looked promising with the class currently studying World War I.

By far, the strangest occurrence of the day happened during lunch. As he was finishing his chicken salad sandwich, a teacher joined him at his table.

You're Russell, did I get that right?"

"Yes, sir."

"Esther Rankin's grandson?"

"That's right," Russell said, eyeing the teacher curiously.

"Mind if I join you for a few minutes? You just keep on eatin'," as the teacher slid into the yellow plastic cafeteria chair directly across from Russell.

"My name's Morris Wilkes." He extended his hand across the table. "I'm your seventh period teacher for home maintenance. I'm also the head football coach here at Pratt. Most students just call me Coach Mo. It seems you were a pretty good football player back in Illinois."

Russell was surprised then bewildered by Morris Wilkes' knowledge. "Sir, how'd you know all that?" he said respectfully.

"Seems I got a phone call yesterday from one of your former coaches." Coach Wilkes pulled out a folded a piece of paper from his shirt pocket, and carefully read, "Ah, a Brad Terrell, remember him?"

"Sure, he was my coach for two years in youth football."

"Well, he sure is a big fan of yours, and he wanted to make sure that you got connected with high school football here at Pratt. He said you were an excellent football player and the best punter he ever saw, a real natural. He knew about your movin' to North Carolina so he did some research and called me yesterday. We must have talked for at least fifteen to twenty minutes. If I might ask, what's Coach Terrell do for a livin'?"

"He works at Juvenile Detention."

Time seemed to be standing still for half the cafeteria's population, especially the boys. Their attention locked on the meeting involving a new student and Coach Wilkes. Russell felt dozens of curious eyes directed their way during the meeting.

"Do you play offense or just defense and punting? What did you play last year as a sophomore?"

"I played linebacker and strong safety. On offense, I played tight end. Plus, the punting."

"And you varsity lettered last year as a sophomore?"

"Yes, sir."

"That's impressive. What was your team's record last year?"

"Not very good. We were two and seven." Slightly shaking his head, Russell added, "We had a weak senior class, only five seniors."

"Well, as the head coach here, I'd sure like you to play for us next fall. We sure could use you and based upon your play in Illinois and Coach Terrell's comments, I think you'd help us a lot."

"It's hard for me to say since I don't know how long I'm going to be living here."

Both Coach Wilkes and Russell were oblivious to student movement in anticipation of the horn ending the lunch period. As the horn sounded, Coach Wilkes said, "Hey, look, Russell, we'll pick this up after class this afternoon if you have the time. That sound OK?"

"I can spend a few minutes, but then I have to meet my grandmother at her job."

As they entered a busy hallway adjacent to the cafeteria, Coach Wilkes said, "We'll make it work."

* * *

As school dismissed and the last students left the home maintenance classroom, Coach Mo continued his earlier discussion with Russell.

"Russell, you said you might not be living here that long. I guess I'm sorta confused by that. I just thought you moved down here to live permanently with your grandmother."

Growing uncomfortable, Russell paused giving his answer careful thought. "I've got some family problems back in Illinois, and neither one of my parents can take care of me right now. Living with my grandmother for now seemed like the best plan."

Coach Mo considered Russell's answer then apologized. "Son, I was out of line there. I had no right to probe like that. I'm sorry. Really none of my business."

"It's OK, Mr. Wilkes. I don't mind."

Coach Mo gave a winning smile. "You mean, Coach Mo."

"Coach Mo," Russell said with a shy grin.

"Russell, I hope this doesn't sound like I'm rushin' anything, even though I probably am, but I'd like to throw the ball around with you and some other players after school, see what you got, see that puntin' game of yours up front. Would you be OK with that?"

"Sure, when do you want to do it?"

"How does tomorrow after school sound, around 3:20 or so? You can change clothes in the boys' locker room, which should still be open. Be sure to wear a heavy sweatshirt as it's supposed to turn cold tomorrow. I might have a few boys join us. Meet me in the gym down the hall here, and we'll go from there, thirty minutes or so, forty-five tops, maybe, dependin' on the weather."

"I'll need to check with my grandmother, but I should be able to make it work. I may need some sweats, though."

"No problem. I'll take care of that. Oh, one more thing, what size shoe do you wear?"

"Eleven, eleven and a half."

"OK, I'll have a few pairs for you to try on."

Extending his hand in gratitude, Coach Mo said, "I'm glad we had our talk, son. Welcome to Pratt County High School."

11

MARCH 4, 1982

————

RUSSELL'S first week in Pratt County was a blur of new faces and new places. Overall, he was pleased with his adjustment to his new high school. The response of the students to his presence had been mixed. There was no marked hostility shown, just a mainly wait-and-see attitude. The girls seemed friendlier than boys.

Coach Mo had encouraged some football players to welcome Russell on their own. Upper classman Jonathan Hunt had taken the lead approached Russell at his locker prior to homeroom on his second day. Jonathan appeared formal yet genuine with his introduction. Several other football players greeted Russell after that; however, these half dozen seemed more obligated to Coach Mo than self-motivated.

As suggested, Coach Mo held a workout Thursday after school on the practice field adjacent to the varsity football stadium. The afternoon was cold and blustery, which cut short Coach Mo's unofficial practice. Five players assisted including Jonathan Hunt, fellow juniors Clinton Emory, Stan Pitts, Neal Reynard, and sophomores Wade Hunter and Jonny Hopkins.

After a short and hurried attempt at calisthenics on a field dampened by a late-morning shower, Coach Mo and Jonathan Hunt conducted a limited passing drill. Short passes were thrown to Russell and the remaining players as they ran designated routes. From this limited exposure, it was clear that

Russell was a tight end prospect because of his size, large hands, and pass-catching abilities.

During the passing drill, Russell caught everything thrown to him including one intentionally errant pass tossed by Coach Mo. Russell's overall speed was also a pleasant surprise. The question that remained was whether Russell could block. Coach Mo conjectured that he could. But, he wanted to see the boy punt as much as anything.

As the clouds darkened and a mild rain began to fall, the workout shifted to defensive agility skills in which Russell outperformed all others within the group. Coach Mo instinctively knew the difference between natural ability and forced performance, and as the drills progressed, Russell's athleticism quickly surfaced. Coach Mo shook his head and softly whispered to himself, "Nice feet, nice, nice feet."

With the weather continuing to worsen, Coach Mo grabbed a canvas ball bag and asked for volunteers to field punts from Russell.

"Russell, I know the weather is not the best, but let's see what you can do, just the same; let's at least get a few kicks in. I'll do the snaps."

Russell's first few attempts were disappointing, and despite observing several sub-standard punts, Coach Mo witnessed form that displayed good potential. After Russell badly shanked his fifth kick, Coach Mo responded, "I know the weather isn't helping, but…."

Russell interrupted, "It's the shoes."

"They don't fit?"

"It's the shoes."

Coach Mo looked puzzled as Russell shook his head. "The shoes? What am I not understandin' here, son?"

"I don't wear football shoes when I kick. I wear soccer shoes."

Coach Mo walked closer to Russell. Wincing his brow in marked confusion, he asked, "Soccer shoes? Really?"

"Yes, sir."

Readjusting his baseball cap as if to improve his understanding, Coach Mo said, "Let me get this straight, soccer shoes? Right? Why soccer shoes, son?"

"They have a smoother surface. I get better contact."

To the mild amusement of the students, Coach Mo scratched his head and responded, "This is a new one for me, Russell. Smoother surface?"

Russell eventually broke seconds of silence by taking off his right shoe. "Maybe this will help. Snap me some more."

"You're going to punt without a shoe, just a sock?"

"Coach, just snap me some more."

Shaking his head, Coach Mo returned to his hiking stance and, on cue, threw Russell a crisp ball. Russell responded by launching his first true spiral, causing punt returner, Wade Hunter, to back pedal and badly misjudge the kick. The punt left Russell's right foot with a resounding, deep thump, as if shot from a cannon.

"Much better, *much* better," Coach Mo said with a big smile. "Boys, you hear that thump? When you hear that thump, then you've got somethin'. Let's try a few more, then we'll get out of here."

Redirecting his attention, Coach Mo bellowed, "Hey, Hunter, you're not winnin' any awards back there. Let's try to actually get in the vicinity and catch the ball next time, OK? That's what punt returners do, you know?"

Subsequent punts continued to improve in overall distance and form while interested players, a delighted head football coach, and a frustrated sophomore punt returner looked on. Russell's final kick, set against darkening, purple clouds, was a monster pure spiral that pierced through rain and swirling wind.

Coach Mo estimated Russell's final punt to have carried fifty-five to sixty yards on the fly in the worst of conditions, well carrying over Wade Hunter's range.

In less than thirty minutes, Russell had established credibility with the head football coach and potential teammates. Coach Mo had seen enough, well more than he had anticipated. He thanked all boys for their participation and directed them to return to the locker room.

As the rain continued, Coach Mo offered consolation to Wade Hunter. "Hey, Hunter, don't feel bad about trying to field those punts. That was like *Mission Impossible* out there. If we ever have conditions like that in a game and you're our punt returner, you don't try to catch anything, hear? Just get out of the way, keep your distance and let the ball land and roll, land and roll. Understand?"

"I get it, Coach. Never seen anyone kick like that in high school. That new boy's got some foot."

"No argument from me," Coach Mo replied.

In a welcoming gesture, Wade Hunter introduced himself to Russell on the short jog to the locker room. As they left the practice field, they passed a small padlocked cinderblock storage shed at the end of the field, which housed blocking dummies and other assorted football gear.

With a chuckle, Hunter motioned over his shoulder toward the shack. "That's a place where you need to be careful. Rumor has it that Coach Mo found a three-foot copperhead in there last year resting up in a rafter. There's kids on the team that won't go near that place."

As Russell changed to street clothes, Coach Mo tossed him a dry pair of athletic socks while he sat on a locker room bench. Intentionally playing down his enthusiasm, Coach Mo concluded, "Russell, thanks for your time this afternoon. Pretty ugly out there. Son, you certainly have a place on this football team should you be around next fall. You sure could help us."

"Yes, sir. Hey, Coach, is it true about you finding a snake in that storage shed?"

"Hunter got to you, didn't he?"

In leaving the locker room, Russell smiled and said, "Thanks, Coach, for the practice."

Before Russell was off school property, Coach Mo was on the phone to Brad Terrell back in Lancaster. This conversation would last half an hour, proving more deliberate and focused than the initial contact. The conversation confirmed everything that Coach Mo had witnessed on the practice field.

Coach Mo had definitely found himself a football player. *Damn*, thought the coach, had he ever.

1 2

MARCH 6, 1982
PRATT COUNTY, NC
EMERSON COUNTY, NC

———

RUSSELL awakened Saturday morning sensing his grandmother was already up and readying herself for the day. To his surprise, he had slept well his first three nights in his new home, so much better than the restless nights in juvenile detention where he'd done enough worrying to last a lifetime.

His mind had barely kept pace since Monday with the sweeping changes thrown at him. Despite all of the challenges, he remained preoccupied with concerns for his ailing father and absent mother.

His father's health was worse than he had imagined. His mother's abrupt disappearance was even more unsettling. To Russell, no words of consolation were effective in softening Loretta's callous decision to abandon her two children.

Equally haunting was Loretta's status in the world. Where was she? What was her intended destination? How would she support herself? Was she safe? Was she still with Dominic?

In short fashion, Russell had grown trusting and comfortable with Grandma Esther and Aunt Helen as genuine and concerned family. Nonetheless, he wondered how long his stay with Grandma would last. If and when would one of his parents be able to care for him and his sister? And where did Rachel fit into the equation?

A polite tap on his bedroom door softly broke Russell's thoughts. "Grandson, are you awake in there?"

"Yes, ma'am. I'm awake."

"Good. I thought you were probably stirrin' at least. We've got a fair amount we need to do today so we best get started. May I come in?"

"Sure."

Esther entered Russell's bedroom dressed in more relaxed attire, a burgundy turtleneck and jeans.

Russell was taken aback. "Grandma, who helped you with your hair?"

Almost blushing and clearly flattered, Esther answered, "No one helped me. I did it myself, been braidin' my hair all my whole life. Now, how soon do you think you can be ready, you know showered and dressed and everythin'?

"Twenty minutes."

"Good, we're goin' to eat at Grandpa Lester's favorite place for break-fast—McBride's. It's on the way."

"How'd you sleep last night?"

"Like a rock. I think it was the storm last night 'cause I love thunder-storms. They don't bother me at all, almost like they do the opposite. I might wake up, but then I go right back to sleep."

"You ever sleep in a house with a metal roof before?"

"No ma'am."

"I'll bet that's part of it. When it used to rain like it did last night, your grandpa used to call it 'a liquid lullaby'. It had the same effect on him."

By 8:15, Esther and Russell were en route to McBride's. With little traffic to complicate the drive, they passed through the section of Pratt County known as the Orchards Region, home to almost a dozen fami-ly-owned and -operated apple orchards. Esther proudly gave a narrative of the area as if serving as a professional tour guide.

"Grandma, can I ask you a question?"

"Sure enough."

"When I learned that I might be comin' to live here, I did some readin' in an encyclopedia about North Carolina. It said that there were bears up in the mountains."

"They're around but usually in the more remote regions of the county, away from people. I've probably only seen a dozen or so black bears around here my whole life. Your grandpa once saw one on our road, but that was years and years ago. They're nothing to fret about. You're goin' to see deer, some wild turkey, an occasional fox, but no, don't worry yourself about any bears."

Esther switched subjects. "All this talk reminds me that I need you to clean out the birdhouses over the weekend. It's gettin' close to spring. Uncle Andrew will need to help you since he knows where there'll are located. We need your help 'cause he's supposed to stay off ladders because of some recent dizzy spells. Your grandpa built 'em all … they're all handsome and unique."

"Sure thing."

Taking advantage of a convenient parking space, grandmother and grandson were soon seated for breakfast. McBride's was a family restaurant serving breakfast, lunch, and dinner six days a week. The restaurant was already near capacity. Esther acknowledged two waitresses; however, the teenage girl waiting their window table was new. The young waitress seemed instantly interested in Russell, making no attempt to hide the attraction.

After both being served cups of coffee, they placed their orders. During the wait, Esther prompted Russell to share comparisons between his old and new homes. Russell proved more relaxed and talkative than was his pattern on the drive from Illinois, and he was full of observations.

The twosome ate quickly upon being served. Esther washed down her "Rise and Shine" selection with another cup of coffee. Russell devoured his "Hungryman's Skillet."

As Esther paid the bill at the cash register, Russell observed business cards and flyers posted on a bulletin board in the restaurant's foyer. Some of the events posted included a spring car wash, a library bake sale, the upcoming schedule for the Colby and Southern Railroad, a church rummage sale, the summer racing schedule for the Emerson County Speedway, and a listing of Easter services offered by area churches.

Back in the car, Esther said, "Grandson, you sure woofed down that breakfast."

"Yes, ma'am. Sure was tasty."

"As I said before, your Grandpa Lester loved McBride's." Esther smiled and nodded. "Seems like you two might have a lot in common."

Esther and Russell's Saturday morning sojourn took them south to adjacent Emerson County, which sported terrain more hilly than mountainous.

"Russell, this is Emerson County, and it has Sexton, the county seat and the biggest town 'round these parts, where we're doin' your clothes shoppin'. We're on the outskirts already. Sexton has a Thirlby's Department Store; they'll have what you need."

Russell was used to major Midwest department stores located in Lancaster's Prairie Center Mall. Thirlby's appeared as something frozen in time from the forties or fifties, a stand-alone store in a declining, forgettable neighborhood that resembled a more industrial setting than commercial.

Esther wasted no time in ushering Russell into Thirlby's. Referencing a list torn from a small spiral notebook, $170 worth of clothing was bought within thirty minutes.

Russell was pleased with the purchases and impressed by his grandmother's bargain-shopping ability as she took advantage of a major spring sale on young men's clothing. He was especially grateful for new athletic shoes bought to replace his tattered, tight-fitting Nike's.

After covering the sale by check, Esther began the return trip to Pratt County. However, on this occasion, she took an alternate route. She headed for Rex, Pratt County's second-largest municipality. On a winding and lightly traveled highway, Esther and Russell journeyed through rolling countryside interspersed by woodlands and fields intended for forage crops and beef cattle.

"Grandma, where're we goin'?" Russell asked.

"I thought it would be helpful for you to see where your Aunt Helen and Uncle George live. Do you remember him at all? Your Uncle George?"

"I don't think so."

"Well, they live on Roy Street in Rex with their two girls, Charlotte and Grace. Helen works out of the main library in Colby and the southern branch that is in Rex. She lives so close to the Rex Library that she can walk to work if she has the mind to. Your Uncle George sells insurance."

Esther drove through the town, giving Russell a five-minute tour. Finally, she came to Helen and George's red brick ranch home resting on a raised lot.

She then retraced her tracks and drove west to a small village known as Osgood where she followed the sign to Aldan Meadow State Park.

"Pratt County's got two state parks, Aldan Meadow and Mt. Wilcox up north, that's the mountain you can see from downtown Colby. I'm kind of partial to this one because it was a favorite place for your grandfather and me."

Russell noticed that visiting Aldan Meadow emotionally roused Esther. Her voice softened and sometimes quivered as she told stories about picnics and quiet walks with Lester near a gentle waterfall area known as the Cascades.

"I'm sorry, Grandson. I didn't think I'd get so emotional passin' through here, but it's been a while since I visited." She lightly dabbed her eyes with a crumpled tissue. "Mercy. This place sure brings back a lot of wonderful memories."

"I understand, Grandma. I'm glad you showed it to me."

"You know, Russell, we hardly know each other, but you seem older and wiser than most fifteen-year-olds."

Russell smiled shyly. "You're starting to sound like Momma. She used to say I was born old, my daddy too."

Having completed a short loop through Aldan Meadow, they headed north to downtown Colby.

"I'd hoped to get you to Kelso's last Wednesday," Esther said, "but we just didn't get to it. We'll take care of that now, then you can take it easy the rest of the day. Maybe you and Uncle Andrew can get to cleanin' those birdhouses."

Kelso's Barber Shop was a local institution based in downtown Colby within close vicinity of the county courthouse. When Esther and Russell arrived, proprietor Kelso Whitaker, tall and thin with meticulously styled milk-white hair, was winding down a busy Saturday morning, finishing up a haircut for a customer Esther did not know.

Without skipping a moment's attention to his customer, Kelso smiled and motioned for Esther and Russell to take a seat in the vacant seating area.

"Esther, what-cha know? I'll be with you right quick, just finishin' up with Mr. Gicking."

On the drive to Colby, Esther had briefed Russell about Kelso, one of Colby's better-known citizens, and his shop, which had been at this same location for thirty-seven years.

Russell was struck by Kelso's overall appearance and alert affect. A World War I army veteran, he was eighty-four years old and still barbering, with no plans of retiring. Kelso more resembled a man in his early seventies than a man born in 1898. A widower of twelve years, he remained an active member of Esther's church.

Kelso's shop was representative of the era. The shop was dated with worn seating and out-of-date, dog-eared hunting, fishing, and sports magazines littering a small wooden coffee table.

A dusty and ignored portable television sat in the waiting room corner away from the entry door. Stale tobacco aroma hung in the air.

After cashing out his customer, Kelso turned and warmly greeted Esther, "Always a pleasure seein' you, Esther." Turning his attention to Russell, Kelso said, "So, this must be the grandson." The out-of-nowhere comment caught Russell off guard.

Esther interjected, "Some church folks knew of your likely movin' down here. Kelso was one of them."

Kelso gave Russell a strong, welcoming handshake. "Pleased to make your acquaintance, Russell. Did I get that name right, Russell?"

"Yes, sir. Nice meeting you."

Kelso escorted Russell to one of the shop's two barber chairs, recognizing that Russell was "home barbered" as he called it. Responding to suggestions elicited from Esther and Russell, Kelso quickly went to work on Russell's overgrown mane. Using a combination of electric clippers and scissors, this was Kelso's biggest challenge of the day. The finished product pleased both grandmother and grandson.

Upon leaving Kelso's, Esther drove to the Colby Village Market, the town's only major grocery store, managed by Russell's Uncle Daniel.

"Your Uncle Daniel is workin' the store in Broadwater today. He actually manages two stores, this one in Colby and the other one north of here in Broadwater. You can learn more about your job tomorrow at Sunday dinner."

It was early afternoon by the time Esther's car came to its final rest for the day under the carport. As they gathered up the shopping bags of clothing, Russell said, "Grandma, I didn't thank you proper back at the store. Thank you for everythin' today—breakfast, all these clothes, Kelso's."

Esther smiled, squeezed Russell's arm, and answered, "You are more than welcome, Grandson, my total pleasure."

Esther was tired from the day's activities, and after sharing tuna salad sandwiches with Russell, Esther retired upstairs for an afternoon nap.

Russell retreated to his room after letting Maddie and Gus outdoors. He pulled the shades to darken the room and lay down to rest but not to sleep.

Both Rachel and Daddy came to mind, and Russell realized he needed to call them both to catch up on their situations. Most of all, he needed to ask Rachel and his maternal grandmother about Loretta's status.

* * *

After washing and drying the dinner dishes, Russell sat with Esther at the kitchen table.

"Grandma, I need to ask you something."

"What is it?" She recognized the earnest nature of the question to come.

"I need to make some phone calls to Grandmother Packer and to Daddy. I need to know if there's anything new about Momma and how Rachel's doin'. I need to check in with Daddy, too. I'd like to call tonight, if that's OK?"

"Grandson, if you had not brought it up today, I planned on suggestin' you do just that. It's not too late if you want to call tonight. I've got your father's number. What about Grandmother Packer?"

"I have her number in my wallet."

"Well, let's get started."

With assistance from Esther, Russell was soon talking to Grandmother Packer long-distance. While it was reassuring to hear a familiar voice, the message was sad and disappointing.

"Russell, I wish I had better news to share. We've heard nothing so far from your mother, absolutely nothing. I'm just so angry with her. This is not like her. I just can't believe this is happening."

Grandmother Packer shifted direction. "You sure have been through it. When I spoke with that probation lady from Lancaster, there was just no way to say yes to your living here because of the fire. I hope you understand. Things are so cramped here right now that Rachel's actually sleeping on the sofa in the living room. It's just not good here. Everyone feels so bad for you, but I always thought your father came from good people from the way he talked about his upbringing. So, how are you doin'?

Russell was gallant in response, although Grandmother Packer sensed reserved answers. "I'm doin' OK. Things are workin' out so far."

In order to divert attention away from himself, he asked to speak to Rachel, who he could hear clamoring to talk in the background.

When connected, Rachel was sobbing. "I miss you so much, Russell. It's so unfair that I couldn't see you before you left. How long do you have to live down there? When can you come visit me and Grandma? When can you come back up here, when?"

"Rach, Rach, slow down, just slow down. It doesn't work like that. I'm doin' good, really. How are you doin'?"

Gaining some composure, Rachel answered, "I'm all right. If I had to be anywhere other than with Momma, this is where I should be. It's just so cramped because of the fire."

"What are you doin' about school?"

"Nothin' for now. We're just sittin' and waitin' for Momma to show up. I just hope she didn't marry that creep."

"Momma hasn't called or written?"

"Nothing, just nothing. I can't believe it. This is all Dominic's doin'. You know that."

"Rach, I can't talk much longer because I still got to give Grandma Packer my phone number down here. Stay strong, Rach. Things are goin' to get better for us once Momma returns."

"I'm glad you called," she said as the sobbing returned. "I love you, Russell. I miss you so much. I love you, big brother."

"I love you too, Rach. We'll talk longer once I'm more settled in. You'll always be my favorite sister."

They both laughed. Russell had often shared this response when Rachel was troubled or down.

When Grandmother Packer returned to the line, Russell shared Esther's phone number, knowing future phone calls from Illinois would be unlikely due to the family's financial worries. Regardless, Russell closed the call with a dramatic plea, "Grandma, if you hear anything at all from Momma, you call me right away. Please, right away. Do that for me." Upon acknowledgement of Russell's request, Grandmother Packer ended the brief phone call.

The news from Chicago was disheartening to Russell. The longer Loretta remained missing, the more anxious and hopeless Russell became.

Loretta's latest caper was a stretch even to Russell's and Rachel's exposure to their mother's erratic behavior. Loretta's recent actions as a mother were reckless, irresponsible, and startling cold. This was child abandonment, with the act serving as a harsh and crushing blow to both children.

Russell decided to phone his father the following day. For now, the discouraging update from Chicago needed time for processing.

"So, how'd it go, Grandson? You look troubled."

Having been completely oblivious to Esther's return from the second floor, Russell sat up and straightened himself at the kitchen table.

Russell stared at the floor. He answered as Esther took a seat. "Not good. Still no word from Momma."

Esther leaned forward for emphasis. She cupped Russell's hands with hers. "Russell, I never knew your Momma well so it's real hard for me to judge all that's happened up there." After a meaningful pause, she continued. "I do know this. You have a warm bed, a roof over your head, home cookin', and someone who loves and cares for you. You're as much a grandchild to me as all the others. Always remember that.

"Grandson, you're at a real critical time right now. I know you're hurtin'. Mercy. Who wouldn't be with the news you're dealin' with?" A short silence followed.

Esther rose from the table and moved to stand next to Russell's chair. She tenderly put her arm around his neck and shoulder.

"This house has been cold and empty since your grandfather died three years ago. Just by your presence, you've warmed it up. I thank you for that. I know I'm being selfish when I say this to you, but you give me pleasure just from your bein' here."

Russell rose to hug his grandmother in gratitude.

Breaking the embrace, Esther said "You've got a big day tomorrow with church and then Sunday dinner, a lot of new faces. Service is at ten, but we'll leave here around nine, as I need to practice some music. You'll be sitting with Aunt Helen and Uncle George and your cousins during the service. You can stay up and watch TV, but for me, Grandson, I'm headin' up to bed."

She softly kissed his cheek in parting, "We'll get through this together with God's help. Remember, you're never truly alone, never."

As Esther climbed the stairs to the second floor, she summoned Maddie to join her. The portly beagle obliged and trudged up the stairway to take her reserved space at the foot of Esther's bed.

Despite her tiredness, Esther ended the day reading a fuller volume of familiar scripture than usual.

13

MARCH 7, 1982
COLBY, NC

———

RUSSELL was not surprised when he slept poorly that Saturday night. He was unable to set aside the troubling news from Chicago. Loretta had thrown a number of curves at her children, but this was easily her most drastic act. The potential permanence of his mother's behavior dominated Russell's mind as he lay in his bedroom. Never had he felt so alone and lost.

The update from Illinois reopened wounds from his three-week stay in juvenile detention including his last contact with his mother, that brief, awkward visit where Loretta appeared distracted and disconnected. It now dawned on him that perhaps his mother, during that final visit, knew full well of her intention to renege on her maternal role at this crucial point in Russell's life.

Loneliness consumed Russell, and despite his comfortable physical surroundings, he felt a prisoner in his new bedroom. He also felt unbridled hatred toward Dominic for the man's sinister manipulation of his mother and despicable role in orchestrating the abandonment. However, it was Loretta, who had committed the unthinkable and regardless of any history to follow, an unmovable wedge was now staked between son and mother.

The illuminated electronic alarm clock read 6:27 a.m. He recalled that Grandma wanted to leave for church by nine. Not wishing to disappoint,

Russell rose from bed, quickly showered, and dressed for church in clothes that were an upgrade from what he had worn to school.

A cause for anxiety this morning was Russell's complete unfamiliarity with church protocol. His parents had not been churchgoers or active with any religious faith during his upbringing. Loretta's childhood involved limited exposure to a small urban Baptist church. Russell knew that his father had been raised Methodist in North Carolina, but Peter held no interest in formal religion, an indifference passed along to his two children.

Russell's only exposure to church was Loretta's attendance with her small children to a pair of Christmas Eve services at a Lutheran church in one of their former neighborhoods. In reality, all Russell knew of organized religion in America was what he'd gleaned from television.

After making his bed, Russell joined Esther in the kitchen, taking a seat at the venerable kitchen table

"Well, Grandson, you look mighty handsome this morning. That haircut sure did the trick. That's a good outfit that you chose for church. Good for you. How'd you sleep?" an upbeat Esther asked.

"Not so good," Russell, said, denying eye contact.

"That's understandable in light of the news you got last night. But there's some things that just can't be fixed, at least not right away. That's why patience is so important, but I know that's not very helpful to hear right now."

Esther redirected her attention to serving Russell his breakfast. He soon received a plate of scrambled eggs, fried potatoes, and patty sausage.

She paused behind Russell's chair and lightly placed reassuring hands on his shoulders.

"You may think you're alone in all of this, but you're not. What's important is that you stay busy. School, church, and work at the market are going to help. I know this is hard. Lord knows how much I've traded shoes with you and prayed on it. You're a smart, sensitive young man, and you're going to get through this. "Things are going to get better and more familiar, just you watch."

* * *

As Esther pulled into the church's parking lot, she announced, "I keep forgettin' to tell you this, but your first probation meeting is scheduled for Friday afternoon at home. And your appointment with Dr. Bower is set for tomorrow after school." Russell nodded acceptance.

Colby United Methodist Church was a traditional red brick building having a raised concrete entrance, white trim, eleven handsome stained glass windows, and a modest, unassuming white steeple.

As Esther parked the car, she explained, "The church has a lot of ground." Motioning with her right hand, Esther continued, "There's a cemetery about a quarter mile down yonder. That's where your grandfather is buried."

Besides the sanctuary and cemetery, the long, rectangular property included a children's playground, a small picnic area complete with grill and shelter, a softball field, and a long-standing open structure with a wooden floor that was previously used for revivals and outdoor prayer meetings.

Esther and Russell entered the church through a side door and were soon outside a basement office. The placard on the door read Rev. Philip Dancy. Esther knocked softly on a partially opened office door, at which time, she was encouraged to enter. A thin, bespectacled man, who looked older than his thirty-two years, rose to greet them.

"Good morning, Esther. This must be Russell."

"Yes, Preacher, this is my grandson."

Extending his hand in greeting, Rev. Dancy said, "Russell, what a pleasure it is to meet you, son. Welcome to North Carolina, this church, and our community, our little spot on the map."

"Thank you, sir."

"What's it been so far, Esther, just a few days now?"

"Yes. Russell started school this past Wednesday."

"Well, that's a good thing, son. I know for a fact that you're in the best of hands here with your grandmother. She is as good and kind a person as there is in this whole county. I understand how upside-down and strange everything is for you being away from your family up north and all. Every day will be a little bit better, a little bit more comfortable, but thank God for your grandmother."

Unusual to his nature, Russell only nodded recognition of Rev. Dancy's words as he nervously stared down at the new brown shoes that were cramping his feet. Rev. Dancy held a short prayer with them, further ramping Russell's anxiety level.

"Well, Preacher, we'll let you be. Reverend Dancy likes time to himself prior to service to prepare, and I need to practice some music, so we'll be on our way."

The reverend rested a hand on Russell's shoulder. "Russell, welcome once again, son, to Colby and our community of faith. I look forward to getting to know you."

Reestablishing eye contact, Russell smiled and quietly thanked Rev. Dancy for his time.

Esther and Russell climbed a short flight of stairs and then entered the sanctuary.

Not being familiar with church interiors, Russell was struck by the church's simplicity; for some reason, it was not what he had expected. Esther took her position at the piano.

"Russell, come sit with me as I practice until your Aunt Helen and Uncle George join us with your cousins." Straightening the sheet music, Esther continued, "Two of the three hymns I could play in my sleep, but this one here I'm not so familiar with."

Having joined Esther on the piano bench, Russell confessed, "Grandma, you need to know somethin'."

Esther dropped her hands to her lap, giving her grandson full attention. "Russell, what do you need to tell me?"

Almost whispering, he said, "I've never been to church before."

Surprised, Esther leaned toward Russell, "You've never been to church before—really?"

"Never, not like this. Momma took me and Rachel to a church at Christmas time, when we were little. That's all."

"Mercy. I had no idea. I'm sorry. I just assumed wrong."

In stride, Esther dismissed the news. "Well, nothing to worry about. This is a small church, but it has a big heart. Just follow what your Aunt Helen and Uncle George do as far as sittin', standin', and singin'. Are you all right with Reverend Dancy welcomin' you to the service? He usually asks if there are any visitors. When he announces your presence, all you need to do is stand, turn to the congregation, smile and wave. You OK with that?"

"Sure. I'm just worried that I'm going to mess up and embarrass everyone."

With confidence, Esther noted, "No one's gonna mess up."

At that moment, two wooden doors opened to the sanctuary. Aunt Helen, Uncle George, and Russell's younger cousins, Charlotte and Grace, approached the altar. Esther and Russell left the stage. Aunt Helen greeted them, and after introductions were made, Russell remembered his Uncle George but not so much his younger cousins. The family took their seats in the third pew near the center aisle with Russell on the end.

During the drive from Illinois, Russell had developed a fondness for his aunt, and he now better understood his father's affection for his sister. Aunt Helen smiled and patted Russell on his knee. "Don't you look grand in your Sunday, church-goin' clothes, and Kelso sure did flattering work on your haircut."

Light chatter followed between Russell and Aunt Helen as the church began to fill. Aunt Helen inquired the most about school and was pleased to hear of Russell's sound adjustment to his classes and teachers.

By the time the service started, the church's one hundred and eighty seats were two-thirds full.

REV. Dancy followed a six-member choir into the sanctuary from a side entrance as Esther played the intro to the opening hymn, *Guide Me, O Thou Great Jehovah*. Self-conscious, Russell mouthed the words but did not sing.

Rev. Dancy presented the call to worship that was followed by a choir member singing a solo, *Jesus, Remember Me*.

The welcome greeting followed, and Russell was introduced to over a hundred fellow worshipers, who responded with warm applause.

General announcements followed including reference to a recent trailer explosion and fire in adjacent Wheeler County, which had hospitalized two young children.

Rev. Dancy conducted prayer followed by the Lord's Prayer. Collection was quickly coordinated.

A veteran churchgoer presented scripture.

Rev. Dancy's well-honed sermon was oddly entitled "The Lenten Roller Coaster."

O Day of Rest and Gladness served as the closing hymn prior to benediction.

As the congregation exited the church, additional church members lingered, making a point to welcome Russell, who now recognized two students from his school in the crowd.

Esther and Russell parted from Aunt Helen and her family in the church parking lot and headed home. Pulling under the carport, Esther said, "You need to call your daddy first thing after you change clothes."

In less than twenty minutes, father and son were on the phone.

"Daddy, this is Russell. Are you OK? You got me worried because Grandma told me this morning after church that you were taken to the hospital. What happened? Are you OK?"

"Whoa, slow down, son. Slow down. I'm all right. People here just overreacted and gave your grandma the wrong idea. I had a little flare-up with my liver, nothin' serious. Everything's under control. It was just a short trip to the emergency room, that's all. No ambulance or nothin'. I'm just tired, that's all. Enough about me. How are you doin'?"

"They still haven't heard from Momma."

Peter delayed his response. "I'm so sorry, son," Peter said with a mix of regret and disgust.

"This is such a mess with me laid up and unable to help, your mother runnin' off to who knows where. You and Rachel deserve better than this. I'd do anything to fix this thing if I could. But answer me—How are *you* doin'?"

With stoic pride, Russell said, "I'm OK, Daddy. Grandma has been great. We've hit if off real good. I've only attended three days of school so far, but that's goin' good too. Most of my teachers are good. I've even met the football coach and some of the players."

"I'm happy to hear that. You need to take some credit here, Russell." A lull in Peter's response took place. "None of this would have happened without, without your cooperation, you havin' the right attitude. None of it."

"Whaddya think of Colby?"

"It sure is different. Hey, Daddy, one of my teachers said she went to school with you, same class and everythin'."

"Who was that?"

"A Mrs. Jennings, but she said her name in high school was Celia Frost."

Peter's answer was again delayed. His speech was slower than normal. "Who would've figured that happenin'. My memory is so foggy anymore. I've been gone from there for so long that, that I can't place a lot of names with faces anymore. Maybe if I saw her picture I might remember her. Hold on, Russell … I need a sip of water."

Thirty seconds elapsed. "Daddy, are you all right?"

"I'm tired and sorta short on breath. I think it's the new meds. I'll be all right."

Shifting the conversation, Russell asked, "Hey, Daddy, my high school's the same as yours, right?"

"Sure is."

"Wow. They really do need a new high school."

Father and son shared a laugh.

"Son, can you hand the phone over to your grandma? I need to talk to her. Russell, you keep doin', you keep doin' what you're doin'. Proud of you, son. We'll lick this thing."

Upon Peter's request, the phone was given to Esther who talked with her eldest son for less than ten minutes. Upon hanging up, Esther was more concerned than ever about Peter's health.

After eating a light lunch of leftovers, Russell retreated to his room to complete weekend homework assignments while Esther tended to Sunday dinner preparations. With dinner plans under control, Esther withdrew to her bedroom for a brief nap, while Russell, having completed all assigned homework, watched college basketball on TV.

* * *

Russell was in awe of his grandmother's calm efficiency. In less than two hours, five adults and six grandchildren would invade her home for Sunday dinner, an established family tradition, which rotated on a weekly basis between Esther and her children and their families.

Helen had suggested starting the activity shortly upon her return from two years of graduate study in Boston. She had learned of the custom from a fellow grad student and her family.

The Sunday dinner model was simple. Every Sunday, Esther and her local offspring and their families met for 5:00 p.m. dinner, with the meeting site rotating among family members. The host was responsible for the main meal, which was generally a meat or poultry dish, although there were exceptions such as chili, venison stew, and lasagna. Whoever was not responsible for the main meal brought a side dish or dessert. Most times, Esther prepared additional dishes to enhance the menu.

A family member could also bring an announced guest, although that option was rarely practiced. Esther's younger sister, Libbie, was the frequent exception.

A well-defined protocol was in place for portioning leftovers and cleaning up while children resorted to indoor or outdoor play after the meal.

There was one exception to the schedule. Youngest sibling, thirty-four-year-old bachelor, Andrew, never hosted the event. His small home adjacent to his auto repair shop was viewed as a poor setting for entertaining. When Andrew's turn came around, Esther provided the site while Andrew covered the main meal.

For many reasons, Esther's house was the favorite gathering spot. It was the most comfortable, and it was Esther's children's only home. The size of the property also encouraged outdoor play during warm months for the grandchildren and occasionally adults before and after dinner. Fires in the stone fireplace were a staple in fall and winter, with Uncle Andrew responsible for supervising.

"The Homestead," as it was referred to by Rankin siblings, provided a welcome and reassuring haven, complete with decades of warm memories. The siblings had already decided the home was never to leave the family after Esther's passing; on that sensitive point, there was unanimous agreement.

Esther was a meticulous housekeeper, and she welcomed Russell's presence to assist her and Uncle Andrew in readying the house for Sunday dinner. Guided by Esther's clear direction, Russell and Andrew repositioned the dining room table, allowing two card tables to be set up at one end.

Due to tightness of quarters, dinner was served buffet-style. The main dish and hot side dishes were set on the kitchen table. Cold dishes, salads, and the main dessert were organized on the kitchen countertop. The main meal tonight was a large pork roast provided by Andrew and cooked by Esther.

Andrew was the first to arrive for Russell's inaugural Sunday dinner. Russell had remembered Andrew as overweight and unkempt, but on this occasion, he proved just the opposite. Russell was taken aback by the clean-shaven, well-groomed, thinner version of Uncle Andrew. He was further surprised by Andrew's exuberant greeting and bear hug embrace.

"How's my long-lost nephew?" he greeted.

Aunt Helen, Uncle George, Charlotte, and Grace arrived next, carrying side dishes of a mashed potato casserole and a homemade Lady Baltimore cake.

As mealtime approached, final preparations fell into place. With established precision, Esther directed preparations. Tablecloths were spread, and individual table settings arranged with an assortment of china, cutlery, and glassware.

Russell learned there was little pre-meal socializing since the focus, at least in Esther's household, was preparation. Socializing would occur during the meal and afterward as adult family members relocated to the living room, while the cousins occupied themselves with board games and other activities.

Arriving last, as was their custom, were Uncle Daniel, Aunt Janice, and their four children: Mitchell, Morgan, Benjamin, and Florence or Flossie, as she was known within the family. The warmth that Russell had felt from the rest of the family was clearly lacking as Uncle Daniel and Aunt Janice entered the home. The greetings toward Russell were staid and formal, seemingly void of any genuine concern or warmth. The couple's four children appeared mildly curious about reconnecting with a distant cousin, but they too kept their distance.

Russell sensed immediate tension between Aunt Janice and the other adults.

She looked disinterested to the point of boredom, avoiding any meaningful conversation. She was cold and distant, in sharp contrast to the other adults. Uncle Daniel was not as aloof but still reserved.

A little past 5:00 p.m., Esther said grace and the meal consisting of roast pork, gravy, fried cinnamon apples, mashed potato cheese casserole, coleslaw, tossed salad, green peas, and cornbread was eagerly consumed.

The conversation focused much on Russell's relocation and adjustment to life in North Carolina. Bits of family information were exchanged, especially pertaining to Esther's other grandchildren. The Whitlock children were appropriate at the meal; however, on several occasions, Morgan and Benjamin Rankin's behavior needed to be checked by their father.

After dinner, the regimented caring of leftovers and kitchen cleanup took place.

Aunt Helen's Lady Baltimore cake was the highlight of the evening. Russell was amazed that the cake was homemade. "Aunt Helen, this is so good, so good. You made it yourself?"

To his surprise, his comment drew much laughter from adults.

Uncle Daniel said, "Don't you know about your Aunt Helen? She's not just the county librarian. No, sir, son. She wins blue ribbons all the time at the North Carolina State Fair. She's met the governor and everythin'. You want anything baked, get with your Aunt Helen."

"Oh, hush up, Daniel. I learned everything I know about baking and cooking from Momma." It was Aunt Helen's signature custom to deflect credit.

Awkwardly upsetting the moment, Aunt Janice announced, "It's time for us to leave. The children do have their bedtimes."

As coats were gathered and gratitude expressed for the meal, Uncle Daniel took Russell aside and said, "I'd like you to start working at the market next Saturday, a full day startin' at eight. You OK with that?"

Somewhat taken aback, Russell answered, "Sure, sure thing."

Uncle Daniel smiled and nodded, tapping Russell on the shoulder. "I'll see you then." He quickly hugged and kissed Esther and Helen as he hurried out of the house to join his wife and children already seated in the family station wagon.

14

MARCH 12, 1982

———

NEAR the end of Russell's first full week in Pratt County, he was scheduled to meet his probation officer. He remembered Ms. Bohars explaining that a probation officer in North Carolina would supervise his case. Russell was more curious about the meeting with probation than nervous. The first meeting would occur Friday afternoon at home.

In scheduling the meeting, Esther learned that North Carolina did not use the term juvenile probation officer but instead used the job title of juvenile counselor in supervising a youth's probation. The job duties and responsibilities were identical, just different titles.

Gary Harris, Russell's supervising juvenile counselor, arrived a few minutes early, carrying a thin manila folder, a legal pad, and an appointment calendar.

Mr. Harris was a tall, three-year veteran of the North Carolina Division of Juvenile Services. Among his multiple duties, he supervised all transfer cases in and out of the county.

Upon arriving, Mr. Harris introduced himself and shook hands with Esther and Russell. To Esther's surprise, Mr. Harris arrived at the house wearing a tie and sport jacket. For some reason, she expected Russell's juvenile counselor to be dressed in a uniform. Counselor Harris had done his prep work and impressed Esther and Russell with his knowledge of the case and the cast of characters. The thirty-minute meeting was conducted in the living room.

Mr. Harris' initial goal was simply to become acquainted and establish expectations of supervision. He also appeared interested in the status of Russell's parents and sister.

"Russell, when cases are transferred from one department to the other, state to state, there's a lot of paperwork involved and sometimes the person on probation can get lost. I've talked with Ms. Bohars twice, plus I have all the documents from Lancaster County. But first, tell me what's happening with your mom and dad."

Russell dropped his head, delaying his answer. Regaining his composure, he reported, "No one knows where my mother is. No one's heard from her." He shrugged his shoulders. "She's just disappeared."

"And your dad?"

"He's still in rehab outside Lancaster."

Mr. Harris said, "Holcomb Valley?" again demonstrating his knowledge of the case.

"Yes, sir. That's it, Holcomb Valley."

"Does your dad have a discharge date?"

"I don't think so. He's got a lot of medical problems."

"Liver and heart troubles, maybe May or April for his discharge," added Esther.

"I ask these questions because, as I understand it, you're living down here temporarily. It looks like the court's intention is for you to return to Illinois once a parent is able to care for you and your sister. Do I have that correct?"

In unison, Esther and Russell both nodded.

"The situation is unusual and unfortunate for you both, but my job is to make certain that Russell follows the conditions of his court order and the rules of probation. Most of all, we don't need any additional contacts with police."

At this point, Counselor Harris reintroduced a copy of the probation order.

He requested that Russell and Esther review the order again. In an effort to eliminate any potential misunderstanding, he asked Russell to initial all individual conditions of his probation as listed on the order.

Next, he proceeded to give Russell a list of potential worksites for the completion of his community service work, explaining the protocol to schedule his hours. It would be up to Russell to select a site from the list that would work best for him.

Since this was Russell's initial exposure to probation, Harris discussed expectations.

"Russell, my goal is for you to successfully complete probation. I look at it this way. I view your success as my success. I get nothing out of your failing but disappointment and more paperwork. I want to assist you in every way possible, but you are the one who must live by the probation conditions set by the judge back home. Understand? You are the one who needs to make good decisions. Let me ask you a question. The conditions that we just went over...."

"Yes, sir."

"Do you think they're fair and reasonable?"

"Yes, sir."

"Mrs. Rankin, how about you? Do you think Russell can meet these conditions?"

"Yes, sir. I do."

"Good. I've found the key to success on probation being honest and clear communication, which goes both ways between the person on probation and the probation officer. I'll do my very best with that, and Russell, you need to do the same. I need to be aware of anything major happening at school, home, or out in the county. This is true, as well, of any key events back in Illinois involving your mother and father and any potential for you to move back there."

Readying to leave, Mr. Harris asked, "Do either one of you have any questions?"

Russell hesitated but then asked as he stared at the floor, "Is abandoning a child a crime?"

Esther was surprised by her grandson's boldness in raising the question.

"Yes, it's a criminal offense. The laws differ from state to state, but yes, it is considered a crime."

Russell nodded his head in response.

Mr. Harris followed up. "My sense is that you worried about how this might affect your mother. Am I right?"

Embarrassed, Russell responded, "Yes, sir."

"I know her absence is very troublesome for you and your family, but I am unfamiliar with child abandonment laws outside of North Carolina. I'll check with Ms. Bohars to see how those laws might apply in Illinois."

Russell remained silent as Esther offered her thanks. "Thank you for doing that, Mr. Harris."

"Here are some business cards with my phone number should you need to reach me. I'm usually in my office by 7:30 a.m., Monday thru Friday, except Tuesday evenings, which is a late night. We'll meet again next month. How does Tuesday evening sound on April 6th in Probation's basement office in the Courthouse? 6:30 sound OK?"

"That should work just fine," Esther said.

"Oh, by the way, I need to check Russell's sleeping arrangement before I go, department requirement."

After a cursory inspection of Russell's first-floor bedroom proved satisfactory, Harris provided summary.

"Russell, from what I can tell, you've made a very good adjustment so far. Keep doin' what you're doin'. Remember that condition about leaving the state and the need for judicial permission because if anything with your mom or dad creates a need for you to return to Illinois, we have to first go through some legal steps. If that's needed, I'll make it a priority to get permission as quickly as I can. This is very important. Leaving the state without the Court's permission will mess up everything, and place you in violation with the Court. Understand?"

"Yes, sir."

"Mrs. Rankin?"

"Yes, sir."

"My pleasure to meet you both. Thanks very much. Oh, wait, wait, wait … one more thing. I almost forgot. From the materials sent to our office, it looks like Russell needs some dental work done. Isn't that right?"

"Russell had his first dental appointment earlier this week with Dr. Bower.

He's got a couple more to go."

"That's excellent. Well, much obliged. See you next month."

Esther inquired. "Mr. Harris, I do have one final question before you go. I'm just curious. I can tell by your accent that you're not from around here. If I might ask, where's your home?"

"Don't mind at all. I get asked that question all the time. Gettysburg, Pennsylvania, ma'am."

"Then how did you get to North Carolina?"

"Baseball scholarship at Wake Forest."

15

MAY 9, 1982

———

SINCE 1947, the house at 415 Grouse Hollow Road, south of Colby, had served as Esther Rankin's home. With G.I. bill mortgage assistance, Lester and Esther purchased the three-bedroom, metal-roofed, white clapboard home, which became their one and only home during the couple's thirty-nine-year marriage. To accommodate the growing family, Lester expanded the home, with the help of friends, to add an additional bedroom and bath on the ground floor.

The original plat of land, at elevation of two thousand five hundred and ten feet consisted of twelve wooded acres. Mature hardwoods forested the property. Over the years, Lester enhanced the property through assorted projects including the construction of a small barn, a family garden, assorted wildflower stations, a berries plot, an unsuccessful honey bee station, and creation of a meandering, uneven path through dense forest from the house to the property's crown jewel, a rocky ridge known as The Point.

It was at The Point where Lester had fashioned a sitting area that included two hand-built Adirondack chairs. From this lofty vantage, one could view Grouse Hollow's half mile-wide depression six hundred feet below and nothing but Blue Ridge Mountains to the north and west. At this private site, Lester and Esther Rankin had pondered life's events and forged major decisions.

Today was very different. Today was only Esther's fourth visit to The Point since Lester's passing in 1979. The day was sunny and breezy for early April. With little urging, Maddie made the trip as well.

After cleaning off her designated chair with an old dishtowel, Esther settled in and took in the landscape before her as Maddie rested at her feet. Little had changed since Esther and Lester's initial visits to The Point. The peace and tranquility linked to the site remained intact.

Esther had come this evening to process her grandson's progress since moving to North Carolina. Reassurances received from relatives and school personnel matched her own impressions.

As Esther and Aunt Helen had quickly come to learn, Russell was no hardened delinquent. He was also not your typical teenager. Despite a rocky upbringing by self-absorbed parents, he had survived the void of responsible parenting.

The quality of Russell's adjustment confirmed Esther's impressions of her oldest grandchild. She saw him as an intelligent, respectful, mannerly, and mature young man, who was committed in making the transition to his new home a success. She also recognized Russell's shyness and limited confidence. It was soon evident to Esther that Russell was driven to take a path unlike any followed by his parents.

School adjustment had been exemplary. Russell was making A's in all subjects. His counselor, Mr. Cornelius, was mindful of his academic accomplishments and his relative ease in acclimating to new peers and teachers.

Having already completed his twenty hours of community service work at a rural fire station, Russell had earned positive reviews from fire station personnel. His meetings with Juvenile Counselor Harris proved supportive and reassuring as well.

Russell had opened a savings account with his earnings from the Colby County Market, where he worked Thursday evenings and all-day Saturday. In his capacity as store manager, Uncle Daniel provided transportation for Russell to and from the store.

Uncle Daniel had taken a photo of Russell proudly displaying his first paycheck in the amount of $60.90; that photo became a permanent fixture on Russell's bedroom mirror. Russell insisted on giving a portion of his paycheck to Esther to help cover his room and board, money that Esther deposited in turn in a separate savings account intended for her grandson.

Esther had begun to value Russell's potential help around the home and property. Since Lester's passing, she had leaned too heavily on Andrew for tending the garden, stacking firewood, and mowing the yard. With some instruction from Andrew, most of these assignments now fell to Russell.

Life for Esther had become dull and predictable since Lester's death. Her myriad commitments to the church and community had been met but without Esther's usual enthusiasm and satisfaction. Work at Hamilton Brothers had become less rewarding. She had even become less connected to her sister, Libbie, and trusted friends. Esther sought relief and direction in prayer; however, her loneliness remained ongoing.

The unlikeliest of developments had served as the catalyst for change. When Ingrid Bohars first phoned her, Esther had been hesitant to involve herself in Russell's life. However, before she knew it, she was knee-deep in the plan to provide a temporary home to a barely known, out-of-state grandson, recently adjudicated a delinquent minor in juvenile court.

While Russell's progress in North Carolina was encouraging, the news from Illinois was not. Over two months had passed since Loretta's disappearance, and from all indicators, her absence and rejection of any mothering role was no longer considered temporary.

Heaviest on the family was Peter's health. From ongoing phone calls, it was clear that Peter's health was continuing to decline. Russell had received one short, handwritten note from his father that was jumbled and repetitive in content, further exemplifying that his father's health, including his mental functioning, was worsening. Esther and Helen's letters had gone unanswered.

Since their visit to Holcomb Valley in early March, Peter had been taken to the emergency room on two occasions to return later that same day once his liver functioning had stabilized. In Russell's initiated phone calls, his father was now exhibiting shortness of breath.

Esther began to accept that Peter was not physically able to care for Russell or Rachel in the immediate or extended future. Holcomb Valley staff was already working with the VA and other resources to locate an extended care facility in the Lancaster area, since Peter was soon to be discharged from Holcomb Valley. This residential setting was needed to provide round-the-clock medical care.

Russell became quiet and aloof following the short phone chats with his father. Esther had taken the initiative to contact Juvenile Counselor Harris by phone to inform him of her son's declining health.

A growling Maddie, who had been abruptly annoyed by scent or sound, interrupted Esther's train of thought. Esther checked her watch and realized she should soon make her way back to the house. Prior to leaving, she offered a prayer for her son and grandson as they grappled with serious life issues. She also asked for strength and guidance in confronting the challenges that lay ahead. As always, her final act was a prayer to her beloved Lester.

That evening, Esther composed two handwritten letters at the kitchen table, one to Mr. Harris and the other to Miss Bohars. The content was identical. The letters read:

May 9, 1982

Mr. Harris/Ms. Bohars:

My son's health in Illinois continues to worsen, and it appears that he will be unable to care for Russell at any time in the future. Loretta Rankin's whereabouts remain unknown.

My Grandson has made a very good adjustment to my home, school, and the community. He has become a welcome and helpful addition to my home.

I want court officials in Illinois and North Carolina to know that I am willing to serve as legal guardian to care for Russell until he turns eighteen because neither his father or mother appear able to perform that duty at this time.

Thank you for your attention and ongoing help.

Sincerely,
Esther O. Rankin

16

MAY 16, 1982

———

A long-distance phone call interrupted Esther's preparation of a corn pudding casserole intended for Sunday dinner.

The sobering news came from Rita Birch, director of treatment, at Holcomb Valley. "Mrs. Rankin, I have some sad news for you. Peter died earlier today in his sleep. The suspected cause of death was cardiac arrest complicated by liver disease. I know I speak for all center staff in expressing our sincerest condolences. We are so very sorry for your loss."

Peter Wallace Rankin was thirty-nine years old.

The shocking news rocked Esther to her core. A chilling silence followed as she sobbed in soft restraint.

Gradually summoning up the strength and control to speak, Esther offered, "This is all so sudden, all so awful. I'm stunned. I really am. Oh, and to think how Russell's going to take all of this, and his sister. This is just too much for us right now."

"Mrs. Rankin, I understand this is hard for you to accept, and I apologize in advance for being so candid, but there is some reassuring news, to all of this.

Perplexed and troubled, Esther quietly asked, "What do you mean?"

"I don't know all the details, but Peter had some meetings with an attorney last month. The attorney's name is Karl Noble. He's a fine attorney and a good man. He's done legal work for several of our patients in the past. Peter met with him a few times 'to get his affairs in order' as Peter called it."

The importance of Peter's engaging an attorney was lost on Esther in light of the startling news of his passing.

"Mrs. Birch, I do remember you from when we visited Peter last month. You were so kind to us during our visit. Oh, my head is so scrambled right now with this news. You said he died earlier today, is that right?"

"That's right. We usually let the patients sleep as late as they like Sunday morning, but around ten this morning, Peter's roommate suspicioned something was wrong, and the on-duty counselor found Peter unresponsive in his bed. We called 9-1-1, and the county arrived shortly to confirm Peter's passing. They estimated time of death around seven this morning. Peter's body was taken to the county morgue where it remains pending direction from the family."

"Oh, this is so awful. I knew his health wasn't good, but not like this. I guess I just didn't figure how serious everything was. And to think my oldest boy died so young."

"Mrs. Rankin, Peter downplayed his health problems to a lot of people. He was especially careful with you folks because he didn't want you to worry. There is some comforting news to all of this because Peter told us just last week that he had drawn a will with Mr. Noble's help. Peter told me last week in my office that 'all's legal now' in regards to his estate."

After a short pause, Esther said, "Ms. Birch, I need to call my daughter and sister and pray on all of this. I am just overwhelmed at this point, speechless, just shaking my head, my oldest boy dead at thirty-nine? Whoever would have thought? Whoever would have thought?" She once again broke into soft sobs of anguish.

"Please understand that we share your loss. We really do. Peter made wonderful progress here. He really turned the corner. It took a while, but he finally conquered the disease. He was well-liked and respected. Many of our younger patients looked up to him sort of like an older brother, even as a father figure. His opinions, his advice really seemed to matter to them. You should also know that Peter had been talking to the post office about a return date to work until his health took such a turn."

"Mrs. Birch, before I go, could you please give me the phone numbers I'm goin' to need?"

In organized fashion, Mrs. Birch shared the phone numbers for the county coroner's office and Mr. Noble's office and home.

"Mrs. Rankin, I already spoke with Mr. Noble this morning. He'll be expecting your phone call later today or tomorrow. He said you should feel free to call him at his house number later today."

Prior to hanging up, Esther expressed her gratitude to Mrs. Birch and the facility staff for their kindness and expertise in treating Peter's chronic battle with alcohol and drugs.

Mindful of the clock and how events would play out on her grandson, Esther immediately called Helen to share the devastating news. Helen gasped, and cried, "Oh, no, Momma … no, no, no!" announcing through the tears that she would be at the house immediately. Daniel and Andrew were out of town and unavailable; they would learn the tragic news later in the day.

She also called her younger sister Libbie, to share the news. Libbie was equally stunned and offered to drive to Colby to support and console the family. Esther vetoed the plan when she learned that Libbie was due at work at 5:00 a.m. the following day.

In less than twenty minutes, Helen was at her mother's side to mourn their mutual loss. Sunday dinner, which had been scheduled at the Whitlock family home in Rex, was cancelled. The uncomfortable task of informing Russell of his father's death would fall to Esther and Helen.

Mother and daughter cried and hugged in Esther's living room as Esther recounted the news. Esther had lost her oldest son while her daughter had been robbed of her dearest brother. Guilt consumed them both as they confessed their shortcomings in maintaining family relations and their compliance in Peter's drifting from immediate family.

Russell was due home from an extra shift at the market by 4:30 or thereabouts. Mother and daughter quickly agreed that a call should be made to Mr. Noble's home phone prior to Russell's arrival. At Esther's insistence, Helen assumed the role.

Helen connected with Mr. Noble at his home. She was surprised to learn the vision and orderliness of Peter's affairs. Long recognized for his predictable pattern of irresponsible adult behavior, Helen was comforted to learn of an estate plan, which had been carefully devised by her brother.

Recognizing that he would likely rent a small apartment once discharged from Holcomb Valley, Peter had sold his much-burglarized trailer at a loss. His limited personal items had been donated to charity or temporarily stored at Holcomb Valley.

To the astonishment of Helen and Esther, Peter had purchased a life insurance policy in the amount of $100,000 through the post office. Despite Peter's chronic alcoholism, unstable marriage, and periodic leaves from active postal employment, this policy had remained current and intact for almost fifteen years, and it would cover funeral expenses and legal fees. Sole beneficiaries of the insurance policy were Russell and Rachel.

Another surprise was Peter's desire to be buried in North Carolina. The remains were to be airlifted from Illinois to Charlotte for transport to the E.R. Mifflin Funeral Home in Colby, arriving no later than Wednesday of the following week, thus pressing the family to schedule funeral plans. As it was a Sunday, Esther opted to take Monday off to schedule visitation and funeral arrangements with church and funeral home.

A coworker would be bringing Russell home from work. Hastily, Esther and Helen huddled at the kitchen table to prepare, agreeing to be succinct and direct. Esther agreed to take the lead.

As if on cue, Russell entered the house through the back door, and upon seeing the somber faces of his grandmother and aunt, he knew something was very wrong.

"It's Daddy, isn't it?"

Esther motioned for him to take a seat at the kitchen table. Tearing up, Esther reached out and joined hands with him, saying softly, "Your daddy died this morning in his sleep. I got the phone call from Holcomb Valley early this afternoon."

Russell gazed at the floor, motionless. Aunt Helen clasped his hands for support. Esther did the same.

Helen said, "Russell, this is a horrible blow to the whole family, but we know it hits you especially hard at a delicate time in your life. You don't deserve any of this, Russell, but as a family, we will meet it and get through it together."

Silence followed with Russell continuing to glare at the aged wooden floor. "Does Rachel know?" he asked after a minute.

"Not yet, Grandson. We've only known for a few hours ourselves. Darlin', we're so sorry for you. You just shouldn't have to be going through all of this at your age."

Russell did not cry but remained motionless and dazed while Esther disappeared for a few seconds. She fetched her worn Bible from its natural resting place on a living room end table.

The trio held hands for several minutes while Esther read comforting passages underscored by blue pencil, in her Bible, which she had referenced often after Lester's death. Both Esther and Helen offered tearful prayers. Russell appeared numb and disinterested in Esther's readings and the offered prayers.

He eventually inquired about the funeral, and like his grandmother and aunt, was surprised to learn about the funeral and burial being staged in North Carolina. To their complete bewilderment was Peter's desire to be interred in a reserved plot at the Colby Methodist Church cemetery.

"Rachel needs to fly down here for the funeral. I don't have enough money saved for her ticket, but she needs to be here. I'll need some help buying the ticket, but that's just the way it's got to be. I'll pay back what I can't pay for right now," Russell said.

"That's not a problem. We agree and understand. We'll take care of it tomorrow after we call her tonight," Esther said.

Russell then announced, "I need time to myself right now before we call Rachel," he said.

Esther and Helen nodded approval and embraced Russell before he retreated to his bedroom for an hour of solitude. As he approached the bedroom door, he began to sob in short, soft waves.

Russell insisted he be the one to break the news to Rachel. He made the call to Chicago shortly after 7:00 p.m. The call lasted fifty-three minutes.

17

MAY 19-20, 1982
COLBY, NC
CHARLOTTE, NC

———

UNCLE Andrew and Russell made the drive from Colby to Charlotte's Douglas airport in two hours. Andrew had a tendency to stretch the speed limit. This excursion proved no exception.

As Russell knew little of his youngest uncle on the Rankin side, Uncle Andrew volunteered a brief biography as his Chevrolet station wagon began its descent to the Piedmont.

"Like my brothers and sister, I was born in Colby at Pratt County General. Did all my schoolin' here and graduated from Pratt County High, class of 1966. Played some football, drank a lot of beer—don't tell your grandmother that. My junior year, I started workin' part-time at Uehler's Garage in Waverly. Your grandfather knew a lot about cars, especially engines, and he passed a lot of that knowledge on to me.

"I've always loved workin' on cars and trucks. Nothin' I'd rather do. I started my own shop ten years ago next to the laundromat, just behind the courthouse. Business got so good that I hired another mechanic six years ago. Couldn't hired a better man than Bud Harold. Likely that I may be hirin' a third mechanic part-time before year's out.

"Oh, yeah ... I've never been married. People say I'm too busy to get married; they're probably right.

"Say, your Aunt Helen says you're some football player. If you stick around long enough, maybe you can play for Pratt next fall."

Russell had already grown to like his Uncle Andrew seeing him as personable, practical, and reliable.

To Uncle Andrew's surprise, Russell continued to explore Rankin family history.

"Tell me about Grandpa Lester."

"What would ya like to know?" responded Uncle Andrew.

"Start at the beginnin', ya know."

"Well, he was born in Wheeler County, just three miles from the county line. He was the youngest of seven kids. Daddy was two years older than your grandma. His people was more mountain people, raised tobacco and corn, had some dairy cattle, pigs, chickens. Don't know exactly why, but they moved to Pratt County when daddy was about ten … mighta had somethin' to do with Grandpa Rankin takin' a job at the furniture company.

"Daddy graduated from Colby High School before the name was changed to Pratt County High. He was workin' as a mechanic at a highway department garage when he met your grandma. Met her when he was buyin' his first car at Colby Chevrolet where she worked."

Russell interjected, "But what was he like?" Andrew paused and collected his thoughts.

"What was he like? Oh, I see what you're getting' at. Well, daddy was a real hard worker, honest, and dependable. He could do most anything with his hands. He said he learned everythin' about construction during his Seabees days in the navy during World War II."

Russell was puzzled. "What's a Seabee?"

"They were construction units that played a big part in the South Pacific.

"Once an island was secured, the Seabees came in to build airstrips, roads, barracks, latrines, and the like. That's why he was so handy. Daddy did most of the improvements to the house himself, sometimes with help from friends.

"He had a strange practice of drinkin' a beer as soon as he came home from the post office. What was surprisin' was he hardly ever drank on the weekends. Maybe after some big project he might pop one, or at a barbecue or picnic, or maybe when playin' cards, but as a rule, he wasn't much for drinkin.'"

The conversation lagged. Andrew broke the silence. "We're about twenty minutes from the airport."

After parking in short-term parking, Andrew and Russell checked into the assigned Delta gate and soon learned that Rachel's flight was delayed due to inclement weather around Chicago. This was Rachel's first trip in an airplane, and while the need for her journey was sobering, she was excited about her initial flight.

As they waited, Russell thought about the hectic activity since his father's death. Grandma Esther and Aunt Helen had taken time off to coordinate the services that would be held Friday evening and Saturday morning. Adding much comfort to the family, attorney Karl Noble had been responsive and helpful about the settling of Peter's estate. What came as no surprise was Rachel's frenetic reaction to the news of her father's death. Russell knew, despite his age, how to approach and present the ugly news to his sister, but he also accepted that preparation and delivery would not matter. Rachel was caught off guard and was overwhelmed by the announcement. It took every ounce of Russell's patience in calming her over the phone to process the news of their father's sudden death.

She cried through the majority of the phone call, and her thought patterns turned nonsensical and destructive. Her initial response was to run away from Grandmother Packer and somehow join Russell in North Carolina; she even entertained a shallow thought of suicide. Rachel had been in denial of her father's medical condition; in the mind of a twelve-year-old girl, her father's declining health was temporary and no cause for alarm.

As Rachel began to accept the news, Russell suggested the need for her to attend the funeral services. The prospect became more intriguing to her once he told her she would need to fly to North Carolina at his expense.

Russell's thoughts were interrupted and shifted to Rachel's pending arrival at Gate 12. For the first time in almost three months, Russell and Rachel met as she was escorted to the gate's waiting area by a Delta flight attendant. The greeting was teary-eyed and long-lasting. Rachel stubbornly refused to end the embrace. After assuring their identity to the flight attendant, Russell introduced her to Uncle Andrew, who gave his niece a warm, welcoming hug.

Andrew was thrown off by the initial meeting. He barely remembered his niece, and for some reason, he was ill prepared for the physical non-resemblance between brother and sister. Unlike Russell, Rachel was chubby with a round, yet attractive face. Her hair was a dull brown medium length.

The trio departed for baggage claim, Rachel firmly grasping Russell's hand.

With Rachel's suitcase collected, they headed home to Colby. Andrew suggested a favorite fast-food stop on the way since Andrew and Russell had disregarded dinner on the drive down. As Rachel talked from the backseat about her circumstances in Chicago, the threesome consumed barbecue, hushpuppies, and soft drinks as Andrew drove the route home.

Fifteen minutes into the drive, Rachel's eyes began to well up. "I never knew Daddy was so sick. I still can't believe he's gone. Russell, what'd Daddy die from, a heart attack or somethin'? But he was so young, just not fair, just not fair," she mumbled between sobs.

Russell turned toward the back seat to better address his sister. "Rach, Daddy died in his sleep from a heart attack. He also had a bad liver."

Rachel grew quiet as Russell continued. "Grandma Esther and our Aunt Helen have been working on the funeral. You'll be with them tomorrow for most of the day while I'm at school. They'll give you an idea about what's scheduled for Friday and Saturday."

"Russell, have you ever been to a funeral? I haven't. I'm awful nervous about all of this. I don't know how it all works. All I know is what I've seen on TV."

"This is all new to me too."

Traffic started to slow on the interstate for a police traffic stop ahead. Uncle Andrew remained quiet, although riveted to the conversation between his nephew and niece.

Rachel changed the discussion. "Russell, do you like school down here?"

"It's OK. I have some good teachers. Most people have been real nice."

Rachel shifted topics. "I just think that any day now Momma will show up, and we'll move back to Lancaster 'cause that's our home. Do you think she's comin' back, Russell? Do you?"

"I don't know, Rach, but I wouldn't bet on it. What does Grandmother Packer say?"

"She's confused like everyone else. She's really, really pissed, real angry and embarrassed about how Momma's treated us."

Silence followed as Rachel's eventful day caught up with her.

As an exhausted Rachel slept soundly, Andrew lowered his voice and said, "You know I used to make this airport run a lot years ago. It was a nice easy way to make some extra cash away from the garage. I got jobs pretty much by word of mouth in Colby and as far south as Sexton. I had business cards printed up and everythin'. But as I got busier and busier at the garage, I had to give it up. Hey, when do you start taking driver's ed? Next fall?"

"I don't really know, but I don't turn sixteen until August."

"You pass that course and get your license, I'm going to have to work on getting you a car. We can go to some Saturday morning auctions if you'd like?"

"I need to save some money first. I'd have to work out somethin' with my hours at the market, but I'd like that. Daddy used to talk about car auctions, but I've never been to any."

With a confident smile that cut through the dark of the night, Andrew winked and replied, "Then, let's make it happen."

Just short of 11:30 p.m., Andrew and company arrived home in Colby. Esther welcomed a very tired granddaughter, who was quickly taken to the vacant second-floor bedroom. Lights were out just prior to midnight but not before Esther warmly fussed over Rachel. As Andrew turned to leave, Russell hugged his uncle in gratitude.

* * *

Esther and Helen had risen to the occasion in coordinating Peter's funeral services. The response from Mifflin's Funeral Home had been exceptional as was the expectation since the families had known each other for over three decades.

Peter had left basic funeral instructions that attorney Karl Noble shared by phone with Esther.

Visitation was scheduled for Friday evening and Saturday morning at the funeral home. The funeral service was to be conducted at Mifflin's on Saturday morning, beginning at 11:00 a.m., with Rev. Dancy officiating. Interment would follow at the Methodist Church cemetery across the street within sight of Lester and Esther's gravesite.

Despite leaving instructions, Peter also left unanswered questions. Why North Carolina for the services? Why no military presence? Why no services held at the Methodist church?

* * *

As Russell attended school on Thursday, Rachel split time between Esther and Helen. Normally, Rachel would have been anxious about being in the company of new and unknown family, but Russell's opinion carried soothing influence with her.

Grandma Esther and Aunt Helen agreed in advance that a hair appointment was appropriate for Rachel prior to funeral events. Rachel's hastily scheduled hair appointment proved more necessity than a gift. Rachel was flattered by the offer to have her hair cut and styled at the salon frequented by both her grandmother and aunt.

As a loyal customer, Esther had called in a favor from the salon's owner and friend, Sally Cox, who had started the day earlier than usual to oblige the need.

Esther accompanied Rachel to a small stand-alone, three-chair salon on the north side of Colby. Sally went immediately to work, shampooing, cutting, thinning, and styling Rachel's thick and uneven hair. The treatment included some curling and Rachel's first exposure to a hair dryer. Rachel had admitted that her hair was usually home cut and was delighted with the attention provided at a professional salon. Her hair had not been professionally cut since early grade school.

The result bordered on spectacular. In less than an hour, Rachel resembled a totally different girl, one who now beamed with pride and self-confidence.

After Esther made payment, which included a handsome tip, grandmother and granddaughter were off to Thirlby's. Esther had inspected the clothes packed in Rachel's suitcase and decided she needed newer, better-fitting clothing for the upcoming services.

During the eighteen-mile drive, Esther told Rachel many of the same things she'd shared with Russell during his trip to Thirlby's. However, she made no stops or alterations to the route—no breakfast at McBride's, no side trip to Rex, and no sentimental tour of Aldan Meadows State Park.

The visit to Thirlby's was timely and productive. A navy-blue corduroy dress with a white Peter Pan collar was chosen, proving a perfect fit. Black Mary Jane shoes were fitted as well as white socks. This outfit would be worn on Saturday for the morning visitation, funeral service, and internment.

Rachel and her cousin, Charlotte, were the same age, and Helen was certain that Rachel could wear one of Charlotte's outfits, possibly with some last minute altering by Esther, for the Friday evening visitation.

Esther also bought a navy blue and maroon striped tie for Russell since Lester's ties had been donated to charity.

Prior to leaving Sexton for the return drive home, Esther called her daughter from a gas station pay phone to provide an update. They agreed that Rachel would stay with Helen for the afternoon.

Helen arrived before noon, taking off a half day from her library duties while Esther returned to Hamilton Brothers to work on payroll. In less than ten minutes, Helen and Rachel were on their way to Slappy's, Colby's only fast food restaurant.

Slappy's was legendary because of the owner and operator, Earl "Slappy" Combs, a lifetime Colby resident, who had opened the restaurant in the mid-1950s. One of the town's more colorful characters, Slappy always cracked jokes and traded harmless insults with customers, never seeming to run out of material.

The small restaurant had no indoor seating; one either ordered take out at one of two sliding windows, or your order could be eaten at one of two picnic tables adjacent to the limited parking.

On this balmy May afternoon, Helen and Rachel ate their cheeseburgers and fries at one of the tables, and to Rachel's delight, the meal included milkshakes.

When they were done, Helen gave Rachel a brief tour of the county. They went to the high school, the county fairgrounds, the depot for the Colby and Southern Railroad, the library, and the Orchards Region.

Throughout the tour, Helen provided historical and cultural narration, Rachel listening attentively. On numerous occasions, Rachel commented about how different Pratt County was from Lancaster and Chicago, "It sure is quiet. No traffic. No graffiti. Everything seems real slow. I'll bet you don't have much crime either?"

"You're right about that. That's one of the wonderful things about living here. I guarantee you one thing, Rachel. Pratt County is nothing like Chicago."

"WHERE do people work around here?"

"Good question. Recession's hit this area hard. We lost two factories within the past five years. One was a small textile factory, the other a factory that made outdoor furniture. Those closings really hurt the local economy. For jobs, a number of people commute to other towns. Quite a few people work down in Sexton and Sandersville. For Pratt County, most jobs are in agriculture or small local businesses."

As Helen took a shortcut on a less-travelled county road, Rachel caught a brief glimpse of a dilapidated trailer situated close to the road. On its rickety wooden front porch sat a disheveled gray sofa with its back facing the road. "Jesus Died for Your Sins" was crudely spray-painted in red on the sofa's back.

* * *

Rachel and Russell spent much of Thursday evening talking in the living room, while Esther and Helen worked at the kitchen table on final details for the services. Russell was taking Friday off from school so he and Rachel could meet with Rev. Dancy that morning.

The closeness between Russell and Rachel became obvious to Esther at dinner Thursday night as brother and sister shared many memories, good and not so good, of their father.

After dinner, Russell and Rachel retreated to the living room where, at first, the discussion focused on Loretta.

Rachel said, "That's all they ever seemed to talk about – Vegas, Vegas, Vegas. They didn't talk about it as much when you were around."

Russell and Rachel agreed that they held no confidence in Loretta's ability to maintain her relationship with Dominic. Her track record with men was abysmal. Since her divorce, Loretta's life had consisted of an ongoing, disappointing parade of failed relationships with men of questionable character. In Russell's and Rachel's minds, Loretta had hit rock bottom pairing with Dominic DiNardo, as he was assuredly the catalyst for Loretta's abandonment of her two children.

Rachel read Russell better than he imagined, and she knew her brother lacked confidence in Loretta's return. Despite all indicators, Rachel refused to withdraw all hope.

Based on their Thursday evening talk, Russell recognized his sister's unhappiness with Loretta's family in Chicago. He sensed that her presence there was an unwelcome burden to maternal grandparents, who were stretched financially. And while brother and sister would be present to attend their father's funeral, Rachel appeared distracted beyond the event due to her less-than-ideal living arrangement in Chicago.

18

MAY 21-22, 1982
COLBY, NC

———

REV. Dancy appeared at the Rankin home Friday morning as planned. He met with Russell and Rachel in the living room, allowing opportunity for them to process the passing of their father and to reflect on their father's positive qualities. "Tell me about your father," was his simple starting point.

Rachel periodically cried through their time together, but there was laughter too, especially when Russell and Rachel recounted fun and lasting memories of their father. Rev. Dancy was amused to learn that, "Don't get preachy on me," was one of Peter's most favorite sayings.

The reverend smiled. "I will do my best and try to honor your father's wish and not get 'preachy'. Russell, I am always available for counsel and prayer at any time. Remember that."

He handed Rachel a piece of paper containing a name and phone number. "Rachel, I know you've just moved to Chicago, but here's the name of a Methodist minister whose church is near where you're living in Chicago. Should you need to speak with someone, you can call Rev. James McCabe at St. Robert's Methodist Church at this number. Your grandmother said it was OK for me to share this with you."

Near the conclusion of their time together, Rev. Dancy gave them a pamphlet. "This has some passages from the Bible that are comforting during times of losing a parent. I've added some verses that I've found especially consoling in the past."

The visit ended with a prayer for strength and healing. Prior to leaving, Rev. Dancy spent time with Esther at the kitchen table, offering additional spiritual guidance and consolation.

★ ★ ★

Fifty-two people attended the Friday evening visitation for Peter Wallace Rankin. The vast majority of the attendees were linked to Esther and her three surviving children. Hamilton Brothers Hardware and Lumber employees came out in force. Several of Lester's former postal workers, many still in uniform, attended the service. Esther was especially touched that two good friends of Lester's, J.T. Granger and Caleb Moore, paid their respects to the family at the visitation.

Russell expected no one to appear on his behalf; however, he was surprised when Coach Morris Wilkes, Counselor Rob Cornelius, and Algebra instructor Betty Hufnal visited to express their condolences.

Aunt Helen had done an exceptional job in pulling together dozens of family and school photographs of Peter. Russell and Rachel had never seen the photos and were fascinated by the mounted pictures of their father ranging from birth to high school graduation. The physical likeness of Peter and Russell as teenagers was striking. High school yearbooks were also on display with tabbed images of the deceased.

Rachel and Russell endured the endless hugs and expressions of condolence, although Rachel was especially brittle during the evening, breaking down on several occasions, especially when she drew near her father in the open casket. At these moments, Russell offered brotherly support and consolation as they stood together overlooking their father.

The ravages of liver disease had greatly altered Peter's physical appearance to the extent that many family members and visitors saw little resemblance to Peter. At one point, Rachel said woefully, "I hardly recognize him. I almost think that's not Daddy."

The visitation scheduled for the following Saturday morning was also well attended. Vice Principle Kenneth Hayes paid his respects early in the gathering. April McNaughton, who Russell worked and went to school with, was in attendance, and, surprisingly stayed for both the visitation and the service to follow.

Five minutes before the service, Helen thanked everyone for coming and let all in attendance know that the service would soon begin. The gatherers thinned out, and Russell's and Rachel's cousins now joined their parents for the service. Thirty individuals were present for the funeral service co-conducted by Rev. Dancy and Helen.

Rev. Dancy's address was based upon his close association with Esther and recent contacts with Helen, Russell, and Rachel. He openly admitted his disadvantage in preparing a message since he and Peter had never met.

He thanked family members and friends for paying tribute to Peter. He emphasized that this was a time when the family and community both needed to give and receive comfort and support in the grieving process.

To Peter's children, he said this was a time to "unblock" the emotions and that it was OK to cry since tears were actually God's gift that brought healing and eventually ushered understanding and acceptance.

More than anything, the mourners were encouraged to trust in God's decision to bring Peter home.

"A man's life should not be based upon duration but based upon contributions. Peter was a three-year veteran of the United States Navy, who served two years in Vietnam and was honorably discharged. Upon discharge from the navy, Peter held one job as an adult, and one job only, and like his father before him, that employment was with the United States Post Office, sixteen years of additional public service.

"Perhaps, Peter's greatest accomplishment was his two children, Russell and Rachel, who I know miss him terribly today.

"The pain and suffering that he endured due to alcohol and drugs has finally been conquered as he has gone to God's kingdom, and he has been returned to us in North Carolina as well. With that said, I turn the lectern over to Helen."

"Good morning. My name is Helen Rankin Whitlock. First of all, thank you all very much for attending this morning's funeral service for my brother, Peter Wallace Rankin, born October 2, 1942, in Colby, North Carolina. Peter died last Sunday from cardiac arrest in Shellsburg, Illinois. Peter was thirty-nine years old when he died.

"Representing the immediate family today are our mother, Esther Rankin, Peter's three siblings and their families, and very importantly, Peter's two children—Russell and Rachel, with Rachel traveling all the way from Chicago to be with us for the services.

"I was the only female sibling and the oldest of four children in our family. Peter and I were close in age, just one year apart, and our earliest years were spent with our father, Lester Rankin, away in the navy fighting World War II in the Pacific. With our mother continuing to work full time at Colby Chevrolet, Peter and I spent a lot of time with our maternal grandparents in Wheeler County and other relatives. It was during those years with our father off to war that Peter and I drew close as siblings.

"What was Peter like as a small child? He was always very busy, very inquisitive, and very curious. He had a mischievous side as well. He played well with others and me, but he was also comfortable in spending time alone by himself. He liked to read, especially Landmark adventure books and books about space and science fiction.

"He also took to his father's passion for baseball, and frequent catches between my father and Peter in the side yard remain etched in my memory. He earned honorable mention All-State recognition as a third baseman for Pratt County High School and even received a tryout with the Pittsburgh Pirates.

"Peter was an average student, somewhat lazy, and had to be pushed with his schooling as our mother would agree. He worked part time at the old Hillary's Cafeteria for three years in high school, earning enough money to buy a used car. He dated frequently in high school, and he enjoyed going to shows at the Royal movie house in Sexton.

"After graduating from high school, Peter followed our father's lead and enlisted in the navy for three years, where he earned an honorable discharge, two of those years being spent land-based as a truck driver and munitions' handler in Vietnam.

"When visiting a close navy friend in Chicago a few months following his discharge, Peter landed a job with the post office in 1963, again following our father's lead. However, Peter's postal job was out of state in Lancaster, Illinois. Peter took the Illinois job with the firm hought of eventually transferring to a North Carolina post office. Unfortunately, that anticipated transfer never took place.

"Peter married Loretta Packer in Chicago in 1964, with two children being born of that union, Russell and Rachel Rankin. Peter and Loretta's marriage ended in divorce in 1977.

"Ever since Peter's return from Vietnam, there was a void in our family because of his absence. None of us thought that he would permanently leave North Carolina. We all thought that he would eventually return, but Vietnam seemed to change everything. A failed marriage did not help, but an irony here is that throughout my brother's fight with alcohol and drugs, he remained an excellent employee.

"Because Peter left that instruction, I phoned Peter's boss in Lancaster earlier this week. His name is Sam Infante, and this is what Sam had to say:

> *I could not have had a more dedicated employee. Peter had his issues outside of work with alcohol and drugs, but he never brought them to the job. He was hardworking and loyal, too, and a really good example for others to follow. One thing I'll always remember about Peter was that he made me laugh, but the really funny thing is that he always thought the jokes were funnier than they really were. But he did make me laugh, he really did. I'm going to miss him ... such a sad thing that he died so young ... so very sad.*

"None of us can rewrite the story here. We all wanted a different script, a better ending, but what I hope to do in getting on after Peter's passing is to remember the best of our childhood and teenage years together. My parents gave us a wonderful upbringing, for which I'll always be grateful, with Peter playing a huge part in those forever memories.

"Just this week, I asked Russell and Rachel about their most favorite memories of their father. Russell's were the times that he and Peter attended Lancaster Lancers' minor league baseball games together at Lancaster's Peppler Field. Rachel's fondest memory was attending a traveling circus, complete with outdoor big top and parading elephants, at the DeMooy Park in Lancaster.

"We all need to recognize those favorite recollections of Peter and routinely revisit them, not just now but in the years to come.

"I very much loved my oldest little brother. He was my little brother for whom I have nothing but the fondest memories. I only wish that life had been kinder to him.

"And, Peter, this is for you – you finally did come home after all. Thank you again for your presence here this morning."

When Helen took her seat, two of Peter's former high school class-mates, Gene Henry and Harry Hollister, shared remembrances and favorite memories. Rev. Dancy offered additional biblical passages for comfort, and after a closing prayer, the visitation was dismissed as Mifflin's staff escorted the casket and immediate family to the nearby cemetery.

Russell and Rachel sat next to each other during the service. They held hands throughout with Rachel's head occasionally resting on Russell's shoulder. Russell remained stoic; Rachel sobbed intermittently.

Esther sat motionless and somber throughout the service as younger sister Libbie sat next to Esther, offering her comfort and support. Esther eyes were moist with tears throughout the ceremony. Even during humorous moments, she failed to smile or laugh.

★ ★ ★

The brief interment service was attended by nine family members. Rev. Dancy's final words of consolation were dramatically overshadowed by Rachel's emotional breakdown at the gravesite. Aunt Helen and Russell rushed to comfort her, but the sight of the closed coffin, soon to be lowered into the ground, proved overwhelming, all too graphically underscoring the finality of parental loss.

Esther broke down as well. In providing support, Libbie hugged her older sister with soothing whispers of consolation.

1 9

MAY 22, 1982

———

FOLLOWING a lightly attended chicken-salad lunch in the church basement, the family returned home. Esther was understandably exhausted from the services and the crushing reality of losing her oldest son. She quickly retreated to her bedroom for a lengthy afternoon nap.

With Pratt County enjoying a picture-perfect May afternoon, Russell and Rachel gathered Coke bottles from the refrigerator and sat at the back-yard picnic table recapping events. There was no real agenda; brother and sister simply needed quiet time with each other.

"I'm sorry I lost it at the cemetery. Seein' that coffin put in the ground just did me in. It wasn't all that real until then. Even the time at the funeral home didn't get to me that much because I could still see Daddy and talk to him."

"Rach, you've got nothing to be sorry for; everyone understands. Not many kids lose their father when they're twelve years old."

"Almost thirteen," she corrected with a smirk. A short pause followed.

"I'm worried about Momma, real worried. Now that I think about it, the idea for them taking off seemed to come together when you were in juvie. I'd hear them talking in bed at night. I couldn't hear most of what they were sayin', but I'll bet that's what they were talking about."

"Thanks for the pep talk, Rach," Russell said, continuing to stare through slots in the aged picnic table.

"You know what I mean."

Russell reestablished eye contact and asked, "Did you think anything weird was happenin' when you got dropped off at Grandma Packer's?"

"No, not really. I know that makes me seem dumb and all, but Momma was always a pretty good actress. I was more worried about her marryin' that creep than leavin' us."

Due to Rachel's upcoming return to Chicago, Sunday dinner was moved to Saturday, with Andrew responsible for the main meal. Helen and Aunt Libbie would pull the meal together with the side dishes and dessert. Russell overheard that Uncle Daniel, Aunt Janice, and the couple's four children would not be in attendance because of a birthday party scheduled near Charlotte for someone on Aunt Janice's side of the family.

It was now mid-afternoon. Aunt Helen's car announced its presence on the gravel driveway. She was alone, so Russell and Rachel joined her to assist in carry items in for dinner.

"Let me get some things started in the kitchen. Then your grandmother and I, we'll join you in a bit. We need to talk to you both."

In the past few months, Russell had grown wary of scheduled talks with adults. Too many disappointments and surprises had produced unexpected life-changing results, and even though the request had come from a trusted family member, Russell remained on edge. Rachel seemed unfazed by the announcement.

During the next half hour, Rachel and Russell strolled Grouse Hollow Road from the Rankin home to the road's end at Dr. Dilworth's property.

"Dr. Dilworth's the vet who Grandma says saved Maddie's life, the time she ran into a bee's nest out in the woods. He wasn't at the visitation because he was out of town, but his wife was there Friday night. They're nice people and real good neighbors to Grandma."

The siblings randomly reminisced about happier times as they walked, sometimes hand in hand, heading back to the house, where they joined Grandma and Aunt Helen waiting at the backyard picnic table.

"Grandchildren, your Aunt Helen will do most of the talkin' as I'm pretty empty right now. Your daddy's passin' has been hard on us all. Your Aunt Helen's agreed to share some important news with you. You've seen a lot of comin' and goin' for Aunt Helen and me the past few days, a lot of meetings at the funeral home and with a lawyer. You need to know what's goin' on. We like to think that this is good news for a change."

Russell was instantly relieved since Aunt Helen's affect was clearly upbeat and promising.

Helen began. "OK, here's the important news that you both need to know.

"Your daddy recently drew up a new will. That's a legal document that people write with a lawyer's help that's used when a person dies. It helps divide up property, money, things like that. It can also make it clear who raises the children in a family should the parents not be able. Your daddy did this because he must have reckoned that he didn't have a long time to live. He also made the will because of your momma disappearin'. He knew that there was a chance that neither of them might be around to raise you. So, with your daddy dyin' and your momma's whereabouts unknown, what happens to you children? This gets tricky in the eyes of the law since your mother is still alive. We just don't know where she is. Are you with me?"

Russell and Rachel nodded their understanding.

"Good. To the surprise of a lot of us, your daddy bought a life insurance policy many years ago. The amount of the insurance policy is $100,000, to be split between the two of you upon your father's death. Now, because you are minors, that money cannot be handed over to you directly until you turn eighteen.

"OK? Still with me?"

Somewhat confused, Rachel inquired, "Daddy left us all that money? How'd he do that? Daddy never had any money."

Helen and Grandma both smiled.

"He bought the policy over many years through his employer, the United States Post Office. In his will, he was very specific about who was to care for you, who was to act as your parent. In his absence and your momma's, he named your grandmother, here, to be your guardian, both of you, until you turn eighteen."

Both children were stunned. "Then who are we supposed to live with?" Rachel asked eagerly.

Esther responded, "Me."

Both children were surprised, especially Rachel, who became even more wide-eyed.

Helen continued. "Now all of this has to be approved by the court here in Pratt County. This is not final, but if there are no conflicts or challenges within the family, the court generally follows the plan written in the will.

"Russell, this impacts you a little differently because the juvenile court back in Lancaster is your current guardian. You know, you're here temporarily until some living arrangement was to be worked out with your mother or father. Nothing really changes for you until you get off of probation next year. Then your guardianship will switch over to Grandma. But all of this has to be made official through the court back in Illinois and the one here.

"Rachel, I know this all comes as a shock, but it's important for you to tell us where you want to live. You're with your other grandmother now, but that's temporary too."

Then, if I move to North Carolina, Russell and me can be together?"

Esther responded with a smile, "That's right, sweetie, right here in that house behind us," as Esther motioned over her shoulder.

"We'll, I want to be here with Russell and you all."

Russell intervened. "I understand what could happen with Rachel, but I need to get this right. Because of Daddy wanting Grandma to be my guardian, the court in Lancaster could switch guardianship to Grandma? I'm not going to have to move back to Illinois?" Russell asked.

Aunt Helen replied, "That's my understanding, but I'm not a lawyer. Now, we have an attorney here in Colby who is very familiar with what they call probate law. His name is Perry Erhleman, and he's done legal work for your grandparents and your Uncle George and me in the past. He's already agreed to handle your father's will and file the necessary papers for guardianship with the Pratt County courts.

"I know this is all rushed on the same day as your daddy's funeral, but there's more news here that you need to know today since Rachel is scheduled to fly back tomorrow."

Esther said, "Russell, I recently wrote identical letters to Mr. Harris and Miss Bohars before your daddy died. In them, I said that because of your daddy's poor health and your mother disappearing, I was willing to serve as your legal guardian when you got discharged from probation. Mr. Erhleman is aware of this as well, and I believe he's written a letter to Judge Shield's back in Illinois to that same effect."

Russell asked, "What's all of this mean to my probation?"

Aunt Helen answered, "You're still going to be on probation. It's just that the guardianship part would not change until your probation ends next year. That's all up to Judge Shields back in Lancaster, but as long as you're doing well on probation, my sense is that she would agree to it, but Judge Shields makes the final call."

Esther continued, "Mr. Erhleman needs to meet you both next week to explain the steps involved. Remember, he's the lawyer, and he'll do a better job in explaining all of this legal stuff than I ever could. He's already been in contact with the Illinois lawyer, who drafted your father's will."

"Grandma, you'd do this for Rachel and me?" Russell asked.

"Yes, I would. I always pray on big decisions. That's what I did when the Illinois probation people asked me to take you in. I did the same this time. Grandson, you've been a blessing to me. I look forward to you being in my life every single day. And it warms my heart that you and Rachel could stay together if that's what you want. And Rachel, it'll be nice to have another female in the house to keep an eye on Russell," Esther said with a chuckle.

"Grandchildren, I'm sixty-one years old. I don't move as quick as I used to. I don't have the same energy I once had, but I'd be pleased for you both to live here until you at least turn eighteen. Even though your grandfather has been gone for more than three years, I think he would want this for you too. In fact, I know he would."

In unscripted unison, Russell and Rachel rose to embrace and thank their grandmother. To no one's surprise, Rachel started crying tears of joy. She hugged Russell tightly, evolving into an exuberant yet awkward dance of celebration.

Esther asked in jest, "Well, is that a yes?"

Rachel grinned and shouted, "Yes, yes, yes!"

As the revelry subsided, Esther added, "We need to run the situation by Grandmother Packer tonight after dinner on the phone. We think it may be best for Rachel to finish out the school year in Chicago, then move down here in June, but we should check with them first."

Rachel interjected, "I don't want to go back. I want to stay here as long as Russell and me can live with you, Grandma."

"Rachel," Esther asked, "How do you think Grandmother Packer will react to all of this?"

"Not so good. She doesn't like being told what to do. But, wait a minute, what happens when Momma returns?"

Somewhat troubled by the question, Esther said, "Rachel, that's another good question to ask Mr. Erhleman since your Aunt Helen and I don't know the answer."

Aunt Helen interjected, "Well, we can talk more about this later, but for now I need some assistance fixin' dinner. Aunt Libbie might need some help on the deviled eggs and salad."

"I'll help too," Rachel said eagerly with a broad smile. In turn, she eagerly walked to the kitchen to help.

A subdued Saturday dinner followed.

* * *

The next day, Russell stayed after home maintenance class to inform Coach Mo that he would be available to play football in the fall. The coach was so ecstatic in receiving the news that he gave Russell an embarrassing bear hug.

20

JUNE 1982

———

PETER'S death preoccupied Russell as the school year ground to a close. Even though homework and exams had taken a backseat for Russell, he proudly finished the school year earning all A's in his classes.

Russell did not grieve alone outside of his family. Despite being new at school, some classmates and even some faculty were supportive with comments and gestures. As English class ended one morning, a shy, nearly invisible classmate gave him a note as she left class. The note read:

Russell,

I'm real sorry you lost your dad. I know what it's like. My daddy died when I was twelve.

—Sara Yarnall

Following the funeral, Esther had done her best to control, if not conceal, her emotions. However, Peter's death had unraveled her. She had thought over the years about how unthinkable it would be to bury one of her children. Perhaps it was due to the separation in miles, Peter's failed marriage, her son's ongoing battle with alcohol and drugs, or Peter's aloofness from the family, but in Esther's mind, he'd always been the one most vulnerable to die early.

Peter's death had reopened the wounds caused by Lester's passing in 1979. Lester's death had come without warning, so the shock value had been particularly high. Esther eventually followed a church member's suggestion and joined a bereavement group sponsored by a Methodist church in Sexton. She attended bi-weekly meetings for over two years, her attendance only turning inconsistent in early 1982.

Showing uncommon insight for a teenager, Russell realized from something Aunt Helen had mentioned that his grandmother was grieving on two levels. He, in turn, proved especially attentive to Esther, a role that he extended to Rachel as well.

Rachel proved especially needy as she and Russell adjusted to life without their father. One evening when Esther wasn't home, they talked in the living room after dinner.

"You know, Russell, I cry most nights thinking about Daddy before I fall asleep. I know we didn't see him much, but he was still a part of our lives. You know it just hit me so hard at the cemetery. I just couldn't believe that he was really gone, that Daddy was the one who died, that he was the one dead inside that coffin. It just seemed too much, too much like a bad dream."

Russell nodded but didn't respond.

"When do you think we'll hear from Momma?"

Russell took his time contemplating his answer.

"Rach, I don't have a good feeling about this. I think Momma might be gone for good. You know it's been over three months, Rach—*three months*. If she was coming back, I think we'd have heard from her by now."

A long silence followed.

"Well, if Daddy's dead and Momma's not comin' back, doesn't that sort of make us orphans?"

Russell grew reflective. "You know, I never thought of it that way, but I think you're right."

Rachel began to sob in soft bursts. "I miss her so much, Russell, so much. I just want to hear her voice or see her showin' up at the back door out of somewhere."

Rachel regained some composure. "This never would have happened without Dominic screwin' everythin' up. I hate that son of a bitch."

Russell got up to embrace his sister. "It's you and me, Rach. This is our struggle. You're not the only one cryin' at night."

* * *

In early June, Esther became aware of a female classmate's attention toward Russell. Esther recognized sixteen-year-old April McNaughton as a Village Market employee. On her own, April had attended the Saturday morning visitation and funeral service for Peter. April's presence at the funeral service was noteworthy because she'd been the only nonfamily teenager present.

April was known as an intelligent, driven, and outspoken young woman, likely destined to be class valedictorian. She was sophomore vice president and an accomplished athlete in both tennis and soccer.

Small and compact at five feet two inches, April was athletic, with strong shoulders and well-defined legs. Despite her diminutive size, she was an aggressive and cunning athlete whose abilities impressed her opponents. She also possessed exceptional speed and quickness.

April was an attractive girl, who enhanced her features to maximize her appearance. Her face and body were lightly freckled, a despised trait she had inherited from her mother.

April's best physical feature was her long, strawberry-blond hair that she frequently braided. Her hair coupled with striking green eyes highlighted a demure face accented by a petite nose and mouth.

While popular, her peer detractors saw April as more adult than adolescent, more scholarly and career-oriented than was typical for her age. She was respected more than liked and more intimidating by her intellect than friendly.

Among her peers, April was known for her quick temper and fondness for profanity. She was not hesitant about taking controversial stands with classmates, teachers, or even school administration. She prided herself as a feminist.

April had worked twenty-plus hours a week at the Village Market for over a year. She and Russell shared two high school classes so they were slightly acquainted when Russell started working at the market. April had helped with Russell's orientation and training more than anyone else at the store, and the two often shared work breaks together.

Highly interested in this handsome new boy from the Midwest, April was more than eager to provide a lift home to Russell from the market when schedules aligned.

From April's daily journal entry, she and Russell quietly became a couple in late May. Esther confirmed the emergence of the relationship mostly because of the frequent phone calls exchanged after dinner. Usually, when Russell went out on Friday and Saturday evenings or when not working during the weekend, he was in April's company.

The couple began spending occasional time at the Rankin home under Esther's supervision. With weather accommodating, Russell and April talked privately at the venerable outdoor picnic table. At Russell's urging, Esther introduced the couple to The Point, a locale they enjoyed because of its expansive view and privacy. They also took leisurely walks, usually hand in hand, on Grouse Hollow Road to Dr. Dilworth's property and back.

At sixteen, April was six months older than Russell. She had known one serious boyfriend, Blake Martinson, in high school. In retrospect, she regretted having wasted so much of her sophomore year on this elitist upper-classman, who was best known for his looks, clothes, car, and money. To many, April's pairing with Blake seemed forced and out of place.

The relationship turned ugly at a party following Blake's senior prom. Fueled by alcohol, Blake aggressively sought to consummate the relationship with April in a classmate's vacant basement bedroom. A fierce knee to Blake's groin sent the overaggressive senior reeling off the bed in pain. The couple never spoke to one another again.

Within days after the breakup with Blake, April focused her attention on the new boy from Illinois. April was not alone in her attraction to Russell, but the competition soon waned because of her reputation for getting what she wanted. The proximity of their lockers made meetings at school frequent. April even coordinated her driving to school to coincide with Russell's bus arrival.

The biology project they'd worked on together at the end of school served as a significant step in building the relationship since they were frequently alone, supposedly concentrating on the impact of endangered predators in North America. The project's work sessions started with good intentions, but Peter Rankin's death complicated the assignment's completion, with April readily assuming a fuller load. Due to their frequency in meeting, April also served as a sounding board for Russell's grief, further fostering their ties to each other.

Through this catharsis, Russell and April agreed to a movie date at Sexton's restored Royal Theater the week following Peter Rankin's funeral. April drove them in her 1971 Chevrolet Vega, and the couple agreed to split expenses. On this evening, romantic interest was staked by both girl and boy.

Once the school year ended, Russell and April saw each often, usually daily either at work or on dates to sit-down and drive-in movies, the bowling alley, skating rink, or even Friday night teen dances sponsored by the Rotary Club at the county fairgrounds. Not surprisingly, Rachel resented April's impact on Russell's time and availability.

As the relationship progressed, Russell began spending more time at the McNaughton home. Russell met April's parents, Tommy and Susanna McNaughton. Tommy was a Pratt County native and veteran UPS driver. Susanna, college-degreed in Southern Appalachian Studies, worked out of the house making quilts and craft items indigenous to the Blue Ridge Mountains. Russell was introduced as well to April's curious younger sister, Autumn.

* * *

During summer months, When Russell was not working at the market or working out in anticipation of the upcoming football season, he and April were together. April's cramped Chevy Vega provided freedom and privacy, and to ease his transition to his new community, April took him on tours to parts of the county not yet visited.

She introduced him to Mount Wilcox State Park, the Morgan Mill County Park, and a new foot/biking trail known as the Laird River Trail, still largely undiscovered by outsiders.

On one occasion, April and Russell visited a heavily logged section of land known by the locals as the Timber Region. He was introduced to a seasonal tourist attraction, the Colby and Southern Railroad, which formerly hauled lumber from the area south to Sexton where linkage was made with the Southern Railroad.

With the railroad's logging role supplanted by trucking, state railroad enthusiasts in the late sixties envisioned revival of the existing track and equipment as a tourist railroad. The cumbersome, expensive process took nearly eight years to complete, with the Colby and Southern Railroad offering limited, round-trip weekend passenger service, spring through fall, beginning in May 1977. Unknown to Russell and April, Lester Rankin had served as a volunteer mechanic for the railroad for two years until his death.

During the visit to the Timber Region, April slowed her Vega to stop at an overlook. "We need to get out here. I want to show you somethin'."

Standing before a historical marker, April motioned northward with her finger. "Look yonder at those mountains. At one time, most of the trees there were American chestnuts, and Pratt County had the thickest growth of American chestnut trees in North Carolina. At one time, this county had over three million American chestnut trees."

Russell showed minimal interest.

In mild rebuke, April countered, "It's because you're not from around here. You don't understand the importance of this tree to the history of the mountains and its people." Recognizing April's passion, Russell became better engaged.

"There were millions and millions of these trees in America at one time; now they're near all gone."

April told Russell of a building addition scheduled to open in the next few months at the Pratt County Museum. The addition's sole exhibit was devoted to the history and importance of the American chestnut to southern Appalachia.

"Last fall, Mrs. Gooch had a biologist from N.C. State speak to our class. He helped find grant money and donations to pay for the addition to the museum. He said the American chestnut was the perfect tree. The *perfect* tree. I'll never forget that. Can you imagine that? And now it's almost gone."

"Why'd he call it perfect?" questioned Russell.

"Because the people here used it for most everythin'. They used the chestnuts to feed their cows and hogs. They used the wood for fences, barns, houses, furniture, musical instruments, practically everythin'. And people like to eat them especially at Christmastime. Now chestnuts are wiped out because of a disease brought in from China.

"And I'll bet you didn't know this too. This is big salamander country. Mrs. Gooch said this region is sort of like the salamander capital of the United States. She even told me that UNC is researching some new species of blind salamander right now, right here in Pratt County."

Russell sheepishly admitted, "And I don't even know what a salamander is."

★ ★ ★

With great enthusiasm, April shared a special site that was contiguous to the McNaughton family's five-acre property. The McNaughton land was hilly, bordering the earliest ascent to a small range of foothills known as the Drummond Hills.

Bordering the McNaughton's land was a ninety-head cattle ranch owned by the Bright family. Ben and Ginny Bright were very close to the McNaughton family. They regarded April's parents as their most trusted neighbors; likewise was the relationship of the McNaughton's toward the Brights, who they considered pseudo-grandparents to April and Autumn.

This bond between families allowed April the freedom to explore a section of pasture on the Bright's property where their Black Angus grazed. She considered this stretch of land her backyard, a special place she had visited and explored often since childhood.

The rolling pasture was bordered by forest on all sides. The field's two- to three-foot-wide stream lazily meandered through the sloped land, granting cattle easy access to cool, spring-fed mountain water.

A few isolated hardwoods supplied welcome shade to the cattle during hot summer days. Boulders, many large in size, were scattered indiscrimi- nately across the grassy clearing.

More than anything, April wished to share this place with Russell during this late spring visit. Barefooted, April led Russell down a narrow, worn path from the McNaughton property to the fence line guarding the Bright pasture. Using an adjacent crabapple tree for leverage, they hopped the four-foot wire fence.

"Watch out for the cow pies, Russell. Remember what my daddy says: 'To a cow, the whole world's a bathroom'.

"Don't worry about the cattle. They won't bother us, but we need to check for ticks when we leave since this time of year is when they're real active." April escorted Russell to an oft-visited smooth, rounded rock bor- dering the creek mid-field. "I can count the dozens of times I've cooled my feet at this spot on hot summer days. It's a little early in the season, but stick your feet in, Russell … right now. Go ahead, just do it."

Russell chose not to disappoint, and with his socks and Nike's now discarded, he slipped his feet into the chilly water. "Whoa, this is like ice water. How can you stand it?"

She playfully wrapped her arms around his waist and rested her head on his shoulder. "Don't be such a baby; it's just spring water."

Her spontaneity caught Russell off guard; the warmth of her touch melted his tenseness. They remained silent and motionless, the only sound coming from the water's tranquil movement. Eventually, April broke her embrace, and as she lightly kissed Russell's cheek, she caught his eye, "Thank you for this moment."

With three curious Black Angus now in closer proximity, April said she wanted to reveal another special place. Russell dried his feet as best he could, stuffed his socks in his back pocket, and pulled on his Nike's. Hand in hand, she led him to the field's largest cluster of boulders, scaling almost forty feet in the air.

The couple sat together in silence for a few minutes until April said, "This is one of my most special places. I've climbed up here since I was in first grade."

She turned to him. "Russell, I've never been to Illinois, just seen pictures, but I can guarantee you one thing for sure. You've never seen fall until you've seen it in these mountains. The colors are so big and bold—yellow, green, brown, and dark red. I always wait for the colors to be at their peak, and then I climb up here to take it all in. The mountain air in the fall is so crisp and clean."

With marked uncertainty, Russell stared intently into a crevice between two boulders and quietly announced, "You need to know some things."

"Sure, you can tell me," as April's interest peaked.

"My family's nothing like yours. The whole reason I moved here is because of family problems, just 'the dealin' of the cards' as my daddy used to say. Now he's dead, and no one knows where my mother is. Last February, she just up and left town with her latest boyfriend, didn't say good bye or nothin'." Reestablishing eye contact, Russell concluded, "Grandma Esther's pretty much all Rachel and me got."

"I figured something really bad happened back in Illinois."

Russell took her hand, and they locked eyes, "April, I like you. I like you a lot, but you need to know something else because it'll come out sooner or later."

"What's that? You can tell me."

Hesitating, he shifted his gaze to the open meadow. "I'm on juvenile probation for a year." Russell swallowed hard. "A police officer broke his elbow when he fell in our apartment. He had to have surgery so they blamed me for the injury."

"Why was a police officer at your home, anyway?"

"Because my mother's boyfriend called police to have me taken to a shelter 'cause we'd just had this big fight. Dominic wanted me out. I wouldn't go, and then I lost it and ran—worst decision of my life. The cop fell on a wet floor when I ran by him so they filed charges on me. It's the only time I've ever been in any trouble with the police, ever."

"This makes no sense. I don't understand. You didn't mean to hurt him, right? I know you didn't."

"I swear I never meant to hurt anyone. I was on the run for a day, but then Dominic tracked me down where I was workin' and called the cops."

"This sounds awful, but why were you arrested? You didn't hit anyone."

"When I ran from the apartment, I brushed by the officer, causing him to fall. At least that's what they said happened. I spent almost a month in juvenile detention until Grandma Esther agreed to take me in."

"So, when did your mother disappear?"

"When I was locked up in detention."

April was horrified in learning of Russell's abandonment. She dropped her head on his shoulder. "Oh, you poor thing, you poor dear. This is so awful."

"My probation's been transferred down here. I see a Mr. Harris at the courthouse or at home once a month. He's been real fair so far, but I figured, sooner or later, that someone would see me at the courthouse. So, now you know."

"Thanks for trusting me with all of this. You're right about people finding out. That's the way it is in a small town. Secrets aren't secrets for very long."

Their eyes met again.

"Russell, nothing's changed between us—nothing. In fact, I respect you even more for your trust and your guts. What you shared with me stays with us. I won't mention this anyone. You have my word."

After a short pause, April asked a question she hadn't dared ask before. "Are you still movin' back to Illinois?"

"I don't see that happenin' now with Momma takin' off like she did. I've already told Grandma Esther that I want to stay here to graduate after my probation ends next year. She's agreed to be my guardian then and until I turn eighteen. No, I don't want to go back to Lancaster. Too many bad memories there. This is home now, not Lancaster.

April was elated but attempted to mask her joy. Russell's announcement in the Bright pasture changed everything.

21

JUNE/JULY 1982

———

In June, Esther, Russell, and Rachel met with local attorney Perry Erhleman to have Peter's will explained. Even though Grandmother Packer did not take kindly to Peter's requirement for the children to be raised by paternal relatives in North Carolina, she accepted the will's directive, offering no resistance.

The inheritance intended for the children's care would be tapped in small monthly amounts to assist Esther in covering expenses associated with her unexpected role in the raising of two grandchildren. Any early retirement plan for Esther had been placed on hold. Mr. Erhleman also explained the separate details in Esther attaining guardianship for Russell and Rachel. He was optimistic that both requests would be approved providing that Loretta Rankin remained missing and uninvolved. Attorney Erhleman also explained his fees and itemized funeral expenses. Later that month, the guardianship request for Rachel was filed with the Pratt County Court. A hearing on the guardianship request was scheduled for late July.

* * *

By mid-June, school had been out for over two weeks. The emotions and drama produced by Peter's death, while still present, were beginning to lessen. For Esther, it was difficult to imagine life returning to normal because she was now raising two teenage grandchildren.

Russell's summertime was occupied by working lengthier hours at the market, conditioning for football, and spending time with April. His network of friends, while still small, was football-based, and included Wade Hunter, Jonathan Hunt, Jamie Goetz, Tommy Gleason, and Nate "Scooter" Monroe, one of the few African-American players on the football team, who also worked part-time at the market.

Sunday dinner continued serving as a regular opportunity for Russell and Rachel to better acquaint themselves with relatives. It came as no surprise that Rachel had quickly bonded with Aunt Helen, while Russell grew close to Uncle Andrew. Rachel spent considerable time that summer at Aunt Helen's due to her fondness for her cousins Charlotte and Grace.

In early summer, Russell continued to observe distance, even tension, between Uncle Daniel's family and Esther and other family. The source of the discord appeared to be Aunt Janice, a Charlotte native, who rarely displayed interest in the Rankin family members. Even through Russell's limited observation, a disconnect existed. Rachel even caught on, and at one of her earliest Sunday dinners, she motioned toward Aunt Janice, and whispered to Russell, "What's her problem anyway?"

* * *

As a protective older brother, Russell watched over Rachel's adjustment. Rachel had spent only two weeks in her new middle school in Colby, but the last half of her school year in Illinois had been unproductive marked by disciplinary infractions and poor grades. Aunt Helen and Esther knew that events beyond Rachel's control had caused her to stall academically.

As a boost, Aunt Helen enrolled Rachel in the library's summer reading program, which provided incentives to participating students based on volume of books read.

Esther enrolled Rachel in a new six-week summer program at church called Operation Reload, run by a retired elementary teacher. The program was scheduled to run for six weeks, Monday through Friday from 8:30 a.m. to 12:00 p.m. in a basement classroom of the Colby Methodist Church.

Volunteer high school students from Pratt County High School's Future Teachers of America Club would assist remedial tutoring of language arts and math to underachieving sixth- to eighth-grade students, who, due to poor grades and poor attendance, were considered high risk for dropping out of high school. The program was free to county residents within the Pratt County School District.

Rachel initially balked at the program but caved when Russell declared that her attendance was "a done deal." Transportation would be tricky, with Aunt Helen and Uncle Andrew juggling the duty.

* * *

The relationship between Russell and April deepened during the summer, and through increased exposure, Russell quickly grew very fond of the McNaughtons. Russell had been well received by April's parents and was a welcome visitor to the McNaughton home. He found April's parents to be kind, stable, and nonjudgmental adults, who served as attentive parents to April and Autumn.

The McNaughtons enjoyed camping on summer and fall weekends. Tommy, as a native of the region, knew the better, less-congested campsites in national forests and state parks located within the northwest section of the state.

April's work schedule cut into the McNaughtons' plans for weekend camping trips. So, for the first time, her parents agreed to leave April on her own at home while they went camping if she couldn't trade hours with another employee. They started planning an early-July trip to a recently opened state park in southwest Virginia, which would give April her first night at home alone without having to babysit.

2 2

JULY 1, 1982

———

ON an early July Thursday, April and Russell worked identical hours, and once off work, they devoured a Slappy's order before heading to Mt. Wilcox State Park. Here, April sought to escort Russell on a trail to Dunn Falls, one of her favorite destinations in the county.

Upon their arrival, only three cars were parked in the lot designated for picnicking, access trails to Dunn Falls, and the park's fire tower. Russell and April sprayed each other with insect repellent before beginning the half-mile hike to the falls. April cautioned Russell that the hilly trail might be muddy due to Wednesday evening's heavy rain, and such was the case. Several times, the couple joined hands to help each other maneuver during the more challenging and slippery sections of trail.

April said, "We're getting close, just about a hundred feet now." Then the sound of cascading water greeted them. The couple emerged from the forested canopy, which had shielded them during the majority of the hike.

Dunn Falls was a pleasant surprise for Russell with which he had nothing to compare. The flow of water, at first gentle, appeared one hundred feet up a smooth, slightly rounded stone face, with a shallow coat of clear mountain water descending forty feet in width. The water hugged the exposed stone, glistening as it rolled. More than halfway down, it gained speed and narrowed to form a deeper, thirty feet-wide flow that wildly careened off the mountain, crashing into a waist-deep pool below.

The couple had seen two families on the trail returning to the parking lot, but for now, Russell and April were the falls' lone visitors. Still hand in hand, April escorted Russell to a wooden park bench that granted a full, frontal view of the falls. A minute of quiet reflection followed.

April chose to break the silence. "Well, just don't sit there. Whaddya think?"

"It's not what I expected, more peaceful. I like it."

"This is another special place for me. I can't tell you how many times I have come here. I came here after your daddy's funeral service when you and your family were at the cemetery and the church afterwards. I did a lot of thinkin' that day."

"Thinkin' about what?" They reestablished eye contact.

"You, me, and us. I thought there could be something really special between us, but that it had to be a 'two-way street' as my Granddaddy McNaughton would say."

Additional silence took hold.

Avoiding April's gaze, Russell focused on the cascading waterfall before him.

He looked inward.

"I still can't believe all that's happened since February. It's so unreal even now. None of it has been fair, none of it, but I didn't have any choice, just dealt with it as best I could. I feel like one of those snow globes, ya know? Rachel had one of them when she was younger that she kept by her bed, that when you shook it, it started snowin'."

Turning his attention to April, he continued. "But for me, the snowin's never stopped, it's never let up—being in juvie, going to court, my mother up and leavin' Rach and me, the move down here, a new school, Daddy dyin' last month. Sometimes I think my head's gonna explode."

After a short pause, Russell smiled and offered a mild laugh.

"What are you laughing at?"

"It just hit me. So weird, but Momma used to say the same thing when she had a migraine."

"Say what?"

"That her head was goin' to explode."

Russell paused then continued in a milder tone. "A lot of times I just don't know what to think."

April tightened her hold on Russell's hand.

"Rach and me had a talk awhile back, and she said something that's stuck with me. She called us orphans. I never thought of it that way until then."

Russell swatted away a mosquito.

"I wasn't that shocked when Grandma and Aunt Helen told me about Daddy dyin'. I really wasn't. I could tell by their faces. The news wasn't that big a shock. But Momma's disappearin'? That's somethin' way different.

"A lot of times, she did the best she could. We had some good times together watchin' TV, goin' to movies at the dollar theater, and goin' to city parks for picnics and free summer concerts. So, how could she just pick up and leave? I know Dominic was the reason."

Russell grew visibly angry. "How I hate that motherfucker and what he did to us."

April was surprised by Russell's choice of words.

"I don't know if I'll ever get over her leaving. I really don't. Never would I think that Momma would just pick up and leave us. Never. That's what's so hard to deal with. Since my parents broke up, it was pretty much just Momma, Rach, and me. We'd go months and months without even seein' Daddy, and he was always late on child support, which made life hard for all of us. Momma always said that Daddy chose drinkin' over us."

Russell continued to speak softly, staring at the wood chips on the ground. "But that's not the worst part."

Confused, April inquired, "What do you mean?"

"The worst part is not knowing where she is, how she's doing. Momma's not strong. Men take advantage of her; they use her just like Dominic did. They may not even be together right now. So I don't know where she is, if she's OK, still with Dominic, homeless, in jail, or passed out in some sleazy bar or what.

"Even though Daddy dyin' has been hard, I understand it. I can accept it.

"We're all going to die. Daddy's time just came earlier than most. I get that. I can deal with that. But not knowin' about Momma just eats away at me. Every day, I hope for some news, any news, but looks like that's not going to happen now, maybe ever. I just want to know she's OK, that's all. Otherwise, that sick feeling's never going to go away."

The couple sat in silence staring at the falls.

"Has anything good happened since you moved down here?"

"Yeah. Grandma's been unbelievable, Aunt Helen too."

April had hit a raw nerve. Russell continued as they locked eyes, "You're a big part of the good too," as Russell tightly gripped her hand.

"You've helped me since I moved here more than anyone by just being there, by listening. April, I've never had much of a family, but I feel like you've never judged me or my past. I don't really know why but it seems like you've been in my corner since we met at the market."

They kissed and held each other in lengthy embrace. Using the silence to craft a better response, they both swatted at mosquitoes. "We need to get out of here. We're gettin' all chewed up, but you need to know something else. I turn sixteen this summer, and I've never had a girlfriend, a real girl-friend before. This is all new to me. I've never even dated before 'cause dating takes money, and most of my restaurant money went to Momma to help out. Plus, we didn't have a car."

"That's all in the past now, Russell; we own the future."

2 3

JULY 16, 1982

———

AFTER a busy day at the market, Russell and April were relieved when they punched their time cards at 6:00 p.m. They hadn't decided what to do that evening. To save time, Russell quickly showered and changed clothes at home, while April, Grandma Esther, and Rachel casually chatted at the kitchen table.

Upon arriving at April's house for a change of clothes, Russell noticed the station wagon was gone. "Where're your folks, anyway?"

April nonchalantly responded, "Oh, they're camping in Virginia with Autumn this weekend."

The boldness of April's intention caught Russell off guard. The couple had naturally grown intimate, but April was clear that intercourse, for now, was off limits. Nonetheless, this orchestration of an unsupervised evening in her home was welcome but not expected.

In discovering Russell's lack of confidence in matters sexual, April had been the aggressor in introducing intimacy in the early stages of the relationship. While her sole reference was the selfish behavior of her former boyfriend, she longed for more mutual sexual play. April and Russell had been hampered by the lack of privacy with April's Vega being a poor choice for staging the opportunity. In light of the presenting opportunity, this Friday evening proved tantalizing.

As soon as they were inside, April eagerly walked Russell to her bedroom, all thoughts of an evening meal suspended. Drawing the curtains to her bedroom's windows, she playfully kissed him on the lips. "I'm going to take a quick shower." She lit two scented candles, started a window fan, cut the overhead light, and turned on a portable stereo, which was primed to play a series of classical LPs. April had carefully planned the couple's evening down to the last detail.

As Russell lay in April's single bed, he loosened his shirt from his jeans and kicked off his shoes. His thoughts raced and his body tensed in anticipation. This was his first time in April's bedroom, and he took everything in. The room was small, painted a muted pink, with worn, creaky hardwood floors covered by small throw rugs.

The room included a tiny closet, a standup oak dresser, a low bookshelf housing the stereo, and a compact desk complete with portable typewriter. The walls were decorated with posters, family photos, and a bulletin board dominated by quotations.

April appeared at the door after her shower, wearing a short white terry cloth bathrobe, and eagerly joined Russell on the narrow bed where they lay relaxed and entwined for several minutes.

"Are you OK with the music? I know all we've ever listened to or talked about before was country and rock, but do you like it, or do you want me to shut it off? It's OK and everythin' if you want me to turn it off."

"It's fine. It really is."

The tall, aged trees that surrounded the McNaughton home combined with the setting sun to darken the room. April appreciated Russell's patience for the ambiance to further develop, but she sensed his nervousness with what was to come.

"You know, Mr. Rankin, I think it's acceptable for you to take off your shirt and pants." Giggling, she assisted with Russell's disrobing. April swept back the bedspread and sheet, stood and turned her back while dropping her robe to reveal her total nakedness. She joined Russell again, and they kissed deeply, fondling each other as Russell shed his underpants.

Even though she had repeatedly admonished that intercourse was not to happen, she worried as to how both she and Russell would handle the privacy afforded to them by her family's absence.

With hands and mouths, the couple explored each other's bodies short of intercourse. Despite his limited experience, Russell proved a quick and adept learner as he followed April's encouragements.

The young lovers pleasured each other in known and new ways, both bodies becoming bathed in sweat. Exhausted by the intensity, the couple lay entwined, catching their breath.

"That was incredible. Just incredible. Whoa, you really are somethin'," said an exhausted Russell.

Nestling her head on Russell's shoulder and after a sustained pause to rest, April said, "You were wonderful too. I knew you would be. Russell, you need to understand something. I don't want you to get the wrong impression. I'm not experienced either. I wouldn't let Blake do much of anything. That's what pissed him off so much. I know more than most girls because I've read a lot."

"Well, where do you get books on sex, anyway? I don't think my Aunt Helen is checking them out to teenagers at the Rex Library."

"You're real funny, Russell, real funny. Hey, don't be knocking your Aunt Helen. My mother volunteers at the Rex Library a lot with special events, and she loves your aunt, just loves her, thinks the world of her.

"OK, I'll tell you a little secret. Susan Beverly and I have been best friends since the fifth grade. We know each other so well that we're like sisters. Anyway, we were both chosen for a weekend trip last February, right before you moved here, to Chapel Hill for future applicants with excellent grades. We roomed together in an old dorm."

Russell twirled a lock of April's hair as the story continued.

"During the day, we went to lectures and presentations, but Saturday evening was left open so we could explore campus and the stores and restaurants along Franklin Street, stuff like that."

"We're on a side street near Franklin Street, and Susan says that we should go into this bookstore. Hardly anyone's in the store. There's just one creepy employee, an older guy with a greasy, gray ponytail, about sixty. We're just lookin' around when Susan quietly motions me to join her.

"She found a book on the *Kama Sutra* with illustrations and everything. Well, we couldn't believe our luck, but the book was expensive, almost twenty dollars. We barely had enough money to pay for it, and I was going to use my money to buy T-shirts for Autumn and me."

Russell shifts his body to establish eye contact. "What's a Karna Sutra anyway?"

April grinned. "*Kama Sutra*, silly, *Kama Sutra*, not Karna Sutra."

"OK. *Kama Sutra*. Go on."

"The *Kama Sutra* is a Hindu love classic that describes the techniques of making love. It's the most famous book on sex ever written. It even has drawings and instructions for sixty-four sexual positions. Most of the illustrations are in color. That's probably why the book was so expensive. The main focus of the book is about sexual pleasuring.

"We decided that Susan would buy the book 'cause she looks older. She was wearing a Carolina sweatshirt under her jacket so the creepy guy with the ponytail could mistake her for a Carolina student. I left the store, and in less than five minutes, Susan ran out the door carrying a bag with this big smile on her face saying under her breath, 'We did it! We did it!'

"The only bad part of the deal was the old creepy guy at the cash register staring at her when she paid. Anyway, it was getting cold outside. So, we ran back to our dorm to look at the book, and I mean we ran. We stayed up 'til 3:00 a.m. devourin' the whole thing."

"So, where's the book now?"

"Susan's got it. We rotate it every two weeks. Hey, the music's stopped. Do you want me to...."

Russell interrupted. "No, leave it off. I'm more interested in you right now," he said, drawing her close.

The ambiance had grown more complete within the past hour, and the couple took advantage of the mood to return to their lovemaking.

As they clung to each other during a second lull, April gently whispered, "Russell, something's happened here tonight. I feel like I've never felt before, and I know it's because of you and nothing else. You're strong and kind. You don't force anything. There's a sensitivity about you that is very attractive."

Russell acknowledged April's words by caressing her and holding her tight.

He whispered, "Tonight is your doin', April. We owe tonight to you."

In the dim light of her bedroom, she stared into her boyfriend's eyes and thought, *Russell Rankin, I'm falling in love with you.*

AUGUST 6, 1982

———

ON a whim, Esther decided to do something out of the ordinary for Friday dinner. A new restaurant, the China Gate, had opened three weeks ago, and it had received positive reviews from Helen and Andrew. Esther stopped on the drive home for a takeout order.

She took the food home and ate at the kitchen table, leaving leftovers for Russell and Rachel, who were both occupied with evening activities. She looked at the kitchen, empty of family, and noting the silence, was motivated to go to The Point, a destination not visited since spring. On a muggy summer evening, she grabbed the required basics and headed out under Maddie's supervision.

Over the years, trips to The Point had served many purposes. During her married years, Esther and Lester had discussed a myriad of topics at this location, which Lester dubbed "the office." Those meetings had been valuable when the couple disagreed on a significant event or an important decision. The peaceful setting most always helped clear the vision and reconcile differences.

During her early days of widowhood, Esther sought The Point's privacy to process and soften her grief. Here she had addressed her thoughts and feelings about Lester, his absence, and her future alone.

Unashamedly, the solitude encouraged her to talk out loud with her fallen partner as she sought Lester's insight and direction. It was at this locale that the pangs of loneliness seemed to lessen as life inched toward a new balance. Esther knew that the site was key because Lester's soul always seemed present there and in the peaceful hollow below.

With Russell and Rachel's arrivals, Esther had served more as a mother than a grandmother in her role as caretaker. Daily practical decisions had to be made about school, schedules, meals, transportation, activities, and the like. Life was no longer predictable and smooth; it now contained more energy and enthusiasm.

Russell was adjusting well. Despite his shyness, he had connected with peers, especially April McNaughton, the bright classmate, who he professed was his girlfriend.

Esther smiled and proudly reflected upon Russell's respectful manner within the home. He was helpful around the house when called and frequently volunteered to help out in any way possible. Uncle Daniel gave him high marks as a part-time employee at the market.

She had few complaints, however, Russell tended to overextend his time with April. Curfew was too often challenged on nights out, a point that stressed Esther due to the link with probation requirements. Of greatest concern to Esther was Russell's growing tendency to lessen his attention toward Rachel, again due to time spent with April out of the house.

Russell had saved almost $200 from his part-time job at the market with the intent of buying a car once he completed driver's education in the fall and passed his state driver's test. Unknown to Russell, Uncle Andrew was already on the hunt for a vehicle. Esther had thought to ask Russell's juvenile counselor, Gary Harris, if any probation restriction was in place about Russell having a driver's license.

Russell was eagerly anticipating the upcoming high school football season by committing to a demanding conditioning and weight-lifting regimen during the summer.

Not to be ignored, Rachel came to mind. Rachel was needy and less secure, requiring greater attention and guidance than her brother.

Her reaction to limited enrollment at Pratt County Middle School last spring had been unremarkable. She had been aloof and unmotivated, making little effort to positively interact with teachers and new classmates.

On a positive note, Rachel had established a popular babysitting service through the church that served as a positive outlet and unexpected source of income.

Esther was pleased that the guardianship request for Rachel had been initiated with the court earlier in the summer as planned. Another positive note was Esther's eligibility for a state program designed to financially assist grandparents assuming a caretaking role for their grandchildren.

Taking respite from her review, Esther lost herself in a trio of turkey vultures drifting above as they surveyed the holler below. She stroked Maddie's head, recognizing that her loyal companion, at age seven, was beginning to slow down. The portly beagle was now less active, less adventuresome, and more inclined to stay closer to home than demonstrated during her younger years.

The caretaking role of Russell and Rachel had forced Esther to postpone any thoughts of an early retirement. Dr. Ray Willis would attest that Esther's physical health was excellent. Her weight was appropriate. She had never smoked and was a light drinker. Her sole vice was daily consumption of four to five cups of black coffee every morning. She also slept long and well, taking in seven to eight hours a night on the average.

Distant lights began to flicker in the holler below, urging Esther to begin the hike home. As a brilliant sunset began to fall, she said a heartfelt prayer to Lester, which was her custom.

"Let's go, Maddie. We're burnin' daylight. And those skeeters are sure sendin' a message."

With lit flashlight in hand and Maddie as her noble sentry, Esther began the trek home, carefully avoiding some gnarled, raised tree roots along the narrow, wooded path. On the short journey back to the house, she was reminded of a troublesome topic that she had unintentionally avoided during her reflective time this evening—the growing discord in Daniel and Janice Rankin's marriage.

2 5

DIARY ENTRY—AUGUST 13, 1982

For the first time in my life, I made love tonight in a beautiful special way to Russell. Tonight's lovemaking took place in my bedroom with my parents and Autumn out of town on a camping trip.

Tonight was planned after we pledged our love for each other earlier this month. I wanted it special. I wanted it memorable and not in some hurried and cheap way. Tonight had to be perfect with someone special because this memory would be with me the rest of my life. When Russell and I got off work at the market, we went straight to my house. We took separate showers. This just raised the excitement. My room was hotter than usual, so only one candle tonight. I turned on my stereo ... Schubert and Ravel.

What I'll remember most about tonight was Russell's patience and concern for me. He was such a gentleman. That's what I love so about him. He kept saying that he didn't want to hurt me, that he would stop if I was in pain or uncomfortable in any way. That never happened. The foreplay helped.

I gulped as he entered, but there was no pain. Momma had always thought that my hymen had been broken years ago from sports. She must have been right. Russell asked me if I was OK. I'll never forget that. He was so sensitive, so sweet and concerned about me.

These were heavenly, tingling feelings that I had never known before, but it was special because of Russell, the boy who I love with complete heart. It was so important to me that he be the first. I will never forget tonight. I will never forget the young man who so gently introduced me to womanhood. I'll always remember both his strength and his gentleness.

Tonight was more than I ever hoped for. How I love this boy and how he loves me!

For now, it is our special secret ... our lasting memory. And yes, I want more and more.

—ALM

2 6

SEPTEMBER 17, 1982

———

FOR as long he could remember, Ray Willis had aspired to be a small-town doctor. Hailing from mountainous northeast Georgia, Dr. Willis had practiced as a family physician in Colby for over thirty years.

This was Doc's eighth year as the team physician for Pratt County High School's football team. To no one's surprise, Doc accepted no payment for his services, in large part due to his two sons playing football for PCHS in the mid- to late-sixties.

Doc was average in stature with thick, course gray hair. His voice was brusque, yet respectful. He was renowned in Pratt County as a knowledgeable and caring physician. He knew when to refer to medical specialists in Charlotte or Winston-Salem when the case demanded.

This fifth game of the season matched Pratt County versus the visiting Mitchell Marauders, a team deep in talented players. With Mitchell leading 13-6 in the third quarter, a violent collision took place between Russell and Mitchell's star running back James Newsome. Doc instantly sprang into action.

Russell's head had soundly whiplashed when he hit the turf; Newsome's fall to the ground was awkward, helmet and right shoulder pad hitting the ground simultaneously in one graceless, downward thud.

As both players lay motionless on the ground, Doc surmised Russell's injury to be more severe, so Russell was attended to first. Before Doc could even examine Russell's eyes, he summoned veteran EMT Charlotte Gillen to apply gauze and pressure to the bridge of Russell's nose. Blood from a half-inch gash was trickling into Russell's left eye.

Doc's examination revealed both pupils dilated, confirming what he highly suspected—concussion and most likely a severe one.

Doc cracked open a capsule of smelling salts, and with calm reassurance, Russell was conscious in a minute, although restless and disoriented. Doc was relieved to see that Russell possessed movement in all extremities.

EMT and Mitchell personnel attended to James Newsome, who was awake but in significant pain. Within a few minutes of the collision, Newsome was sitting up, leaning forward while clutching his right forearm. He sobbed quietly, while lead EMT John Fergusson and an assistant coach hoisted him from the ground. On wobbly legs, he was walked to the waiting ambulance. Generous and heartfelt applause erupted from both teams and respective fans.

Fergusson reported, "Doc, we're taking the Mitchell boy to County. I suspect we might have a broken collarbone here, concussion as well."

"Got it. When's the backup getting' here? We're gonna need it. We got a concussion here, too," Doc said.

"One's already on the way, Doc … it should be here in about two minutes."

"Hey, and no silly sirens, John, in either wagon. Neither one of them needs the noise."

While awaiting the arrival of the second ambulance, Doc made a calculated decision to remove Russell's helmet. Feeling confident of no spinal injury, he carefully removed the helmet, much to Russell's protest.

The helmet had cracked between the strap lock screw and the lower edge of the helmet. The facemask had broken as well, in close proximity to the strap lock screw.

Doc and EMT Gillen carefully applied a neck brace, and Russell was slowly shifted to a backboard.

Doc and Coach Mo, who had joined the scene, continued giving Russell simple explanations. "Son, this is Dr. Willis. You've had a nasty whack to the head in a Pratt County football game. What's important is that you're OK, but we need to take you to the hospital for some follow-up medical work. Remember, son, you're OK even though you don't feel OK, right now. You're in good hands. You're going' to be fine."

Russell was unresponsive.

Coach Mo intruded, "Hey, Russell, this is Coach Mo. You hang in there, and I'll see you after the game. I think we may have them on the run because of you." Doc rolled his eyes but said nothing.

Since the game-stopping tackle and to get better vantage, Esther had moved down from the home stands to the cyclone fence that separated the stands from the track and football field. She was visibly shaken. She had attended the game with local judge Harlan Ballard, a friend through church.

In this small town and tight community, there was a long-standing bond between Judge Ballard and Dr. Willis. They were Thursday night poker buddies and were known to occasionally share glasses of Kentucky bourbon at Judge Ballard's home. Doc, noticing Esther and Judge Ballard's nearby presence, motioned for them to wait until Russell was loaded onto the ambulance.

At Doc's direction, Russell, still prone, was lifted onto the litter and rolled to the second ambulance. During his transfer to the ambulance, Russell groaned, attempted to sit up, and then vomited off the side of the litter. Once at the ambulance's rear door, he was lifted into the ambulance to a rousing applause from teary-eyed Pratt cheerleaders, players, and spectators, representing both high schools.

Doc gave John Fergusson emphatic instructions, "Remember, no sirens."

Referees resumed the game while Doc spoke at the fence to Esther and Judge Ballard. A sobbing April McNaughton and two supportive girlfriends soon joined them.

April interrupted and said, "Dr. Willis, is Russell going to be all right?"

"He's gonna be fine." Doc turned his attention to Esther and Judge Ballard. "He's got a pretty good concussion. They'll need to suture that gash at the bridge of his nose and do a more thorough medical exam at the ER. The real concern is the concussion. Dr. Price is the ER doctor workin' tonight, and she's a good one. She knows her stuff. Don't be surprised if Russell's kept overnight for observation. That's pretty standard in situations like this; he'll likely be discharged in the morning. I'm obligated to stay here 'til the game is over, but afterwards, I'll follow up at the ER. This is what I know for now. Esther, any questions?"

Esther looked downward and shook her head without voicing a word.

"Esther, look at me."

With eye contact now fixed, Doc said, "Russell's going to be all right. He might miss a football game or two, but in the long run, he'll be just fine. I suspect you'll want to get to the ER for now so I won't keep you. I still have a job to do here. OK, y'all better get on your way."

Esther and Judge Ballard offered their thanks and left the stadium for the adjoining parking lot. Esther's final words before leaving were to April. "I'll call your house later tonight when I know more, I will. Don't worry, sweetie, Russell's gonna be OK."

Still sobbing, April was comforted by girlfriends as they sought privacy in a remote corner of the stadium grounds.

* * *

Tonight was Doc Willis's first exposure to the construction and remodeling taking place at Pratt County General's emergency room. The area was in major disarray, with all phases of the operation disrupted by downed walls, plastic sheets hanging as room dividers, inoperative bathrooms, and a displaced waiting room, which now occupied a narrow hallway.

Fortunately, the emergency room's only patrons at that moment were Russell and Mitchell's injured player James Newsome. Doc Willis immediately checked in with Dr. Price, "What d' ya know, Beth?"

"Evenin', Ray. The Mitchell boy just came back from X-ray; he may have a collarbone break or at least a deep bruise. His concussion is milder than Rankin's. He's oriented, and he can go home tonight as long as he continues to stabilize."

"What about Rankin?"

"He certainly got the worst of it. Suturing his nose was a challenge because he was so restless. He's got a major headache, still nauseated and vomiting. His cervical x-rays were normal. I'm keeping him tonight for observation. He may have some broken fingers, but we'll deal with that in the morning when he's not as restless. He's with his grandmother now."

"Good. Monday, I'm going a call a medical school classmate to set up a neurological next week at Bowman Gray."

"Yeah, I totally agree with that. I'll show you to his room in the midst of our mess. By the way, if all goes to plan, I'm going to discharge the Rankin boy tomorrow morning when I'm relieved. The construction crew starts up at eight and that's the last thing he needs is all of that noise." Doc nodded in agreement.

Doc moved to the bay housing Russell. "Hello, Raymond," said Esther. "Glad you came by."

"How you doin' Esther with all of this?"

"I'm OK. It's just so hard seein' my Grandson hurtin' this much." Tears welled in her eyes.

As Esther remained seated, Doc stood aside her and gently massaged her shoulder. "The good news is the worst is likely behind us. Russell's had a major trauma to his brain, and it simply needs time to settle down and heal."

"I understand, Raymond, I do."

"He's going to miss some school. Plus football is totally out of the question for now."

Esther nodded in agreement.

"Where'd Harlan go, anyway?"

"He ran home to let the dog out. He's comin' right back."

At this point, Russell was resting quietly in his hospital bed. The fidgeting had stopped, and a previously administered injection had helped quell the pain and counter his upset stomach.

Doc sat in an empty chair. "Esther, Dr. Price is in agreement with me that a neurological exam should be scheduled next week. This is just a precaution, nothin' to be alarmed about. I know a neurologist in Winston, Dr. McConnell, an old med school buddy of mine, and I'm pretty certain that I can arrange for him to see Russell sometime next week. Perhaps Helen or a friend could help you drive down there and back?"

"I'm sure I'll be able to work somethin' out," Esther said with a forced smile. "By the way, Raymond, did you see the Mitchell boy's parents when you came through?"

"No, I must have missed them."

"I had a nice chat with Mrs. Newsome. She was so kind and supportive. I think their boy is going home tonight. Looks like he may have broken his collarbone."

"Yep, we certainly have two beat-up boys, right now. That's for sure. That was one terrific collision. Are you goin' home or stayin' the night, Esther? You know you could go home and get some decent sleep before Russell's discharged tomorrow mornin."

"No, I'm not goin' anywhere. You know me. I can sleep anywhere. I'm needed here." Doc chose not to challenge.

Now both standing, Doc and Esther hugged.

"Now, now, Esther, as I said from the start, your grandson's goin' to be all right. He just needs time to mend. Give my best to Harlan, now, hear?"

Esther nodded. "And I still need to call April."

Doc checked in to confirm facts with Dr. Price before leaving. A gentle, misty rain was now falling, with fog likely to follow as Doc left the hospital for the short drive home. Warmed-up meatloaf and mashed potatoes would be waiting for him as a late dinner.

27

SEPTEMBER 18, 1982

———

RETIRED educator Roy Henry had overslept and was running late. Fortunately, his wife had reminded him of the Saturday morning commitment as they washed dishes the night before. The last thing he needed had he missed Saturday breakfast was to serve as fresh fodder for J.T. Granger.

Thankfully, Roy had to drive only a few short miles to Colby. He turned into Connie's parking lot with a few minutes to spare.

For almost four years now, four 1928 graduates of Colby High School met the third Saturday of the month for breakfast at Connie's Courthouse Diner. Connie's was a fixture in Colby, at one time the only sit-down restaurant in town.

The restaurant consisted of two large rooms, front and back, as they were known by familiar patrons, connected by a narrow hallway, which accessed the men's and women's bathrooms. Front-room seating included a counter and ten stools, eight square tables, and six roomy booths. Kitchen personnel were easily visible behind the counter area.

The interior walls were faded red brick, adorned with a jumbled collection of photos, local paintings, metal signs, framed letters, maps, and other assorted memorabilia. On the wall behind the cashier's station, framed photos of active and retired military were displayed.

The idea to establish a monthly breakfast tradition to "stay better connected during our senior years" was born from a discussion at a fiftieth Colby

High School reunion. Both Caleb Moore and J.T. Granger claimed credit for the concept, a point of ongoing, good-humored contention between the two. Connie's was the obvious choice for breakfast due to its familiarity, central location, and excellent, home-cooked food.

When Roy arrived, George McLemore was already seated, reading an edition of *The Charlotte Observer.* George was a tall, thin man in excellent physical shape. Despite his partial baldness and snow-white hair, he more resembled a man in his early sixties than seventies. George was a navy veteran and retired commercial airline pilot.

Roy and George had barely greeted one another when Caleb Moore joined them. Caleb, a Pratt County native, army veteran, and contractor, was short and stout. He prided himself being a lifetime bachelor. Caleb had lived most of his life near the small, unincorporated town of Waverly in a house that he built himself.

The threesome ordered coffee from a familiar waitress, exchanged pleasantries, and snickered at J.T. Granger's tardiness. "Oh, J.T. will be here, for sure. I saw him just yesterday mornin' at the post office, and he was all pumped up about last night's football game. Rest assured, he will be here," Caleb said.

As coffee was served, cattle rancher J.T. Granger, barreled into the restaurant, as was his custom. Larger than life, J.T. walked with a slight limp, an injury sustained at age thirteen in a car accident. The injury proved devastating to him as it disallowed interscholastic sports in high school and military service during World War II.

Extroverted, loud, and frequently profane, J.T. was well known as a sage and successful cattle rancher and breeder and one of the town's more colorful characters. He'd suffered a serious personal setback two years prior when he lost his high school sweetheart and wife of forty-six years, to breast cancer. J.T. was still lively and boisterous but not to the degree before his wife's death.

By designed agreement, all glanced and tapped their wristwatches with raised eyebrows to mock J.T.'s tardy arrival.

Ignoring the snub, J.T. questioned, "Did you hear?"

"Hear what?" Caleb asked.

"Our boys beat 'em. Coach Mo and the boys whipped Mitchell. Can you believe it? This is huge. This is just so huge. Just Pratt County's version of David and Goliath, that's all."

Clearly, J.T.'s breakfast mates were not fully appreciative of the significance of Friday night's victory.

The group took their seats at a back-room table. J.T. continued his game coverage.

"When's the last time Pratt County ever played Mitchell? Never, right? 'Cause Mitchell's a powerhouse, that's why, and a much bigger school, and it's in Virginia. When do we ever play anyone out of state? Never," J.T. said emphatically.

"Hold up, J.T. Just hold up. Don't have a heart attack. What was the final score anyway?" Roy asked.

"We beat 'em, twenty to thirteen. Mitchell's ranked number six in Virginia with an all-state running back who we knocked out of the game. Mitchell brought over sixty players; we have twenty-nine on the team. Their championship band is five times our size, and they brought seven school buses. Can you believe it? They probably had as many fans at the game as we did. Fortunately for us, they drove back home to Mitchell sadly disappointed," J.T. said with an impish grin.

Interrupting the foursome appeared Ruth Ann, a feisty, middle-aged waitress, who was somewhat of a female version of J.T. "J.T., what are you so excited about, anyway? Shoot, we can hear you blabberin' all the way back to the kitchen."

"Darlin', talkin' about the big game last night 'cause our boys whooped the number-six team in the whole state of Virginia, twenty to thirteen, that's all. Little Pratt County beat the boys from Mitchell and their snooty coach," J.T. said, beaming.

"Well, good for the Ridge Runners. I'll bet my grandson was at the game. You know, come to think of it, I did hear some talk up front earlier when we first opened about last night's game. J.T., coffee?"

"Sure thing, darlin'. Thank you much."

"Seems two boys got sent to the hospital, that right?" Ruth Ann said.

"Yup, their all-state running back and Esther Rankin's grandson on our end. More on that later. Let's order some breakfast."

Switching gears, Ruth Ann got down to business. "All right, gentlemen, what be your likin' this fine mornin'?"

In predictable fashion, Caleb and J.T. ordered biscuits and gravy. Roy settled for a western omelet, while George opted for Belgian waffles, an item only available on Saturday's menu.

Ruth Ann collected the menus and smiled. "Y'all continue with your spirited discussion."

Before J.T. could continue, Roy said, "J.T., something's missing here that I don't get. Now, I only coached high school baseball, mind you, never football, but what is Pratt County doing playin' a larger school from out of state? All that's likely to happen is for us to get our butts kicked." Shaking his head, Roy asked, "Why was the game scheduled in the first place?"

"Roy, that's a long story, and I won't bore you boys with all the details. But Coach Mo and the Mitchell Coach Vance Eddy go back a ways. They both played together at Skyline where they had a bad fallin' out after Skyline lost the championship game their senior year, somethin' to do with a fumbled snap that proved critical to the outcome. Let's just say they don't feel too kindly toward one another."

"OK, there's got to be more to this," Roy said.

"You bet. They both attended a coaches' clinic at Wake Forest a few years back. In the parking lot after the clinic, Eddy got on Coach Mo one more time. It got so heated with Eddy's rantin' and ravin' that some Wake Forest assistant coaches had to intervene. The end result was Eddy, right there in the parking lot, challenging Coach Mo to a game in Colby between Pratt County and Mitchell. Coach Mo accepted on the spot."

"Whoa, that's some story, J.T." Roy said. "Eddy sounds like someone who shouldn't be coachin' or teachin' anywhere. How's he getting away with crap like this?"

"The Eddys are a well-known, influential family in Mitchell, come from railroad money, with the family's biggest asshole being a business teacher and head football coach at Mitchell High School."

Breakfast orders are delivered, but the discussion again turns to last night's game. J.T. is on a roll and has his classmates fully engaged.

George chimed in, "J.T., you were the only one of us at the game. It seems like the odds were all stacked against us. How did Pratt win the game anyhow?"

"There was no question that our kids were pumped. We were 3-0 goin' into the game so there is better talent than in '81 or even '80. Russell Rankin, you know Esther's grandson, has been a huge addition, and he plays both ways. Jonathan Hunt has improved at QB since last year, plus the defense is more experienced and playin' real good as a unit. God damn, did they ever play good last night."

Even Caleb Moore got into the questioning, "But really what happened last night, J.T.? What was the difference? Talent wise, we don't match up with the likes of Mitchell."

"I'm gettin' around to it, Caleb, just be patient. I'm gettin' there. One major play changed everythin' in my mind. I learned when my Chris and Dan played that some teams play up to their talent level, while some teams play down. I think that happened last night. Mitchell played down, and we played up.

"Second, I think some of that Virginia arrogance got in the way, that Mitchell thought they could simply strut down here and walk away with an easy win.

"Third, we played a near perfect game. They had three turnovers in the fourth quarter; we had zero turnovers in the whole game. We had nineteen first downs; they had fourteen, most in the first half. We had two penalties; they had nine with one unsportsmanlike conduct penalty called on their asshole head coach. And there was this monster play where both teams lost their best player."

At this point, all breakfast orders, save for J.T.'s, were being readily consumed. All eyes and ears remained riveted on J.T., who was yet to touch his biscuits and gravy.

"Mitchell's all-state running back is James Newsome, black boy. He's a real stud at six feet two inches and 210, a Virginia state high school finalist in the one hundred meters. He's had a boatload of major offers including Virginia Tech, Tennessee, and Clemson, even Penn State. He's committed to Navy."

George McLemore jumped in, "Whoa, whoa, whoa. You said Navy. Navy? Did I get that right, or has my hearin' gone bad?"

"Yup, I can't figure it out either, but that's what I heard from a Mitchell fan as I was gettin' barbecue. Somethin' about the boy wantin' to captain submarines."

Caleb joined the discussion. "How does this big play figure into everythin'?"

"Lookin' back, you really had to be there to 'ppreciate it, but one play did change everythin'. It's 13-7 at half-time, and most folks are just surprised that we're even in the game. That defense I mentioned did a good job of bottling up Newsome even though he did score both of Mitchell's touchdowns.

"Mitchell got the openin' kickoff, with Newsome almost takin' it back for a touchdown, but Esther's grandson knocked him out of bounds with a fierce tackle that Newsome took issue with. Newsome started glarin' and finger-pointin', which our boy Rankin just ignorin' it all. Of course, Coach Eddy, the cock rooster that he is, was jumpin' up and down, demandin' a penalty for a late hit. It was close to a penalty, I'll say that, but the refs didn't call it. Maybe home field advantage, I don't know, but it was one nasty tackle."

At this point, Ruth Ann returned to freshen their coffee. The group remained locked on J.T.'s narrative.

"I got a great view of the play because I don't sit in the stands. I bring a folding chair and sit behind the southwest corner of the end zone with disabled vets Petey Newby and Everett Bennett, who are in wheelchairs.

"Anyway, on second down and twelve with the ball on our thirty-eight-yard line, Mitchell runs a draw play with Newsome carryin' the ball.

"It was as if the Red Sea had parted. I swear, you could have driven a truck through that hole, yep, a truck. I'm not kiddin'. There was no one on the field in position to stop Newsome 'cept Rankin.

"Rankin plays safety, but he really plays more like a linebacker. Anyway, as soon as Newsome burst through the line, you saw the potential for the showdown. Newsome seemed to head straight for Rankin, almost like he was drawn by a magnet with Russell bidin' his time, cautiously waitin' for the perfect time to strike. And strike he did. God damn, did he hit that Mitchell boy!"

The others remained mesmerized by J.T.'s narrative.

"Boys, I've watched a lot of high school football in my day, but I've never seen anythin' like this. Newsome made no effort to fake or sidestep Rankin. He seemed intent on punishin' him, like unfinished business, for the earlier tackle on the kickoff. Rankin positioned himself just right and sprung, just like some cobra, at the perfect moment with the fiercest head-on tackle I've ever seen. That boy buried his helmet into Newsome's chest, and BAM! Newsome's helmet came flyin' off his head from the impact. The sound from the tackle was enough to scare ya. God damn! I just wish Lester could have seen it. He would have been so proud.

"You could hear a gasp from both stands, and the whole stadium went dead-quiet. Both boys lay motionless on the field; I thought for a second one of them, or both, might be dead. Doc Willis is the team physician, you know, and as I live and breathe, I never knew a sixty-year-old man could run so fast. After the tackle, hell, that wasn't a tackle; it was like two runaway freight trains collidin'. Doc ran from our bench already motionin' for the paramedics to assist him on the field. Both head coaches rushed to join the medical staff around our twenty-five-yard line.

"The stadium remained dead quiet. Everyone in the stands was on their feet. Not a soul was sitting down from either side as the players were treated on the field. Even the concession stand and barbecue truck stopped sellin'. The ambulance positioned itself on the track closer to Russell and the Mitchell boy. Both boys showed movement, which was a good thing."

Said George McLemore, "Well, J.T., who do you think got the worst of it."

"I'll bet they both got concussions, Rankin for sure. Rankin got the worst of it in my mind. He also had a cut over his nose that was bleedin' pretty good. With some help, Newsome walked to the ambulance. He kept clutchin' his left arm. Here's the crazy thing—he never fumbled the ball. I'll give that boy credit. The football was still clutched in his right hand as he lay on the ground."

"Russell was then lifted on a stretcher."

Roy intervened with a question. "Hey, J.T., how'd you get to know Esther anyway? She was a few years behind us wasn't she?

"Esther and Cora Lynn became good friends through their volunteer work at the library. Cora Lynn and Lester, Esther's husband, were both raised and schooled in Wheeler County where their families were acquainted. Both families tobacco-farmed so I know Esther from her ties to Cora Lynn. The four of us played cards a lot for years. That's how I got to know Lester. Now there was a hell of a good, good man. Caleb knows."

Caleb nodded in agreement.

"OK, I understand that Mitchell's big star was out of the game, but being state-ranked and all, Mitchell had more guns than, what's his name?" George said.

"Newsome," J.T. said. "That's the damnedest thing. Things seemed to shift our way. After the injury, Mitchell got the ball to our four-yard line. They failed to score on a fourth down pass. You should have seen Coach Eddy's clipboard flyin' in the air when that pass failed. We then go ninety-six yards in seventeen plays for the tying touchdown. That Hunt boy was so damn good leading the team. You know he's goin' to West Point. He was so cool, so in control runnin' the Wing T to perfection. And you've got to credit Coach Ernie Mack for callin' the offensive plays from the press box because Mitchell just had no answers for us on defense."

Having finished his western omelet, Roy said, "You know, you've done so much yappin', J.T., that you haven't even taken one bite of those biscuits."

Realizing that his biscuits had cooled, J.T. quietly motioned Ruth Ann to the table as he hoisted up his plate, "Darlin', could you please heat up these biscuits for me under one of those warmin' lamps? I appreciate it."

Seizing a perfect opportunity to spar with J.T., Ruth Ann responded with a snarl as she took the plate, "You serious? You know if you stopped runnin' your mouth and ate your breakfast like normal people, this would not be necessary."

"Thank you, Ruth Ann, thank you darlin'." J.T. countered with his signature wink.

Having captivated his breakfast mates with his account of the game, J.T. smugly sat with folded hands as he talked of the fourth quarter.

"The big difference was that Mitchell had three turnovers in the final quarter that killed any hopes of them scorin'. I think it was two interceptions and one fumble, but Tommy Gleason, you know Hazel Gleason's grandson, recovered a fumble, and two plays later, Scooter Monroe caught the winning touchdown pass with about four minutes left on the clock."

Caleb Moore then broke his silence. "J.T., I think you missed your callin', you should give up on those cows and start doin' TV announcin' for the ACC or the NFL."

J.T. chuckled in response. "I'll stick to cattle, thank you."

At this point, Ruth Ann returned with J.T.'s warmed plate, "Here you are, Your Majesty." She dumped the plate on the table with a mild thud.

"Thank you, sweetie," responded J.T.

George returned to the game. "Well, how did the game end? J.T., our boys must have gone crazy."

Alternating bites of biscuits with delayed dialogue, J.T. resumed his analysis. "It was somethin'. The Mitchell players and coaches were stunned, like they couldn't believe it. The Pratt boys held their helmets high, jumpin' up and down, screamin' their heads off. The cheerleaders joined the players on the field. Students hopped the fence and rushed the field. In the middle of all this, the Pratt players and coaches shook hands with Mitchell's kids and coaches, whose heads were down, slowly walkin' to their buses. Oh, yea, our parents were having their own celebration in the stands."

"Did you notice the meeting between Coach Wilkes and the Mitchell coach, what's his name?" Roy asked.

"Vance Eddy. You know, Roy, that's funny you should ask because I was caught up with the scene as well as were Petey and Everett. But, in the midst of all of this, I saw their meetin' perfectly.

"Considerin' their history, it wasn't what I expected. They had a long handshake, with Eddy patting Coach Mo on the shoulder. Eddy did the talkin'. He seemed genuine and contrite with his congratulations, as he looked Coach Mo square in the eye. I was surprised, real surprised, not what I expected."

Caleb followed up. "Well, what was Coach Wilkes' response?"

"He looked stunned too. I suppose not what he expected either."

Ruth Ann returned to refresh coffee mugs and to clear J.T.'s plate. "I hope you got enough fuel from those biscuits because you sure were an attraction this mornin'."

J.T. intentionally chose not to spar, and with restrained poise said, "Thank you, Ruth Ann, thank you very much for your waitressin'."

Twenty minutes of general chatter followed, with the mandatory health checks dominating the discussion. Caleb's worsening arthritic knees received most attention.

"Gentlemen, I gotta run," Roy said. "Beth and I have a wedding to go to in Lenoir so I need to get back home to pick her up and make the drive down there."

"Yeah, I got a fence to mend, seems like that's all I do most of the time, mend fences," J.T. growled with disgust.

Caleb was encouraged to take it easy.

Hands were shaken. Shoulders patted. The next meeting date was confirmed.

J.T. calmly announced, "I got the tip."

"Well, that's a first. Don't be stingy now," George said.

"I never am, George. You know that," J.T. said with a devilish smile.

After the four had departed, Ruth Ann noticed an extremely generous gratuity as she wiped off the table for the next customer. Her eyes softly brightened, knowing full well the source of the gift.

SEPTEMBER 18, 1982

———

RUSSELL was up Saturday just after 6:00 a.m. X-rays were taken of the fourth and fifth fingers of his left hand. They proved positive for fractures. After taking a shower supervised by a hospital orderly, Russell dressed and met with Dr. Price, who bandaged and splinted the two fingers together.

Due to Russell's condition and the likelihood that he would retain little medical advice upon discharge, Dr. Price updated Esther and Aunt Helen in a hallway. The conversation shifted to Russell's bay where he lay resting in bed. He was dressed in shirt and jeans delivered earlier in the morning by Aunt Helen.

Dr. Price presented discharge orders. "We're going to let you go home, Russell, but you're not out of the woods yet. Your grandmother and aunt have been given instructions about your diet and pain medication, which you should take until you are pain-free. For now, a lot of liquids and nongreasy foods, nothing that might upset your stomach.

"You may not remember it, but you suffered a major concussion last night at the football game. I can't stress this enough. The most important thing for you is bed rest in a quiet, darkened room. You need simple bed rest to heal, peace and quiet. No TV, no radio, no reading, no studies. Your brain needs time to rest and heal. And no visitors over the weekend, none. And you already know about your busted fingers. Any questions?"

"What about school?"

"No school until later in the week. Oh, and by the way, you had a gash over your nose that we needed to suture. Dr. Willis will need to take the stitches out in about a week. You may get a black eye or two as well. That lump above your nose will eventually go away, but it will be sore for the next couple of days."

Russell offered a simple thank you. As he rose to leave, Dr. Price handed him a pair of inexpensive black sunglasses. "These may help. It's a very sunny October morning out there. Consider it a gift from our lost-and-found department," she said with a smile.

"Mrs. Rankin, this is very important. If symptoms persist or return over the weekend, best to call Dr. Willis right away."

With written discharge orders in hand, Esther moved her car to the makeshift entryway. Aunt Helen assisted Russell into the car.

Living five minutes from the hospital, Esther drove slower than usual with Aunt Helen following behind. In entering her driveway off of Grouse Hollow Road, Esther's Chevy slowed to a halt over the crackling gravel. With both vehicles parked, Esther escorted Russell from the car to the backdoor.

To Esther's surprise, Russell went directly to his bedroom, doffed his shirt, jeans, and shoes, and went straight to bed. She closed the shade and drew the curtains.

In her predictable, kindly manner, Esther inquired, "How're you feelin', Grandson?"

"Weak and beat up, the headache, my neck, too."

"You sleep as long as you need to. I'll heat up some pot roast soup so that'll be waiting for you with home-made biscuits when you're hungry enough. For now, just get some rest." She gently kissed his forehead, tightening his covers.

"Thank you, Grandma."

"You're welcome, Grandson. The pleasure's all mine. Love you."

"You too, Grandma."

Esther joined Helen at the oak table, a permanent fixture in the family's kitchen for over three decades.

"I was just thinking, Momma. I've never known this house without this old table. How'd you and daddy acquire this piece, anyway?"

Esther smiled, easily recalling the memory. "Your daddy got it at a farm sale near Remington."

"Remington? Way down there?"

"Yep. We'd only been married a year or two. It was on a Saturday, I recollect, late winter or early spring. Your daddy was so happy and full of himself. He bought the table and six chairs for twenty dollars. I wasn't near as enthusiastic back then. That was a lot of money to us, and the table, and especially the chairs were in sad shape. They needed a lot of fixin' and refin- ishin'. We didn't have the barn then, so your daddy had to wait 'til spring to start repairs and refinish outdoors."

Esther smiled with confidence. "Your daddy did good work, didn't he? Good work."

"You know, Momma, I just marvel at your memory. How do you remember all that, four kids later and everything?" Helen poured two cups of coffee, one black, one creamed and sugared.

Fondly cradling her coffee cup, Esther cast a soft smile, gazing at Helen, "The best memories are always the easiest ones to hold on to."

Esther changed direction. "Russell's likely to have an appointment next week in Winston-Salem with a specialist. We should know the date on Monday. I can handle this on my own so no need to worry about helpin' out."

"Momma, I can certainly help."

Esther politely tapped on her daughter's hand. "Helen, you've taken enough time off. I can handle this; in fact, I want to handle this."

Rising from the table, Esther hugged her only daughter, who remained seated. "Thank you, sweetie. Thank you for understandin'. You are such a treasure to me."

Esther disappeared briefly to check on Russell.

When she returned, she said, "That boy's weak as water, just plumb knocked out, dead to the world. Oh, I guess that's a poor choice of words."

Just then, they heard the familiar sound of an arriving car on the driveway and thought it odd considering the hour. Rising to greet the visitor, Esther and Helen stepped outside to discover April McNaughton.

"Hey, Mrs. Rankin. These brownies are for Russell and you too. They're still warm. I just pulled them from the oven. Made them from scratch." April beamed with pride.

"Oh, April, that is so sweet of you, darlin'. Mercy. Thank you, thank you so much. I'm certain Russell will love them."

"How's he doin'?"

"Well, we just brought him home from the emergency room. He's doing fine. He had a decent night's sleep at the hospital, but he's pretty 'beat up,' as he calls it. I can't remember if I told you so or not, oh, I'm sorry. This is Russell's Aunt Helen. Helen, this is April McNaughton."

"Pleased to meet you officially, ma'am. I know you from the Rex Library." April transferred the brownie tray to Esther in order to shake hands.

"Pleased to make your acquaintance, April. I've heard a lot about you from Russell."

April was pleased with the recognition.

"Well, gettin' back to Russell. He has two busted fingers on his left hand, plus the concussion, plus the cut above his nose. He's supposed to rest and stay quiet all weekend. I know you'd like to see him, but he's asleep now. Plus doctors were real strict about him not having visitors over the weekend."

"Oh, no. I understand. I do. I did some readin' up on it, and I know he needs rest more than anything. Maybe I can call him tomorrow?"

"Sure. We'll take it from there as to how he's feelin'."

"Good. Well, be sure to tell him that I was askin' for him. I gotta run as I'm workin' earlier than usual today. I'll say hey to Mr. Dan for you," April said with a cute grin.

"Aunt Helen, wonderful meeting you," April hurried off to her car for the short drive to the market.

"So, that's the girlfriend," stated Aunt Helen.

"That's the girlfriend. Plus the future class valedictorian. Ain't she a peach?"

"I know she's been over here a lot, but our paths never crossed 'til now. She certainly is poised and polished for her years. Russell should invite her to Sunday dinner some week"

"Yep, wants to be a children's surgeon. Based on her grades, I think that's a good bet. Like you said, girl has a lot of polish, too, very mature for a sixteen-year-old."

They returned to the kitchen table, and Gus, the orange tabby, wound in and out of their legs as they chatted. Soon, Helen was driving back to Rex after being assured that her presence was no longer needed. Mother and daughter had decided that Helen should break the news of Russell's injury to Rachel, who had slept over Friday night with her cousins, Charlotte and Grace.

Esther now turned her direction to her devotions, as was her daily custom. With Maddie sleeping next to her on the sofa, she revisited familiar passages for comfort and for strength. She was interrupted twice by deliveries of food for Russell, which included a chicken noodle casserole from Susan Emory and a dozen yellow cupcakes with chocolate icing left by two unidentified Pratt County High cheerleaders.

Late morning, Esther took an hour-long nap on the sofa until she sensed Russell stirring.

Upon rising, Russell slowly walked to the bathroom. He pulled the light cord to the medicine cabinet mirror to get a better look at his face. He squinted his eyes and stared critically at the reflected image. He then made his way to take a seat in the living room.

"How are you feelin' now, Grandson?"

"A little better. Still tired and sore. Real weak. I just checked the mirror in the bathroom. I sure don't look too good. Still got that headache, but it's not as bad. My neck is *really* sore. I was out of it in the hospital. I don't remember much of that at all. Did we win the game, or not? I can't remember, Grandma? Maybe, I dreamed that we won."

"No, Pratt County won, Russell. Folks say it was the biggest football win in years."

"Wow. Really? Too bad I don't remember anything about it. What was the score?"

"All I know is that Pratt County won."

"Wow, that's somethin'. I can't believe we won. Are you sure, Grandma? We really won?

"We really won."

"Coach Mo must be so happy. I'm happy for the team, but I'm really happy for him. I just wish I could have been part of it."

"You did just fine, Russell, and just because you don't remember the game doesn't mean that you didn't contribute."

Russell folded his hands behind his head, closed his eyes, and slowly rested his head on the top of the armchair. "Grandma, tell me what happened; how'd I get hurt."

"Well, first of all understand, I'm not much of a football fan, never have been. Never understood the game like I should, but you were involved in a tackle where you and the Mitchell player were injured so badly that you both went to the ER at County General. You suffered a concussion. Now that's enough. You're supposed to rest. You can hear more about the game when you're feelin' better."

"So what happened to the other player?"

"He got a concussion, too, not as bad as yours, but he may have a broken collarbone. Like I said, that's enough for now. How does some soup and a biscuit or two sound? You hungry yet?"

"Sounds good. I think your soup actually woke me up." "Woke you up?"

"The smell, Grandma, the smell," Russell said with a weak smile.

Esther assisted Russell to the kitchen table where a bowl of pot roast soup and a homemade biscuit were consumed and washed down by a glass of milk. Russell ate slowly and deliberately. When Esther offered him seconds, "No, Grandma, that's fine, that's enough. Thanks. I need to go lie down."

He slowly rose from the table and, with Esther's caring escort, returned to his bedroom, undressed, and lay in bed. She attended to the window shades and curtains again to assure maximum darkness for the room. As she leaned down to kiss Russell on his forehead, she heard, "Grandma, what are the brownies and cupcakes all about?"

"Some appreciation from friends. We'll talk about it after your nap. Have a good sleep. Russell, I need to ask; is that C&O station clock in the hallway botherin' you?

"Never heard it."

"I was worried about it troublin' you."

For the rest of the day, Esther caught up on the wash and other household chores. She also held a long overdue phone chat with Libbie.

Helen returned with a concerned Rachel just after 4:00 p.m. so Esther could practice Sunday's selected hymns at the church. More offerings of food arrived during the afternoon: oatmeal raisin cookies, chocolate chip muffins, and a brown sack of freshly picked apples from Moberly Orchards.

Russell rose from his extended nap encountering an apprehensive Rachel at the kitchen table. She was horrified at his appearance.

"Whatever happened to you? You look awful. You got this all from a football game?"

"Uh, huh. That's what they say. I don't remember a thing."

"You know you're getting' two black eyes, Russell. And what's that bandage over your nose for, anyway?"

Aunt Helen joined brother and sister in the kitchen.

"Rachel, your brother got a cut at the top of his nose that had to be stitched up."

"And what's the matter with your fingers?"

"Broken."

Rachel did not offer consolation. Aunt Helen interjected, "Rachel honey, Russell's worst injury is that he suffered a concussion."

"What's that?"

"It's when you get a nasty bump to your head. He needs a lot of rest, peace, and quiet for a few days until he's going to start feeling himself again."

"Sorta sounds like Momma when she got her migraines."

Rachel became distracted by the donated baked items resting on the kitchen counter."

"Aunt Helen, did you bake all that stuff?"

"No, sweetie, I didn't. Some folks brought them over earlier today."

"For what?"

"Well, I think it might represent a way of people showing their concern."

Sensing Rachel's lack of understanding, Aunt Helen added, "You know, concern about Russell's injury."

"Oh, I get it," as Rachel cut a large brownie from April's pan.

29

SEPTEMBER 19–21, 1982
COLBY, NC
WINSTON-SALEM, NC

———

RACHEL wanted some private time with her Grandma Esther this Sunday morning so she was up earlier than expected. She had showered, combed her hair, and found a dress she was certain would pass inspection for church.

Already dressed, Esther prepared a light breakfast of juice, cereal, and blueberry muffins while awaiting Helen's arrival as substitute caretaker. She had checked on Russell when she'd awakened and found him sleeping soundly with Gus, who was nestled at the foot of his bed.

As Rachel took a seat at the kitchen table, Esther said, "You're up earlier than usual and looking so pretty for church. That dress fits you well, darlin'. Good choice."

"I thought you'd say that, Grandma," Rachel said with slightly smug confidence.

"Grandma, may I ask you a question?" "Mercy, of course you may.

"How come you call Russell and me Grandson and Granddaughter all the time?"

"Well, darlin', does that cause you alarm?"

"No, not really. Grandmother Packer never called us that. She always called us Rachel or Russell. I'm just not used to it. Sometimes, I think you've forgotten our names."

"No, sweetie, nothing could be further from the truth. I reckon I call you Grandson and Granddaughter because of the way I was raised around my grandparents. I never thought of it that much 'til now."

"So, you're just repeatin' something you learned when you were a kid, then, right?"

"It's just that some ways of sayin' things are regional and stay with us. I'm sure they're some sayings from Illinois that would sound strange to me. I remember when your Aunt Helen came back home after living two years in Boston, she was using words and phrases we'd never heard of. We had no idea what they meant. Plus, she was talking so much faster."

"People talk slower down here, and they seem to mumble a lot, but I heard kids sayin' that they couldn't understand me too."

"How's everyone today?" Russell said softly, somewhat startling Esther and Rachel by his quiet arrival.

"How'd you sleep, Russell?" Rachel asked. "How you feelin'?"

Rachel offered her unique brand of support. "You sure don't look so good. Those black eyes seem to be gettin' worse."

"Well, I'm gettin' tired of all this sleep. It's all I do, but I do feel better today, better than yesterday. Still real weak, no energy at all. The headache's almost gone, and I don't hurt as much. But I looked in the mirror, and Rach, I sure don't look too good, just like you said."

"I'm glad to hear you're doin' better, Grandson. I'll pass that news along to Dr. Willis should he be in church today," Esther said.

Russell eased onto a chair after pouring himself a cup of coffee.

"Rachel, are you still willin' to help me make the chicken and dumplings for Sunday dinner?"

"Yes, ma'am, I want to learn your secrets," Rachel said with an impish grin.

Hearing the familiar rumble of the driveway gravel, Esther said, "Mercy. That must be Helen. I plumb lost track of time. Rachel, grab your coat. Time to go."

They quickly gathered their coats. Esther kissed Russell on the cheek. "Glad you're not hurtin' as much, Grandson. Every day's going to get a little bit better."

Greetings between Helen, Esther, and Rachel were limited in the backyard since Esther was anxious to arrive at church for hymn practice.

After shedding her coat, Helen joined Russell at the kitchen table asking for an update on his recovery. During Russell's report, she noticed the plates and containers of baked goods on the counter. "Oh, why don't we have a brownie?" she said getting up to grab plates.

Russell nodded and gladly took the brownie from her. "Where's Sunday dinner? I'm not sure I'm up to that yet."

"Uncle Daniel and Aunt Janice are hosting this week. Uncle George and I will take Rachel. Grandma will stay here with you since you're not up for all that. You know who made these brownies, don't you?"

"April?"

"Good guess and are they delicious." Russell agreed.

Aunt Helen had promised herself not to press Russell conversationally this morning, but she'd been hoping for an opportunity like this. Due to their common history, she was closer to Russell than were her brothers, and for months, she'd been wanting to talk to him privately.

After enjoying the brownies, they moved to the living room, Russell lying on the sofa and Helen taking an armchair.

"Russell, I've been meaning to talk with you for a while. I'll keep this short, but there are some things I've been wanting to share with you, some thoughts I want you to know. I hope they prove helpful to you."

He looked at her curiously. "OK. Is something wrong?"

Choosing her words deliberately, Aunt Helen smiled and began, "No, nothing's wrong. It's just, this year has not been kind to you. I shake my head as I think about all you've been through—the whole experience with juvenile court and detention, moving down here, a new school and teachers, losing your daddy before you even turned sixteen, your momma takin' off to Lord knows where. Your grandmother and I sometimes just don't know how you've done it, but you need to know how much we all believe in you and how proud we are of you since you moved here last March."

Russell was taken aback as he shifted his position on the couch. "Thanks, Aunt Helen. That means a lot coming from you."

She smiled in response.

"Russell, one more thing. You've had to make a lot of adjustments moving down here, and through it all, it would have been understandable for you to lose sight of Rachel. It's easy to see that she absolutely adores you, and you need to be recognized for helping her with the move as well."

He nodded. Brief silence followed.

"I just wish she was doin' better in school. She got off to a rough start last spring after Daddy died. Rach can be real stubborn, real mouthy, in your face. She's never really liked school. It seems that my checkin' on her homework isn't doin' any good, either. She's just got to get serious and get to work. She's hangin' with the wrong kids, too, from what I can see. That doesn't help."

Helen seemed surprised but did not comment.

"Headache's back, seems to happen when I move around," Russell announced. He returned to his bedroom after receiving Excedrin from Aunt Helen. Helen tapped Russell's shoulder to reassure. "I hope my words weren't too much for you in light of your injuries."

"No, not at all," he said. Aunt Helen adjusted Russell's covers, cut the light, and closed the door.

Russell napped on and off the remainder of the day. His headache eventually subsided, with a heating pad helping to quell the pain. His soreness remained, especially in his neck, and he noticed at the bathroom mirror that his arms were covered with bruises. His broken fingers continued their mild throb.

That evening, Esther granted Russell a ten-minute phone call to April. The call seemed to comfort and boost his spirits.

Monday morning ushered in a much-improved Russell. For the first time since Friday's accident, he was starting to feel more like himself. He made a convincing argument for Esther to leave him unattended at home with which Esther complied. He watched some morning game shows on TV but quickly lost interest. With the day being unseasonably warm, Russell and Maddie took a slow walk to Dr. Dilworth's house and back, an activity that thoroughly drained his energy. A lengthy afternoon nap followed.

* * *

Esther and Russell drove Tuesday morning to Winston-Salem for Russell's neurological exam. Dr. Glenn McConnell first addressed cognitive functioning and Russell's recall of events with a series of questions. The physical examination that followed tested Russell's visual and motor skills as to reflexes, coordination, and strength.

The previous diagnosis and treatment plan determined Friday evening was confirmed by Dr. McConnell. An excusal note was written for school with Russell permitted to return to school on Friday or Monday at his choosing. Any football participation was ruled out until Dr. Willis approved a return. The travel and morning activity severely sapped Russell's strength, and he slept soundly Tuesday afternoon upon the return home. .

That afternoon, Esther received a phone call from *Pratt County Advocate* reporter Mary Abernethy. Esther and Mary had been friends for almost forty years, having met when they both worked at Colby Chevrolet.

Among her many duties at the county newspaper, Mary covered high school sports. She had attended the Pratt–Mitchell game as reporter/photographer and her article and two photos were displayed in this Tuesday's edition of *The Pratt County Advocate*.

Knowing that the article would be of interest to Esther and her family, Mary agreed to drop off some copies of the paper's current edition on her way home. The front page of the paper included a photograph of Russell tackling James Newsome on the sidelines at the start of the second half. The photograph's caption read: "Pratt County linebacker Russell Rankin forces a Mitchell runner out of bounds during Friday night's 20-13 upset victory."

Mary was not finished. She also provided Esther with a five by seven black-and-white glossy copy of the photograph. The photo would soon adorn Russell's bedroom mirror. Russell had no recall of the tackle depicted in the photo.

30

FALL–EARLY WINTER 1982
COLBY, NC

———

RUSSELL returned to school on Friday, handling his classes well. However, he was not prepared for the response. The cheerleading squad had gone to great extent to decorate his locker, and upon his return, he received numerous well-wishes and congratulations from students and faculty alike. Due to his heroic play against Mitchell, Russell had achieved celebrity status within the school.

Per doctor's orders, Russell did not play or travel to the October 1st game against Wheeler County. As a special treat, Esther invited April to the house for the evening and a steak dinner. Afterward, Russell and April watched TV in the living room, while Esther read upstairs. Fortunately for the couple, Rachel was sleeping overnight at Aunt Helen's house with her cousins.

Despite losing two of their final three games, Pratt County made the playoffs for the first time in four years only to lose to perennial power Stinson Forge by a 27-14 score.

When state all-star teams were announced in December, Russell had earned second team status on defense. His punting prowess was disregarded on the voting, as players could only be recognized in one of three categories: offense, defense, or special teams.

* * *

Russell's classes for the 1982–1983 academic school year included American Literature, Geometry, Physics, World History, Spanish II, Societal Issues, and Driver's Education/Gym. He was pleased with his instructors with the exception of Mr. Grayson in physics who seemed to harbor a distinct dislike for accomplished athletes.

Russell and April shared only two classes during the 1982–1983 school year—Physics and American Literature—and by Christmas break, Russell had secured honor roll status once again. His favorite course was Societal Issues taught by a first-year teacher, Cassandra Barnes, Pratt County High School's third and newest African-American instructor.

* * *

Russell and Rachel's first Thanksgiving in North Carolina was celebrated at the Homestead. Aunt Libbie joined the family to celebrate the holiday, as was her custom.

Esther and Libbie roasted a huge, twenty-six-pound turkey, beginning at 4:30 a.m., with the feast served at noon. The meal was presented buffet-style in the kitchen.

Besides turkey, Uncle Andrew's venison meatballs and a barbequed ham were available as main dishes. Side dishes were abundant. Esther's macaroni and cheese dish proved the most popular. For dessert, Helen brought her popular Boston cream pie, while Aunt Libbie provided Polish apple cake, a handed-down recipe drawn from the maternal side of the family.

Esther blessed the feast, which lasted an hour. As the table was cleared at dinner's conclusion, it was converted to a serving area that would remain open for additional helpings or "grazings," as they were whimsically called, for the rest of the afternoon.

For the remainder of the day, children played assorted games inside and out.

As an active fireplace warmed the living room, men watched football, and the women chatted about their upcoming Christmas plans, which included the annual all-day shopping excursion to Charlotte.

At Esther's urging mid-afternoon, Uncle Andrew escorted Russell to the barn that uncles Andrew and Daniel had helped their father erect in the spring of 1974. The barn more resembled a garage built with salvaged lumber and a unique metal roof fashioned from abandoned boxcar panels.

For a brief time, the barn actually housed the family car, some furniture, and assorted lawn and gardening equipment; however, the true, underlying intent of the structure became known within two years of construction.

As Uncle Andrew unlocked the side door, he flicked two light switches that revealed several large overlapping white drop cloths that covered what could only be viewed as some type of platform that dominated the building's twenty by thirty feet configuration.

"Uncle Andrew, what's underneath?"

"Well, if you'll be very careful and help me remove the drop cloths, you'll see.

Just be careful."

As the first drop cloth was lifted, Russell's eyes bulged, his mouth opened in astonishment, his body bordered on temporary paralysis.

"This is unreal, totally unreal!"

"Consider this an early Christmas gift from your Grandpa Lester."

"But I don't get it. How'd Grandma know that I liked model trains?"

"Rachel."

In another minute, the partially landscaped, multi-level Lionel train layout was revealed. Russell remained in awe.

"This was one of your grandfather's real passions. He planned on finishin' it before he retired, just never got around to it." In making direct reference to Russell, Uncle Andrew added, "He needs someone to help finish and maintain it. As I see it, the track is all installed; all that's left is the landscaping."

Russell learned from Uncle Andrew's account that his grandfather, over the years, had bought and collected a diverse collection of Lionel engines, freight and passenger cars, track, transformers, buildings, and other model railroading stock. Most of the inventory had been bought at local train shows in North Carolina, but on a few occasions, Lester had taken buying trips to Virginia and Tennessee as well.

All in all, the layout included three steam and three diesel locomotives, twenty-two passenger cars, thirty freight cars, and close to forty-five buildings on a platform that totaled a little short of three hundred square feet.

"Russell, I'm not the carpenter your grandfather was, but I can help once you figure out how to finish the landscaping. I can help with any wiring that needs to be done as well."

* * *

Russell and Rachel's first Christmas in North Carolina proved unique and memorable, like nothing ever experienced before. What was new to them was the sense of order and family tradition affixed to the holiday season. The traditions were numerous including outdoor Christmas lights (this year mounted by Uncle Andrew and Russell), a freshly cut Christmas tree from a local tree farm, and tree decorating at an early December Sunday Dinner.

Additional activities involved a ladies-only shopping excursion to Charlotte, baking and decorating Christmas cookies with Aunt Helen, Christmas gift-wrapping, and Christmas Eve service at the Methodist church. Esther loved Christmas music and from early December on, she played Christmas albums on her infrequently used stereo. Her favorite singers included Andy Williams, Perry Como, Johnny Mathis, and Bing Crosby.

Due to Russell's employment and Rachel's booming babysitting service, both children were able to purchase gifts for Esther and Aunt Helen to whom they had grown especially close. Russell also purchased some fishing gear for Uncle Andrew. Aunt Libbie received Christmas gifts as well.

To engage the grandchildren, "Secret Santa" gift selections were drawn at a November Sunday dinner. Rachel had drawn cousin Grace's name, and Russell had selected Benjamin Rankin, his ten-year-old cousin. Grandma Esther insisted on a moderate dollar limit for gifts.

On Christmas morning, Russell lighted a fire in the stone hearth. Russell and Rachel joined Grandma Esther and Aunt Libbie to open gifts under the living room's Christmas tree as Christmas music played in the background. Aunt Libbie was especially touched by Russell and Rachel's inclusion of her in gift giving.

This warm, relaxed atmosphere was a new experience for brother and sister.

Their history was to receive any Christmas gifts unwrapped at the kitchen table, with the majority of gifts donated from local charities and churches.

Russell's gifts this Christmas were limited, since Grandma Esther and Uncle Andrew were intending to secure a car for Russell early the next year. Nonetheless, he received gifts that he had suggested. Rachel was pleased beyond words with her stash of presents. She was especially touched by Russell's present of a gold necklace.

Grandma Esther was overjoyed by Russell's gift of a bound collection of Broadway musical sheet music.

April visited later that morning before she had to leave to spend the bulk of the holiday with maternal relatives in Winston-Salem. Russell gave her a well-received gold necklace.

April's gift to Russell was simple, yet poignant. Because of the couple's participation on *The Chronicle*, the high school yearbook, April was able to secure a copy of a candid photograph of the couple reviewing an assignment. The five by seven photo was handsomely matted and framed. It would rest on Russell's bedroom dresser later that day.

In respect of Grandma Esther, Christmas dinner was not held at the Homestead but instead at Aunt Helen and Uncle George's home in Rex. Dinner included a roast provided by Uncle Daniel, Aunt Helen's legendary au gratin potatoes, and assorted side dishes and salads. Christmas cookies served as dessert.

As was custom, Grandma Esther and Aunt Libbie played Christmas carols and holiday songs on the piano from memory after dinner, family members comprising the chorus.

Upon returning to the Homestead later that evening, Russell and April made a point to thank and recognize Esther for giving them a Christmas like they had never experienced.

31

EARLY 1983

———

RUSSELL rarely thought about being on probation since he had no difficulty following the rules and expectations set in his probation order. The only exception was a few near-miss violations of curfew in returning from dates with April. Juvenile Counselor Gary Harris had been direct and fair with him, and he especially appreciated Officer Harris' respectful tone with Esther.

Mr. Harris had previously hinted that, due to Russell's positive response to probation, he was inclined to submit an early discharge request in early January, and he hoped the judge and probation department in Lancaster County would be receptive of such a recommendation.

Russell was discharged from probation in late January. Through the court approval of guardianship filings in Illinois and North Carolina, Esther now assumed Russell's guardianship, a role she had assumed for Rachel in August of the past year.

Mr. Harris paid his last visit to Russell and Esther in late January to present copies of the official discharge paperwork. Since Russell was now officially off probation, the conversation was short and candid.

Sitting at the kitchen table, Mr. Harris provided some parting words of support.

"I've been doing this job for three years now. If you had told me when I was in college that I would become a juvenile counselor after graduating, I would have called you crazy.

"The toughest part of the job is that we see the worst that society can offer. We can see the ugly side, the underbelly as a colleague of mine calls it. Pratt County isn't Charlotte or Winston-Salem or Atlanta, but there's ugliness here as well, maybe just not as much, maybe harder to see, but it's definitely here too.

"I see a fair amount of failure and disappointment in this job. I try not to take it personally because, often, by the time I get kids on probation, it's already too late.

"The job gets to us sometime because it can be negative and depressing, but, Russell, you were very different than most of the juveniles I've supervised. It wasn't just your response to probation, it was how you handled the move to North Carolina, your mother's disappearance, and your father's death last spring. You have been a refreshing change for me.

"Russell, your adjustment could have been very, very different, but it wasn't because of you, your grandmother, and other family. Mrs. Rankin, you had a major role with this; your stepping forward to care for Russell and his sister was so important. I know this wasn't on your agenda, but thank you for assuming the responsibility.

"To keep going in this job, we need success stories, and Russell, you are one of mine, not because of anything I did but because of the example you set, the smart decisions you made, the discipline that you imposed on yourself."

Mr. Harris stood, smiled warmly, and shook hands with Russell and Esther. "Well, I best be going. I wish you well. Likely that I might run into you around town, but for now, take care."

Upon Mr. Harris' departure, Esther turned to Russell. Her eyes twinkled. "Nice, belated Christmas gift, don't ya think?"

* * *

An expected development in January was Russell's acquisition of a car, a 1974 tan Oldsmobile Cutlass. Uncle Andrew and Esther had agreed that the car would serve as a Christmas gift to Russell from the two of them, but Russell would be responsible for the balance to be paid in regular installments to his uncle. Uncle Andrew would carry the Cutlass on his insurance, but Russell was responsible for covering his portion of Andrew's policy. The car would remain under Uncle Andrew's registration at least while Russell made payments for the next few years.

In late-December, Uncle Andrew had struck gold in locating the Cutlass at an auction in Winston-Salem. It was in mint condition, with mileage under fifty-five thousand miles. From his exhaustive knowledge of cars and after a thorough inspection, he surmised that the vehicle was lightly driven and meticulously maintained. The Cutlass was a steal, and Andrew was thrilled by the find.

Russell had passed driver's ed in the fall, and the state driving test a few days prior to Christmas.

Uncle Andrew asked Russell to stop by his shop to discuss something important one day when he revealed the car and laid out all conditions for him to take possession. Russell jumped at the opportunity and agreed to all expectations. He had saved most of his earnings from the market, so regular payments would not be a problem.

Before the keys were handed over, uncle and nephew made two test runs around the county, one during the day and one at night. The test runs even included some interstate driving at Uncle Andrew's insistence. Andrew sternly admonished Russell that if he ever heard of or saw Russell driving recklessly or under the influence, he would "yank that car permanently" from his possession.

The keys were handed over to Russell at an early February Sunday dinner, which included April as special guest. Russell was ecstatic.

No one would learn to value the Cutlass more than April.

3 2

SPRING/SUMMER 1983
COLBY, NC
DUBLIN LAKE, NC
BROADWATER, NC

THE relationship between Esther and Judge Harlan Ballard rekindled in the spring of 1983. Judge Ballard was a widower. Previously, he was married for twenty-nine years to the former, Frances Van Zandt, who hailed from nearby Laurel, North Carolina. The couple raised one child, Ethan, who now lived and worked in Greensboro.

The judge was readily recognized around the county. He was tall and flat-shouldered. He wore his snow-white hair longer than was typical for a jurist of the time. A bushy white mustache dominated his upper lip. Another identifying feature was his wearing of a black Stetson hat during colder months.

Esther and Judge Ballard had met at church over twenty years ago through committee work. Their relationship had been cordial but reserved during those years.

On a few occasions in 1980, Esther volunteered to help total and credit collections on well-attended services during the holiday season. In appreciation of her efforts, Judge Ballard took Esther to Sunday lunch, usually at a nearby but out-of-county restaurant. In turn, Esther reciprocated with an occasional Friday night dinner at the Homestead.

The relationship maintained an innocent façade. Permanent coupling was unlikely due to their different backgrounds. Esther was conservative in traditional values and attitudes and tied to the Blue Ridge. Judge Ballard was well-educated and well-traveled and had a broad array of interests.

The judge was drawn to Esther's heart, decency, and willingness to serve. She was as kind and humble as any woman he had ever known, and such was her principal appeal to him.

However, during Russell's probation status, Judge Ballard and Esther ceased their sharing of meals together. Judge Ballard had insisted on the restriction to avoid any sense of impropriety or conflict should a judicial ruling be necessary in Russell's probation.

On the surface, Esther accepted the ban with reluctance, but in her heart, she had grown very fond of the judge. During Russell's probation, Esther and Judge Ballard socialized just once when they sat together on the evening of the memorable Pratt County–Mitchell football game.

With Russell's probation ending, Harlan Ballard and Esther Rankin renewed their relationship. In the process, Russell and Rachel became acquainted with the judge, as did Esther's grown children and their families. On occasion, Judge Ballard served as Esther's guest at Sunday dinners held at the Homestead.

* * *

Russell worked full time Tuesday through Saturday at the market during the summer of 1983.

With their respective work schedules being partially compatible, Russell and April maximized their time together.

During that summer, numerous visits were made to the sit-down and drive-in movie theaters in Sexton. Russell and April also attended small house parties held by classmates. They made day and evening visits to the Bright pasture and other favored locations, which usually included some attempt at outdoor lovemaking.

Russell became better acquainted with the county's two state parks and their multiple trails. Picnics and river tubing on the Laird with classmates were popular outings that summer as well. The County Fair was frequented at the Colby-based fairgrounds, and, later, Russell surprised himself by enjoying a weekend bluegrass festival hosted at the fairgrounds.

On warmer days, the public pool in Colby was visited with friends, and a day trip for couples to Caro Winds amusement park in Charlotte was organized.

With probation a distant memory, Russell better attempted to relax and chill as a seventeen-year-old. Coming as no surprise, April's influence was key as she harped from the onset of the relationship for Russell to "loosen up, try to be less perfect" and relax his self-discipline in order to better enjoy life as a soon-to-be high school senior.

Underage drinking was the norm for Pratt County teens, providing instant and ongoing conflict for Russell. He did not expect his peers to understand his need for abstinence, but he did want April to at least respect his stance, as she was aware of the toxic environment in which he had been raised.

This rub between Russell and April over drinking became a source of continual conflict during their senior year, as April wished to party like the majority of her friends. On one occasion, she even barked to best friend, Susan Beverly, "That boy just needs to loosen up. What harm's one fuckin' beer going to do? Why's he always got to be so tough on himself?"

Bowing to pressure fueled by April, Russell gave in, a decision that delighted her. He surprised April and their friends by occasionally having a beer at parties or gatherings. In the back of his mind, he remained conflicted with these decisions because he feared getting caught and the certain hurt and disappointment such discovery would cause Esther.

Nonetheless, as football co-captain, Russell led by example with any alcohol consumption totally off-limits during the regular season.

Russell trained for football through the summer and was especially focused two weeks prior to pre-season practice. April trained with him as she readied for soccer. Training often involved running trails together at Aldan Meadow and Mt. Wilcox State Park.

* * *

With school starting in a few weeks and football pre-season practice already underway, Russell had promised, weeks in advance, to help his Uncle Daniel during a specific weekend at the Broadwater Store. Russell and two other employees were needed to ready the store for construction of a store addition scheduled to begin the following week. This was an important project; the addition's planning had been in the works for almost a year.

As summer recess was growing to a close, news of Russell's weekend commitment did not sit well with April. She had other plans. Time was running out. She very much wished to visit Dublin Lake, a commercial park located an hour's drive from Colby. The lake was especially popular with teenagers and young adults for a rocky precipice, Clifford's Crag, at the lake's southern rim from which those who dared, leapt forty feet below into the lake.

April begged Russell to renege on his commitment, but he refused because of his promise to Uncle Daniel. April had locked into the outing during the coming weekend in large part because she was scheduled off that Sunday from the market. Despite Russell's absence, she gathered some high school friends, and by Sunday noon on the hottest day of the summer, the group was picnicking at the base of the precipice. The picnicking included beer.

Less than an hour later, April's classmate, Brian Cope, was sprinting to the lake's concession stand for assistance. While clowning on the precipice, April had lost her balance and fallen awkwardly into the lake below. Her body had landed horizontal to the water smacking her unconscious. Fortunately, classmate Timmy Branagan, an excellent swimmer and certified lifeguard, quickly retrieved April from the water. Drowning was never at issue.

Through the encouragement of friends, April regained consciousness. However, she was irritable and confused. She was also crying. A slight flow of blood dribbled from her left ear.

A park employee arrived and radioed for an ambulance to transport April to nearby Buehle Memorial Hospital, where April was treated at the emergency room. Tommy and Susanna McNaughton were contacted by phone, and within an hour's time, they joined their daughter at the hospital. April's friends remained steadfast and by her side until the McNaughtons' arrival.

April was released to her parents' care in less than an hour. She had suffered a mild concussion and ruptured eardrum. With eardrops and time, her eardrum would repair itself. Over the counter medication was recommended for pain. She continued to be nauseated on the ride home.

Upon reaching the McNaughton home, April insisted that she speak with Russell. Tommy McNaughton compromised and substituted as the caller while April rested. Rachel answered Tommy's call.

"Hi, this is Tommy McNaughton calling, April's dad."

"Oh, hi, Mr. McNaughton. This is Rachel."

"Hello, Rachel. Listen, I need to speak with Russell. Is he there?"

"He's still at work, but I'll have him call you when he gets in."

"OK, please do because April's had an accident. She's OK, but she wanted Russell to know."

"Oh, this is awful. Is she all right?" as Rachel's concern elevated. "She's OK, resting for now."

"Mr. McNaughton, I'll let him know."

"Thanks, sweetie."

Grandma Esther was visiting a friend recovering from surgery and was not at home. Rachel had no way of knowing how to contact Russell so she had no choice but to wait.

Finishing his work with Uncle Daniel, Russell called home from the Broadwater Store late afternoon.

"Russell, I'm glad you called. Listen. April's hurt. She's been in an accident."

Russell did not answer. He dropped the phone and bolted to his car without saying a word to Uncle Daniel. He jumped into the Cutlass. A sixteen-mile drive to April's house on mountain roads lay ahead.

Before he was even outside the Broadwater town limits, Russell was driving too fast. His heart was racing, the adrenaline flowing. He did not know the highway well between Broadwater and Colby, but he did recognize, even in his heightened state, that he needed to maintain safe speed. A slow-moving senior driver irritated him, and in exasperation, he passed an old pickup truck over a double line.

Forested land opened to pastures for grazing cattle as the highway zigzagged through the countryside. With thoughts of April in mind, Russell lost responsible focus and accelerated over sixty miles an hour. On a sweeping curve, he lost control of the Cutlass, crashing through a pasture fence, briefly going airborne, then traveling over two hundred feet on a slight descent into the pasture. Russell was dazed but unhurt; the Cutlass rested fifteen feet from a narrow mountain stream.

Russell collected himself and proceeded to walk a short distance to the property's farmhouse where he phoned Uncle Andrew, who would retrieve Russell and later drive him to the McNaughton home to reunite with April.

★ ★ ★

The disciplinary response from Uncle Andrew and Esther was swift and sure. Uncle Andrew had made it clear when Russell first received the Cutlass that any history of speeding, reckless driving, or accident would guarantee loss of the vehicle. Russell knew such a penalty would result from Saturday's accident.

Esther consulted with Aunt Helen and Uncle Andrew the day following the accident about discipline. She also sought Russell's version of what had happened.

For his impulsive decision-making and reckless driving, Russell was grounded until the start of the school year. Naturally, this restriction severely impeded his relationship with April, but the loss of the Cutlass complicated pre-season football as well. Russell would have to find a new means of transportation to and from daily pre-season practices and his hours at the market.

Uncle Andrew was not done. He and Russell repaired the pasture fence within forty-eight hours; Russell assumed costs for materials.

Fortunately, the property owner was sympathetic to Russell's plight. He did not notify the Sheriff's Department or his homeowner's insurance of the incident. There was no ticket or hiked car insurance premium.

Uncle Andrew insisted that he inspect the car for external and internal damages. Again, Russell was lucky; with the exception of exterior scratches, the Cutlass had survived the event without damage and was returned to Russell's use by mid-September.

Esther provided closing editorial comment. "Grandson, this was a dumb decision on your part, a really dumb decision on your part. Everyone understands that your response was guided by your concern for April. But you should've gathered your facts first. Now I want you to learn something' about your grandmother. You don't need to go mopin' around the house because of this. It's over. Your Grandpa Lester always used to say that 'there's value to our mistakes if we learn from 'em.' I hope that's what you do, Grandson. Learn from this."

Russell responded, "I'm real sorry for all of this, Grandma. I'm sorry I made you worry, too. I know I let you down, and for everything you've done for me, I feel terrible."

The McNaughtons' reaction was altogether different. Tommy and Susanna felt betrayed. They were not hovering, overprotective parents, and April's decision to drink on the outing could have caused even greater harm. A disturbing crack in trust between parents and child was caused by April's behavior.

Sympathetic to their daughter's need to recover from her injuries, April's punishment was announced days later when medical issues were no longer pressing. Like Russell, April was grounded until the start of the school year. Her parents would transport her to and from the market as required.

April believed her restriction to be harsh and overreaching. Among teenagers and adults alike, news of the events spread like wildfire.

33

FALL 1983
COLBY, NC
HARP, VA

RUSSELL and his Pratt County teammates enjoyed Pratt County High School's most successful football season in fourteen years, their only loss during the regular season coming in the third game against Morgan Raybuck. Russell, who was elected co-captain for a second year, rarely left the field, starring at both tight end and as linebacker. His punting prowess continued to attract collegiate attention on a national scale.

On a cold drizzly evening, the Ridge Runners' season came to an abrupt end in the state regionals when they lost to upstart Central Benton, 27-25. In a losing cause, Russell played his best defensive game of the season, notching eleven tackles and two quarterback sacks. His offensive production totaled two catches including a sixty-four-yard touchdown.

At season's conclusion, Russell repeated as all-conference and all-regional while earning first team, all-state recognition for his punting.

* * *

On an October Saturday morning in the midst of the football season, April, Russell, and fellow high school students across the country took the SAT exam. Having experienced an especially physical away-game victory against Marshall North the previous night, Russell was grateful to April for driving them to the out-of-county testing site.

The good news was that Russell had slept well and was already on his second cup of coffee when April arrived. She had taken the test her junior year and had scored impressively; however, she hoped to raise her verbal score from 680 into the 700s.

April and Russell reviewed SAT study materials during the latter part of the summer. The couple spent the majority of the previous weekend prepping under Esther's supervision.

At the test's conclusion, April felt more confident about her performance than Russell. The couple revisited the exam on the drive home, stopping at Hardee's for lunch.

When the testing results were received in the mail six weeks later, Russell was pleasantly surprised. On his first SAT exam, he had scored a 600 verbal score and a 644 score on math. April's results were positive as well; she had accomplished her goal by upping both of her scores to new highs, 714 on verbal and 740 on math.

* * *

Complicating Russell's college considerations since mid-junior year were the letters and packages received from college and university football programs. The majority of the interest was regional, with the notices coming from both Division I and Division II schools. However, eastern and midwestern colleges and universities had also shown interest.

Russell kept Coach Mo abreast of developments since the very first inquiry.

While many of the inquiries were generic and boilerplate, the Division I interest was, in large part, generated because of Russell's punting prowess.

Coach Mo made it clear that Russell had the talent to earn a Division I athletic scholarship. He also knew that most Division I programs would be focused on his punting. Russell balked at this notion, stating that he "didn't want to just kick a football," insisting he didn't much care if it was offense or defense, but he needed to be on the field, in the fray, in the action.

Before the conclusion of his senior football season, Russell applied to three colleges/universities: University of North Carolina at Chapel Hill (at April's insistence), Highlands State, and Appalachian State University. Russell considered these options primarily because of location and cost.

Russell refused to lean on Esther or other relatives for help; he would rely on inheritance, student aid, and summer employment to cover college expenses were an athletic scholarship not awarded.

By mid-September, Russell was receiving daily mailings and evening phone calls from interested college football programs. West Point cadet Jonathan Hunt had planted a seed with the West Point coaching staff of Russell's abilities, and Army was now hot on his trail.

A new and complicating twist was interest expressed by Ivy League Schools—Columbia, Cornell, and Penn. Two ACC schools, Duke and Wake Forest, were also in the hunt. Further inquiries came from major programs such as Tennessee, Virginia Tech, Vanderbilt, and Northwestern.

Not to be outdone, the Division II notice was substantial as well, including interest from Delaware, Bucknell, Holy Cross, and Davidson.

The phone campaign became so intense that Esther assumed the role of operator, answering all calls during evening hours. She even prepared evening meals in advance in order to best meet her phone duties. Rachel occasionally took on the role touting the same response as used by Esther, "Oh, I'm sorry. He's not here right now. He's studying at the library."

Russell did talk to many programs, but when he did, his desire to play beyond his special teams role as a punter was poorly received by most recruiters. This response substantially curtailed interest. Plus, he wanted to remain close to home. North Carolina had become home, and it made no sense to him to abruptly move to a strange town and distant state in order to attend college.

April was certainly a consideration, although Russell, ironically, had doubts as to whether UNC would be a wise choice for their relationship. The

Carolina coaching staff had soundly dismissed any position role for Russell other than punter.

★ ★ ★

Mid-morning on a December Saturday, Russell received an unexpected phone call from Coach Mo.

"Russell, I know this is last minute, but I have someone at the high school who I'd like you to meet. Can you come to the school right away? I'll prop open the outside door to my classroom. Are you workin' at the market today?"

"Yes, sir, but I don't start until noon."

In thirty minutes, Russell was meeting Everett "Boo" Buellander, head football coach at McClendon College, in Coach Mo's classroom.

"Russell, Coach Buellander here was a coach of mine when I played at Highlands back in the sixties. He'd like to speak with you about playing at McClendon College."

Russell responded with strong eye contact and a firm handshake. "Pleased to meet you, Coach."

Coach Buellander was tall and fit and looked younger than his fifty-two years would suggest. He was a veteran college football coach who played offensive guard at Columbia from 1949 to 1953. Since then he had served as an assistant coach at Columbia, Highlands, and Bucknell and beginning in 1979, as McClendon College's head coach. At McClendon, Coach Boo achieved unexpected, early success for a program that had long languished in the cellar of its conference.

"The pleasure is all mine, son." They settled into wooden chairs, and Coach Buellander asked about Russell's academics, his interests and hobbies, and his potential choice for a college major.

The coach then shifted gears. "I've watched some game film of you this morning, and you certainly have the talent to play on the collegiate level. You're an outstanding punter, son, just outstanding, easily one of the best I've ever seen in high school."

"Thank you, sir."

"Russell, one of the first questions I ask a potential recruit is 'Are you any good?' I like to see their reaction to the question. I'm going to skip all that because that's a question I don't need to ask. Your punting is exceptional, just like out of a textbook as to form and timing. It's hard for me to believe that you haven't had any specific instruction or attended any kicking camps.

"From what I've seen on film, it would be a poor coaching decision on my part to let your defensive or offensive skills go to waste. You're more than a punter, son. There's a lot more to the game than punting and holding for extra points and field goals. There's a saying in coaching that you need to put your best players on the field. If it's up to me, I don't see you just kickin' a football, at least, not where I'm coaching."

Coach Buellander's words were exactly what Russell wanted to hear. Russell's interest grew more intense.

"A lot of coaches would be fearful of their punter playing some offense or defense, and I understand the reservations because they could easily lose a specialist to injury, but I'm willing to take that gamble. In fact, it isn't a gamble to me; it's a responsible risk—something altogether different. You've made it work in high school because of your athleticism, your versatility, your guts. And while it's a big leap to the college game, I'm banking on Coach Mo's knowledge of your abilities and your character that you'd do the same at McClendon."

Russell remained enthralled.

Coach Mo intervened and took a hard look at Russell.

"Russell, my little Ronnie is only seven, but if he has any talent and desire to play college football, there is no better head coach for him to play for than Coach Buellander. Coach Boo is a bad bull-shitter. He tells the truth straight and hard, whether you like it or not. He'll get the best out of you. He's gonna work you, for sure. Plus, he truly gives a damn about academics and his players outside of football, then and after college."

Coach Buellander gathered some papers and materials that he handed over to Russell. "Here's an admission's application, a college catalog, a media guide, and some other materials you'll want to look at to help make your decision. Russell, we'd like you to visit next weekend at our expense. By my math, Colby is slightly more than one hundred miles from campus."

Russell broke his silence, "Whereabouts in Virginia is the school?"

"We're north of Roanoke in the small town of Harp, Virginia—some of the prettiest country you'll ever see."

"Still reeling from the attention, Russell said, "About the visit, I need to check first with my grandmother."

"Son, I understand. You let Coach Mo know, and he'll relay your decision on to me. We'll work out the details"

Standing up, Russell extended his hand in gratitude, "Thank you, Coach, for making the drive down here and everythin', but I need to get to work. I'm due at noon."

What Russell recalled from the meeting was Coach Buellander's handshake. While it was expected to be firm, there was a sincerity and humility to it that Russell could not put into words.

As Russell parked at the Village Market, he was disappointed due to the absence of April's car, recalling that she was not working today. His show of exuberance would need to be delayed 'til quitting time.

* * *

Russell did not make an immediate or impulsive decision to attend McClendon. Due to a conflict, Aunt Helen subbed for Esther the following Saturday when Russell visited the McClendon campus. As a disinterested April had underscored, the school was isolated, resting in a remote site within Virginia's Shenandoah Valley.

As Russell and Aunt Helen soon discovered, the hilly, yet walkable campus included an eclectic blend of buildings, some old and new—some wood, some brick, some stone. The oldest building on campus was the original white clapboard McClendon Mansion, which served as the college's Office of Admissions. The freshman dormitories were adequate but unlikely to win any awards for size and accommodation.

Even on a dreary December Saturday, there was a welcoming and peaceful air to the well-manicured grounds, accented by brick walkways, ancient, towering hardwoods, and long-anchored rhododendrons. Tranquil Brethelkinny Creek lazily meandered through the campus, necessitating the erection of numerous stone and wooden bridges for vehicular and foot traffic. Aunt Helen was awed by the campus' charm and quickly imagined how beautiful the campus might appear in warmer months.

Where Coach Buellander made an obvious impact on administration and the Board of Regents was in the approval of substantial upgrades to the football offices, meeting rooms, and training facilities. Renovations to the existing stadium, Pruitt Field, were underway to enhance capacity to eighteen thousand seats for the 1984 season.

As 1984 rolled in, mailings and phone calls continued as the daily pattern at the Homestead. After Christmas and with Uncle Daniel's support, Russell had taken a two-week absence from working at the market to concentrate on campus visits. He visited two ACC schools, which surprisingly, did not offer any serious challenge to Russell's interest in McClendon.

Russell's attraction to McClendon remained firm despite April's lobbying efforts against. Because of distance and location, she viewed McClendon as a poor choice for Russell and them as a couple.

During a mid-January weekend, Esther and Russell visited the campus for an additional look. Esther stayed on campus in the small College Union Hotel, while Russell bunked Saturday night in Ellister Hall with two freshman football players.

A sophomore business major gave Russell and Esther a personal tour of the campus late Saturday morning. Russell eventually slipped away to display his punting prowess to Coach Buellander, two assistant coaches, and the team's long snapper, Hank Ronalter.

A home basketball game followed, with the McClendon Muleskinners handily defeating visiting Willard State by a score of 70-50. Saturday night dinner was held at Coach Buellander's home located three miles off campus.

Prior to sitting down to a roast beef dinner at the coach's home, Natalie Buellander asked Esther if she and Russell would like to accompany them to Sunday morning services at their family church, Darby's Bridge Methodist. Esther accepted the invitation on the spot.

After a casual walk and chat on campus with Esther, Russell approached Coach Buellander before they left for the return drive home Sunday afternoon. He stretched out his hand and said, "Thanks, Coach, for a fantastic weekend. I've made my decision. I'd like to attend McClendon College and play football here." Russell smiled, "I'd like to wear number four if that's possible."

On the ride home, Esther and Russell took a half hour to process the visit. As they closed out their talk near the Virginia–North Carolina state line, Russell looked his grandmother square in the eye and said, "Grandma, I've never been more sure of anything in my life."

Esther beamed with joy. Back in Harp, Virginia, a college head football coach was beaming as well.

34

1984
COLBY, NC
WHEELER COUNTY, NC

———

APRIL was not happy about Russell's decision to enroll at McClendon College. Rather than support him and celebrate his good fortune, she chose to lash out. She had always thought that Russell "would come to his senses" and stay in North Carolina by picking an ACC school like Wake Forest or Duke, which were both interested in him as a recruit.

"Russell, I just don't understand you. Wake would be perfect for you and us. It's one of the best schools in the South. It's close to both Chapel Hill and Colby. What is the fuckin' matter with you? And then you go and commit to this dinky school up in the middle of nowhere that no one's ever heard of? Could we have at least talked about this before you said 'yes?' Man, they must have fooled you big-time. I don't fuckin' get it. I just don't get it. You're actually movin' farther away from us, not closer. And I'm supposed to be happy with this fucked-up decision? Really?"

Russell had learned of April's temper early in their relationship, and when it went off, it was best to get out of the way. When she lost it, she assumed attack mode with the potential of being cruel and cutting with her words. She had crossed the line with school administration more than once, and in turn realizing the rudeness of her actions, had to sheepishly return to the authority she had offended in order to apologize.

What eventually crystalized for Russell was the self-centeredness of April's tirade. His decision had not fit into her predestined plans for the couple and their post–high school future. The relationship's equilibrium had been rocked, and April, out of anger, recoiled at the loss of control.

Russell was deeply wounded by her callousness; it was a side to April's personality that he had never witnessed in its full fury.

To make matters worse, April hung up the phone on him that Sunday evening, further deepening the ugliness of her reaction while casting doubt in Russell's mind as to the permanence of the relationship. It was impossible for Russell to hide his hurt despite the efforts of both Esther and Rachel to improve his spirits.

Monday morning's initial meeting at school was strained, with April approaching Russell at school's end to apologize by handwritten note.

The note read:

Darling Russell,

I'm so, so sorry. I really am. I had no right to react that way. You're such a sweet boy, and you didn't deserve any of that. I'm not using this as an excuse, but you caught me off guard at a bad time. I just wasn't expecting your decision so quickly.

Please forgive me and accept my apology. Loving you always,
April

The rift between them was the mainstay of gossip within the senior class for the latter part of January and early February. Gradually the ice thawed, and prior to Valentine's Day, normalcy returned.

In late February, April received news from UNC that she had been awarded the prestigious Margaret D. Cull scholarship, which covered all undergraduate expenses at Carolina, providing that she maintain an overall 3.5 grade point average during her four years of college.

In unfamiliar fashion, Tommy and Susanna McNaughton invited Russell to celebrate April's scholarship with them at Sexton's most stylish restaurant, Ernesto's.

The remainder of the school year moved slowly for graduating seniors. Due to the recession's economic impact on families, senior parents were respectfully polled by school administration for suggestions to cut expenses for the senior prom. The outcome was that boys' formal wear was discouraged, although boys were required to wear shirt, tie, and khakis. Girls must wear a dress, although formal wear was not required.

The event was held on Saturday, April 7, 1984, at the County Fairgrounds Exposition Hall. Dee Crawford, a popular radio personality from Greensboro, served as DJ.

During the week prior to graduation, the edition of the 1984 Pratt County High School yearbook, *The Chronicle*, was distributed. It was devoured upon receipt by upper classmen, especially seniors.

Due to their accomplishments, April and Russell were featured in numerous photographs. Their listed accomplishments included:

RUSSELL OWEN RANKIN

National Honor Society Football 3 (co-captain), 4 (co-captain)

All-Regional football 3, 4

All-State football 3, 4

Service Weekend 3, 4

Rex Elementary Big Buddy Tutoring 3, 4

The Chronicle 3, 4

Ecology Club 4

History Club 3, 4

APRIL LYNN McNAUGHTON

Valedictorian

National Honor Society

Tennis 1, 2, 3, 4 (captain)

Soccer 1, 2, 3, 4 (captain)

Debate Team 3, 4 (captain)

Class secretary 1, 2

Class vice-president 3

Pratt Tatt 2, 3, 4

Homecoming Court 4

Service Weekend 2, 3, 4

The Chronicle 2, 3, 4

Ecology Club 3, 4

Graduation was held in late May in the high school's hot and stuffy gymnasium. Dr. Ernest Thigpen, professor of History and Contemporary American Culture at UNC-Charlotte, served as an amusing and inspiring speaker. The Class of 1984's student speaker was April McNaughton, class valedictorian, who provided seven minutes of eighteen-year-old insight and reflection.

Upon graduation, Russell worked steady and long hours at the market. When not with April, he focused on weight-lifting and conditioning for football, knowing that the level of play in college would be a major step-up.

* * *

Rachel's progress during the 1983–1984 school year again produced disappointing results despite Russell's oversight and tutoring. Equally disappointing was the continuation of behavioral problems at school, which included disruption in class and harassment of other female students.

Esther attended two school-requested conferences with a middle school counselor that resulted in mild improvement. At the core of Rachel's underachieving was her association with classmates who were experiencing similar bouts of apathy and disinterest. The majority of these students came from families that did not trust or value education, and the potential dropout rate for these girls was high.

Russell was aware of this influence and did his best to discourage Rachel's questionable choice of peers. At one point, Rachel reacted nastily to Russell's intervention commenting, "Well, if you're so damn smart, how come you're the one that was on probation, Huh? Answer that one."

Esther was amiss and out of her league in attempting to curb Rachel's poor choices. However, Aunt Helen, in her patient and soothing way, continued as a supportive sounding board for Rachel, who listened to her aunt with marked attention.

* * *

After three years of working retail grocery, April had enough; she desired a change and a larger paycheck. Through years of persistence, she was able to finally secure a summer job as a waitress at the county's prestigious Mountain Club community, Vista Hollow. By working set hours in the restaurant and private parties and events, the summer proved lucrative.

Russell and April easily recognized that their worlds, as they knew them, would come to an abrupt halt when Russell reported to McClendon for pre-season football in early August. In light of their approaching separation, the couple maximized their time together, the bulk of which was spent alone. While most of their high school classmates were partying and exploiting the last remnants of their senior year summer, Russell and April chose solitude and each other.

On a humid Saturday evening in late July and at Russell's lead, the couple dined at a romantic, off-the-beaten path Wheeler County hideaway, the Lost Cabin restaurant. They enjoyed a candlelit dinner together, and as evening darkness approached, Russell announced they needed to leave the restaurant because he had a special surprise to share.

A short drive toward Mount Wilcox State Park followed, but after crossing the Kern Creek Bridge, Russell turned off the highway onto a narrow unmarked dirt road.

Russell assured April that all was under control. She knew enough about county geography to recognize that Russell could not drive much farther since the Laird River at this point was straight ahead by no more than a few hundred yards.

"Russell, what's this all about? This is getting' creepy, way too creepy. It's dark out here. Do you know where you're goin? You sure there isn't a Freddie Kruger-type roamin' these woods?"

In a minute, Russell parked the car in a space worn by previous vehicles. "Just a few seconds more. I need to find the lantern and the bug spray."

"Russell, this isn't funny anymore. What's this all about? Please!"

"Here it is," he said, lighting the lantern. "Just be patient."

April could now see the moon's pale reflection on the calm, slow-moving Laird River.

"Follow me," he said as he took her hand.

An exasperated April said, "Oh, sure, you're not going to drown me in the river, are you? You know, there's songs written about this stuff."

Russell responded with a chuckle, "No, no drownin' tonight."

The lantern illuminated a rowboat resting on the riverbank containing two oars and two life jackets.

"Get in," he instructed.

"Russell, what do you know about rowboats anyway? I guarantee nothing. This goofy idea is likely to get us both killed."

"I know more than you might think. I've been practicing with Jonathan Hunt who's home on summer leave. He's going to meet us about two miles downriver and drive us back to the car. Now get in, put on the life jacket, and be sure to use the bug spray." He tossed the can of repellent April's way.

April's apprehension lessened as she was awed by the majesty of a full summer moon illuminating the slow-moving Laird. Hundreds of lightning bugs enhanced the scene on both sides of the river. The dominating sound that humid summer evening was Russell's oars gently slapping the water.

"This is lovely, really lovely. I have to hand it to you, Russell, very romantic, the full moon and everythin'. Goin' to be hard to forget tonight."

"That's the idea."

The boat drifted lazily on the tranquil Laird. Remembrances were shared. Commitment was confirmed.

In less than an hour, the couple viewed a lantern hanging on the east side of the river and then Jonathan's welcoming face as the boat neared the riverbank.

"Well, it looks like no one's drowned. How'd he do, April?"

"Better than I thought. I think it's the instructor."

As the rowboat docked, Jonathan helped April onto shore and hugged her, "April, it's really good seein' you. It's been more than a year, I'll bet."

Jonathan then assisted Russell's exit. They caught up with each other on the brief ride to Russell's car; due to the hour, the conversation was cut short.

By 10:30 p.m., the couple was making love in their favorite parking spot, an abandoned logging road east of Colby.

PART III

———

35

FALL 1984–SPRING 1985
HARP, VA

———

RUSSELL made a smooth transition to McClendon College in the classroom, dorm, and football program. Choosing McClendon was proving an excellent fit.

His roommate was fellow freshman football player, David Booth, an easygoing North Carolinian, who hailed from Deep Gap, North Carolina. Booth played defensive back and was unlikely to be on the field much as a freshman. Russell also forged solid friendships with other team members, especially his fellow freshman players.

Academically, Russell made Dean's List, demonstrating the same well-honed discipline that had been his trademark during high school. McClendon, known for its excellence in the liberal arts, required freshmen and sophomores to take several core courses in the liberal arts until a major was declared late in their sophomore year. Russell aced both history courses under the tutelage of Dr. Lane Feydenhall, an American Civil War scholar.

Russell's accomplishments on the football field surprised no one on the coaching staff. On a mediocre Muleskinners squad that notched an inglorious 3-8 record, Russell was a clear star. The McClendon offense was so sluggish that students actually cheered, much to the athletic director's and football staff's disgust, when Russell entered the game to punt.

Special Teams Coach Alan Pitcher offered little technical suggestion about Russell's punting, intentionally steering clear with the understanding that he was coaching a punting phenomenon. "He's a freak, a bona fide freak. He's never been to a kicking school or instructional camp. He's all natural. I pretty much leave him alone and get out of the way. His hang time is ridiculous. Why mess with perfection?"

Coach Buellander kept his word, permitting Russell to play tight end in eight of the team's eleven games, alternating with junior Will Kennedy. He also gained additional playing time as a holder on extra points and field goals.

However, it was Russell's punting that garnered most attention. As a freshman, he was the third-leading punter in the nation per average on all levels of collegiate football. In the second game, he set a McClendon College record for longest punt, and by season's end, the majority of McClendon's punting records had been shattered.

Russell led his conference in most punting statistics, and at season's end, he made first team all-Blue Ridge Conference. The biggest honor was making first team Division II All-American as a freshman. He also earned Academic All-American recognition.

To Russell's delight, Esther, Aunt Helen, Uncle Andrew, Rachel, and other family members attended several McClendon home games, April traveled to three games as well, staying over Saturday night.

Russell called home at least once a week, and it was not unusual for Esther or Rachel to call as well. Once football season was completed, Russell returned home for weekend stays and scheduled rendezvous with April who would make the trip home from Chapel Hill.

All was well with Esther, but Russell continued to be concerned about Rachel's ongoing issues at school. Rachel had taken her brother's absence hard, and she missed daily interaction with him and the ongoing support that he demonstrated toward her. Her unremarkable grades were in sharp contrast to Russell's high school record.

Russell constantly encouraged Rachel to become involved in extracurricular school activities, a suggestion at which she balked. On a positive note, she generally remained attentive and obedient to Esther and especially Aunt Helen.

Rachel's babysitting service continued as a steady source of income while occupying much of her free time on weekends and even an occasional weeknight.

Russell and April maximized their three weeks together during Christmas break, with Russell working part-time hours at the market. The couple Christmas shopped in Winston-Salem, where April had maternal relatives, reconnected with high school classmates, and spent the majority of their waking hours together when Russell was not working.

Not surprisingly, April aced all of her first semester courses at UNC. She also decided to double major in biology and chemistry as the best preparation to prepare for medical school after graduation.

The couple's relationship continued to progress. Conversations about marriage and children were broached. April remained passionately committed to her desire to become a pediatric surgeon. Russell's career path remained less certain, although the suggestions about a career in professional football were not unrealistic, considering his first-year success at McClendon. Were professional football not an option, Russell was inclined toward teaching history on the high school level.

With Christmas and New Year's now behind them, Russell and April returned to college to the months that April regarded as "the dark months" and her toughest time of the year.

Normally a dependable letter-writer, April's correspondence fell off in February and March as did her phone calls. Russell rationalized the decline was due to demanding courses classes in biochemistry and inorganic chemistry, which were challenging April's 4.0 GPA.

The couple did manage a short weekend together in mid-March where Russell traveled to Chapel Hill because April believed that she could not afford taking time to return home for a weekend away from Chapel Hill. Most of their weekend was spent in study at the UNC library, and even when not hitting the books, April seemed preoccupied, moody, and anxious. Even their lovemaking seemed rigid, incapable of relaxing her enough to enjoy a brief respite from stressful academics.

On two occasions, April broke down and softly sobbed for no apparent reason. Russell associated these spells to fatigue linked to her demanding schedule. He even suggested that she seek medical or psychological help through the university, advice that she shunted aside.

Overall, the weekend was a disappointing one because April was so overwhelmed with assignments and upcoming exams. For the first time since they'd become a couple, their time together seemed flat and less rewarding.

★ ★ ★

Coach Buellander scheduled spring football to be concluded prior to Easter.

McClendon's final spring practice, an intra-squad scrimmage, was held on a Saturday morning in late March, a full week before Easter.

As no surprise to anyone, Russell excelled in the punting game, and with former starting tight end Will Kennedy switching to linebacker, Russell assumed starter status at tight end. In that role, he caught two passes, which amounted to minor gains, during the officiated, lightly attended contest at Pruitt Field. A barbeque for team members and their guests in the college's Azalea Room followed the scrimmage.

Esther was unable to attend the spring game, but a nattily dressed Uncle Andrew visited with his new girlfriend, Christa Spencer.

With hovering fog and steady rain falling by mid-afternoon, a campus tour for Uncle Andrew and Christa was cut short in favor of the couple getting a jump-start on the return drive to Colby. On their parting and with the rain intensifying, Russell checked his Ellister Hall mailbox, and to his delight, he found an overdue letter from April.

36

CHAPEL HILL, NC

———

March 27, 1985

Dearest Russell,

This letter is my sixth or seventh attempt to say what I need to say. I am a coward at heart because I don't have the guts to tell this to you face to face.

When you decided to go to McClendon, I was naïve in thinking that I could handle our separation. The distance between us has been our enemy. I've learned this year that I must have you completely or not at all.

You are a kind and beautiful young man who will forever be my first true love.

I will always hold your memory close. At this point in our lives, I cannot live with this separation any longer. I must let you go since I cannot live this life any longer.

Do not second-guess yourself because you have done nothing wrong. I hope someday that you will learn to forgive me, especially when you find someone more deserving of your love than me. By the way, there is no one else complicating this decision. No one.

I wish you all success, happiness, and love. No one deserves it more than you.

Thank you, my sweet Russell, from the bottom of my heart for the special memories shared during our time together. You will always be with me and in my heart.

And you will always be the first....

Love always,
April

3 7

MARCH 30—APRIL 1, 1985
HARP, VA

———

RUSSELL was blindsided by April's devastating message. He was expecting heartfelt news from her, never anticipating the cold announcement terming the relationship.

Russell's face flushed and his mouth grew dry as he reread the letter two more times in the dorm's lobby.

A familiar yet unnamed freshman interrupted his concentration as he passed by while offering his congratulations,

"Hey, good game, man."

Despite his average performance, Russell answered with a mild nod, "Yea, thanks."

Russell needed privacy, and he knew where to turn. Despite the ongoing rain, he stashed the letter in his coat pocket and jogged to the nearby Sheppard Hall. The sky had further darkened as thunder rumbled across the campus.

Anticipating that a small study room would be empty in the dorm's basement, he entered the vacant room and sat on a worn loveseat where he reread the letter several more times. April was a precise writer who took pride in capturing emotion in the written word. Knowing her as he did, he thought she must have spent hours composing the letter. Looking beyond her words proved frustrating and unproductive.

Russell's stomach remained knotted. His mouth and lips remained dry.

Following minutes of quiet reflection, his eyes glazed with tears.

To avoid the potential of being seen, he moved to a remote, corner table and chair where he could better isolate himself from view on this dreary Saturday afternoon.

Russell remained in denial. Perhaps April's response was fueled by a misunderstanding that could be corrected over the phone. However, Russell knew April well enough to appreciate that such a prospect was unlikely. There was an order and formality to her letter that scared him. He needed to hear her voice and challenge a decision that he could not accept.

Russell had a solid relationship with his roommate, David Booth. They had bonded well since last August. He knew he could never camouflage his emotions before David so that painful disclosure was soon to come. Some delayed reading assignments for two courses added to Russell's anxiety. With the late afternoon thunderstorm subsiding, Russell decided to call April from the dorm room phone that he shared with David. He was surprised to find his dorm room empty.

He called April at 5:06 p.m.; there was no answer. With David's understanding to vacate their dorm room in favor of studying at the library, Russell placed additional calls at 6:20, 7:45, 8:10, and 9:35 p.m. All calls went unanswered.

* * *

Because of his inability to contact April by phone, Russell grew desperate. To no surprise, he slept poorly Saturday night. Two attempts to contact April by phone Sunday morning went unanswered. Russell then concluded that April could be spending the weekend at the beach with college friends and that she would not be returning to Chapel Hill until late Sunday.

Russell even contemplated making the four-hour drive to Chapel Hill later in the day to sit down and resolve any issues in their relationship. Further uncertainty developed. What if April wasn't at the beach at all, maybe she was home in Colby? A call to April's home could not be risked since her parents might then consider the relationship off-kilter.

The upcoming week for Russell was demanding with three tests and an assigned paper. Despite the upset caused by April's letter, Russell refused to jeopardize his grades. He again considered a drive to Chapel Hill as a potential response mid-week when much of his schoolwork was behind him. Contacting April by phone remained the sensible approach, and the sooner the better. Russell's hurt and pain continued overwhelming.

April was not an early riser. She was very proud of the fact that she had registered for spring semester courses that avoided early morning classes. With this knowledge in mind, Russell dialed her number Wednesday morning at 8:45.

After the fourth ring, April answered the phone. "Hello," answered April.

"It's me."

Surprised and instantly recognizing the voice, April sat up from her bed. She was alert but did not comment. She was relieved that her roommate was already showering and out of the room.

"I got your letter Saturday. I've called all weekend. What's this all about? You can't mean any of this, you just can't. This is just crazy. I've never been so surprised in my life."

April said nothing.

Russell's voice started to quiver. "You can't mean what you wrote—you just can't. What's really going on here?" Russell's voice grew more demanding. "April, I sure think I have a right to know."

Again, Russell's words were greeted by irritating silence. "Damn it, April. I need some idea about where this all came from. After all we've been through, this is all I get?"

April again delayed any answer.

"Russell, it's all there in the letter. I just can't live this way anymore with you stuck up in Virginia and me here in Chapel Hill. I was stupid to think this could work, really stupid. I finally see that now."

April's response was cold and harsh. It offered no clues.

"So, after almost three years of bein' together, this is how it all ends?"

April showed agitation. "Don't put this all on me, Russell. I told you our senior year that your goin' to McClendon was the stupidest thing you could ever do, way up there in the middle of fuckin' nowhere, four hours away from Chapel Hill."

April's words became more intense and pointed. "You could have gone practically anywhere on full scholarship, but, no, you threw it all away for some fuckin' reason that I'll never understand. Shit, you could be playin' football in Durham right now or Winston-Salem. If you really, really cared for me, and us, that's what you would have done, but no, you had to go to McClendon, and because of that, you threw us away as well."

Russell was stunned by April's scathing comments. Never had she been so cruel.

"No more phone calls, understand? No letters. No visits. This is over."

Russell did not respond.

"Goodbye, Russell."

38

1985–1988
HARP, VA
COLBY, NC

RUSSELL'S remaining three years at McClendon continued to prove successful in both the classroom and on the football field. In May 1988, he graduated from McClendon with an overall GPA of 3.50, majoring in history and earning a certification to teach social studies and history in high school. Family members continued their loyal support of Russell's football play by attending home games. Surprisingly, Esther became the most devoted family follower of McClendon College football.

Russell's play continued to merit conference, regional, and national recognition, especially for his punting. Russell achieved Academic All-American recognition during all four years at McClendon. He co-captained the 1986 and 1987 squads. He was a first team all-conference selection at punter and tight end his senior year. His proudest accomplishment during the 1987 season was an eighty-yard punt against VMI, which broke his personal best by five yards.

Russell's ongoing success his senior year reinforced NFL teams' interest in drafting the perennial all-American punter, who now stood six feet, four inches, weighing 225 pounds. Another attraction for NFL teams was Russell's limited injury history during his collegiate playing years, missing only one game in four years.

Through professional contacts, Russell was steered to a sports agent and attorney in Chicago, who specialized in negotiating professional contacts with NFL teams. The Atlanta Falcons, Miami Dolphins, Minnesota Vikings, and Philadelphia Eagles appeared the most interested teams and the most likely to draft Russell as high as the third round.

On April 25th in the ballroom of New York City's Marriott Marquis, the Philadelphia Eagles selected Russell Rankin in the third round of the 1988 NFL draft. He received the news of his selection in Coach Buellander's office late morning.

* * *

While Russell had achieved marked success in the classroom and on the football field at McClendon, his social life was lacking during his college years. The breakup his freshman year with April had been devastating to the point where he remained in Harp working summer construction between his freshman and sophomore years, only occasionally returning to Colby for weekend visits.

For several months, he quietly attended a counseling center on campus that provided ideas and suggestions but no real answers as to how to move forward from the breakup with April.

A July weekend contact in 1985 between Russell and April had taken place at a Colby gas pump. The meeting, which included no physical greeting, lasted less than five minutes. Conversation was clumsy and strained. April's nervous aloofness was especially chilling, leaving Russell with the firm impression that the relationship was unsalvageable.

Russell dated his final three years at McClendon, but no meaningful relationship developed. His abstinence from alcohol and drugs, due more to family history than any seasonal restriction imposed by the football program, did much to limit the field of coeds, who might be interested. Even among his teammates, Russell's nondrinking caused a clumsy wedge.

* * *

Back in Colby, Esther retired in March 1988 after twenty-five years of dutiful employment with Hamilton Brothers Hardware and Lumber. Russell was naturally lured back home for celebrations. The timing of Esther's decision was, in part, influenced by Rachel's planned enlistment in the U.S. Navy in 1988 upon her graduation from high school.

That same year, Uncle Andrew married Christa Spencer after a five-year courtship. The couple bought a red brick ranch house three blocks from the high school, where Andrew happily assumed stepfather duties for Christa's two teenage daughters.

However, the biggest news was Esther's remarrying. Judge Ballard had made his intentions clear two years prior to Esther's retirement, but she insisted on delaying the union until Rachel finished high school. With Rachel recently graduating from naval boot camp, a quiet and very private wedding was held in the Wheeler County Courthouse.

Judge Ballard abdicated the honeymoon site selection to Esther, who, after researching destinations at the library, opted for a week's stay on the Outer Banks.

For now, Mr. and Mrs. Ballard would reside at the Homestead.

39

1988-2002
PHILADELPHIA, PA

———

THE Eagles' drafting of Russell was designed to fill the gap created by veteran punter Joel Englander's retirement. While other potential punters would vie for the job at training camp, the job was essentially Russell's to lose.

Russell had never been to any large eastern city. Chicago was the biggest city he had ever visited, but he knew that while similar, Philadelphia would be unique. Their fans were legendary—loyal, passionate, demanding, and highly critical of any underperformance by Philly's professional athletes.

Russell became the Eagles' punter and PAT/field goal holder from 1988 to 2002, marking a productive and record-setting fourteen-year career. Taking a page from Coach Everett Buellander's playbook, Russell was used creatively by Eagles' offensive and special teams' coaches. To the delight of Eagles fans, it was not uncommon for Russell to run or pass for first downs from punt formation.

Early in his career, he also lined up as a split tight end on unique occasions, used more as a confusing decoy, number four netted fourteen catches during his pro career including a game-winning touchdown grab against the Redskins. These heroics further enamored Russell with Eagle fans.

However, it was his masterful foot that brought raucous and respectful applause from the Philly faithful due to his legendary ability to skillfully land punts out of bounds within the opponents' ten-yard line.

Russell became a fan favorite, not only due to his heroics on the gridiron, but also because of his extensive work with charities, much of it behind the scenes. He held a particular sensitivity toward working for causes supporting disadvantaged youth.

While attending a January 1996 banquet honoring volunteers at the Children's Hospital for the University of Pennsylvania, Russell met Sandra Carlsen, the NBC evening news anchor in Philadelphia. As part of the post-dinner program, Carlsen interviewed Russell with prepared and fielded questions from the audience.

CARLSEN: Russell, tell us a little about yourself away from football. What are your interests and hobbies?

RANKIN: I like to stay in shape year-round so I'm usually at the gym at least five days a week during the off-season doing a lot of stretching, yoga, high-rep weights, because groin and hamstring injuries are especially problematic for punters. I run a lot. I like exploring the state's historical sites. I've been to Gettysburg a lot. I have two cats, Ozzie and Inky, and a ten-month-old brown lab, named Boo, who I run with whenever possible.

CARLSEN: Now, a little bird told me that some of your fellow players call you "Professor." Is that true?

RANKIN: Yes, that's true. I've had an interest in American history since high school and it was my major in college. I talked with the history department at Penn, just a few blocks down the street here, and I'm now about halfway through getting my Master's in American History. So, that's where the nickname came from. So, yes, it's true.

CARLSEN: Russell. Now, we only have time for one question, unfortunately, from the audience. Miss, you here in the blue and white striped dress, yes, you. What is your question for Russell Rankin? But first of all, your name and where you're from?

AUDIENCE MEMBER: Oh, sure. Hi. My name's Gwen Ambroz. I live in Lansdowne. My question for Russell is this: Are you single or married? And if you're single, I don't understand.

RANKIN: (After the laughter had died down and now totally embarrassed) No, I'm not married, still single. I just haven't met the right person yet. I came close once, but no need to rush into anything right now since my teammates and I need to stay focused on bringing a Super Bowl championship to Philadelphia.

Upon the banquet's conclusion and in uncharacteristic fashion, Russell wasted no time in approaching Sandra Carlsen. With a polite smile, he thanked her for emceeing the event. He said, "If you're not married or seeing anyone, I'd like to take you to dinner."

And thus began the courtship of Russell Rankin and Sandra Carlsen.

* * *

Sandra's rise within television broadcasting had been meteoric. She was two years younger than Russell, having graduated from the University of Wisconsin–Madison in 1990 where she double-majored in Journalism and Broadcasting. Spurning an immediate job in television, Sandra opted to earn her master's degree in journalism at Northwestern University.

Upon completing her master's, she worked weekend then prime-time news for two years for the CBS affiliate in Madison. A successful one-year news anchor position followed in Indianapolis from which she was hired unexpectedly as the prime-time news anchor for NBC in Philadelphia.

Critics argued that Sandra was too young at twenty-seven, too inexperienced to assume the news anchor slot for such a major market, but Sandra proved her detractors wrong through her preparation, attention to detail, flawless and polished delivery, and a personality that was irresistible to the general public. Her Nordic beauty was a plus as well, being extremely attractive with shimmering blond hair, blue eyes, and lissome figure.

Russell had seen what Philly's general viewership had seen, and from their very first date at Vitale's, Russell's favorite Italian restaurant in South Philadelphia, he saw a more complete side to this beautiful young woman from Wisconsin.

Sandra proved to be a marvelous conversationalist and listener. On many occasions, Russell directed their talks to Sandra, her family, and her career. Through her conversation and actions, Sandra impressed Russell as intelligent, learned, witty, and spontaneous, yet even-keeled. She was also humble and respectful toward everyone, a trait that instantly endeared her to Russell.

There was little not to like, and from the onset of their relationship, Russell liked it all. After the first date, he said to himself but kept secret the prediction that Sandra was the woman he would marry. The only question he held, should the relationship move forward, was how to compatibly balance their respective careers.

Immediate complications with the couple's dating were threefold. First, they were both well-known by the public and easily identifiable in Philadelphia and the suburbs.

Second, Sandra lived and worked in Center City Philadelphia close to the NBC studios. Russell owned a suburban home, which provided easy access to the Eagles' complex and practice facilities in South Philadelphia.

Third, their respective work schedules were incompatible, with Sandra working early afternoon to midnight, Monday through Friday. Russell was preoccupied with football from early summer to December or January, depending on the Eagles' status in the NFL playoffs. He was generally unavailable during weekends from midsummer through early winter.

Very early in their dating, the marked differences in family and upbringing came to the fore. Russell viewed the contrast as a formidable challenge to their relationship. The inevitable "tell me about your family" inquiry would arise at some point. How was Russell to handle the discord and marked family dysfunction in which he had been raised? How could he sanitize the drinking, drugs, criminal records, marital discord, and parental irresponsibility in a manner not to alienate the listener, especially one such as Sandra?

Russell chose not to dodge the bullet when Sandra asked of his childhood. "My upbringing wasn't the best. My father died when I was fifteen. I haven't seen my mother since 1982. I was born and lived in Lancaster, Illinois, until tenth grade, when my sister and I moved to North Carolina to live with my paternal grandmother. I consider North Carolina my real home at this point."

Despite the challenges presented, the draw between the two was instantaneous. In less than a month, they were spending weekends together, as schedules permitted, either in Sandra's Center City apartment or Russell's suburban home. Nearby Cape May, New Jersey, offered frequent weekend solitude after the Eagles' season concluded.

To Sandra, Russell fully disclosed his teenage years with April including the trauma of the breakup. Other than April, Russell had never been in a serious relationship. However, that pattern had changed because of Sandra.

Unlike Russell, Sandra had maintained romances in college and during her professional career. She had been close to marriage, but that relationship was termed by Sandra. In her tie to Russell, there was never doubt or hesitation.

As the couple became more serious, brief trips to North Carolina and Wisconsin were held in order to meet parents and extended family. On Christmas Eve 1996, Russell proposed marriage to Sandra in the same Methodist Church in North Carolina where his grandfather had proposed to Esther in 1940. Sandra said, "Yes" on the spot. Both the Carlsen and Rankin families were thrilled with the announcement.

In order to accommodate the fall–winter NFL schedule, an early June outdoor wedding was held on the Carlsen dairy farm in central Wisconsin. Lutheran minister and long-time family friend, Rev. Frank Conrad, conducted the outdoor service before a gathering of two hundred and fifty guests. Lund Abramsen and the Oompah Rascals provided entertainment at the reception.

Upon marrying and completing a two-week honeymoon in Hawaii, the couple settled into a Center City condominium within walking distance of the television station.

40

2002–2003
PHILADELPHIA, PA
COLBY, NC

RUSSELL retired from professional football after the 2002 season, having accomplished more than he ever hoped for as a professional athlete. In 2001, he earned a PhD in history from the University of Pennsylvania, where he focused primarily on the American Civil War from the Confederate perspective and twentieth-century Europe.

Russell's doctoral thesis was a revealing biography of conflicted Confederate Col. Nathaniel Benjamin who, when physically disabled by battle wounds at Antietam, antithetically chose a clandestine life in northern Virginia as an organizer and conduit for Underground Railway traffic through the Shenandoah Valley.

In their early thirties and with Sandra's career in full bloom, the couple became intent on having children much to the joint encouragement of Grandma Esther and Russell's mother-in-law, Anita Carlsen. The couple also wished to return to familiar rural roots to raise their family so the only question was would it be Wisconsin or North Carolina?

In January of 2003 and in the early months of Russell's retirement from professional football, Sandra took a leave of absence from her position as Philadelphia's premier news anchor to birth their first baby, a boy they named

Roger. Like many new mothers, she was torn about returning to work after her maternity leave had expired.

During Baby Roger's first few months, the couple entertained lengthy talks about their future. Even in her early thirties, Sandra disliked the pressure of evening news and the consistent emphasis on ratings. In Philly, she was at the top of her game, with the only possible advancement being a final leap to a network position in New York or Washington. To the shock of nearly everyone, Sandra was not interested. She was not enthusiastic about ever returning to Philadelphia's NBC newsroom. Motherhood had impacted her beyond all expectations.

Russell thought university or high school teaching would be his next calling. However, could any college or university take the jock-turned-professor seriously? And on the high school level, wouldn't he be viewed more as a celebrity than an overqualified teacher?

On a lark during a summer visit to North Carolina, Russell stopped by his old high school to connect with former staff. Principal Bruce Osborne, who was fully aware of Russell's recent retirement from the NFL, lightheartedly suggested that Russell apply for a vacant high school history position.

"You know, Russell, Ellie Stanley retired last month after forty-two years of teaching high school history. We haven't filled her position yet. You'd have the distinction of having the only doctorate degree in the building."

To the principal's surprise, Russell showed interest, "Well, to be honest, my wife and I have thought of relocating back here or moving to Wisconsin where she's from. Philly's a great town, we'll miss it, but we want to raise our kids in a rural, small town setting either in Wisconsin or down here."

The conversation ended as quickly as it had begun. Russell accepted an application form on his way out.

With Esther and Judge Ballard serving as babysitters for an exhausted and early-to bed Baby Roger, Sandra suggested she and Russell visit The Point, a destination known to Sandra from previous trips. Soon, they were decompressing on weathered Adirondacks after a full day's activities.

"Something strange happened at the high school today."

"What's that?"

"The new principal, a fella named Bruce Osborne, suggested that I apply for a vacant position teaching history."

"Where'd that come from?"

"He said he saw some interview on ESPN about my retirement where I mentioned that I might become a teacher."

"He was serious?"

"Seemed to be."

"Are you? Do I get any say in this?" Sandra asked laughing.

Pointed discussion followed with the hollow darkening below as soft blankets of evening haze caressed the landscape. It was no secret that Sandra was leaning heavily toward becoming a stay-at-home mom to Roger and additional children.

Equally appealing to Sandra was the opportunity to research, write, and produce a documentary on a rugged western Virginia midwife named Nancy Cutter, a colorful figure, who they had discovered while Russell researched his doctoral thesis.

Since her days at Northwestern, Sandra had remained close to a fellow graduate student, Nicholas Meyer, who had become an award-winning documentary producer. Prior to Roger's birth, Sandra had discussed the Cutter project with him by phone.

Nicholas was encouraged about being able to raise funds for the project, but he needed a solid commitment from Sandra toward her involvement in further researching the subject and drafting an outline. Both Sandra and Nicholas agreed the project worthy of pursuit, providing that Sandra retire, even temporarily from broadcasting, to write and co-produce the documentary.

"You know, Russell, if we take this major step, it gets down to a few basics. If I stay at home to care for the children, we need you to provide some income and benefits. I need to be active outside of the children, and the Cutter project seems like a perfect fit even though I wish Nancy Cutter lived and practiced a few miles closer. You're going to have to do some major double duty while I'm away, you know that?"

"You know McClendon is in the same general neighborhood. So what do I do to earn a regular salary and benefits?"

"You know. Teach high school history at Pratt County High."

"But what about Wisconsin?"

"It's just a bad fit right now. What I want and need to do is here, not Wisconsin."

"What would your mother say?"

"Oh, Anita won't like it, but she'll get over it. We'll need to visit more, maybe spend more time up there during the holidays, but she'll get over it. She always does."

A few lights flickered in the hollow below as the couple lost themselves in the serenity of the moment.

"Honey, there's one other thing that's especially important. I never recognized it until this trip. That home back there and these mountains helped heal a wounded teenager years ago. I never want to take that away from you. This is where you need to be. Funny, but I'm pretty certain this is where *we* need to be too."

Still seated, Russell turned to Sandra and held her hand.

"You are amazing, simply amazing. I don't deserve you. I really don't."

Sandra smiled and laughed. "You're right about that. You got the best end of the deal."

After a minute's lull, Russell concluded, "Esther would say that we need to sleep on this. Let's do that and talk about it more in the morning."

The couple stood and caressed. "Russell, I only ask one thing if we go through with this."

"What's that?"

"I pick where we retire."

He smiled. "Done deal. I repeat—done deal."

"Aren't you curious about where that's going to be?"

"Sure. Ask me in twenty years."

41

WINTER 2005
COLBY, NC
LAS VEGAS, NV

———

Pratt County High School received a phone call in mid-January. It was transferred to Russell in his empty classroom as he graded tests during an open period.

"Hello, Mr. Rankin. Is this Russell Rankin of Colby, North Carolina?

"Yes, ma'am. This is he."

"Oh, good. My name is Carol Doherty. I work as a senior nurse for hospice in Las Vegas. I'm calling about your mother, Loretta Packer, who is a patient in our care. I understand that your mother has not had any contact with you since you were a teenager."

Russell was stunned and remained silent.

"Mr. Rankin, are you still there?"

"Oh, I'm here. Just surprised at the news, that's all." Surprised was an understatement.

"Well, I'm calling you because she requested that we attempt to find you. She has been in hospice care here in Las Vegas for the past week at a nursing home specializing in treatment of the terminally ill."

Russell interrupted, "How did you locate me, anyway?"

"One of our employees is very good at finding lost relatives. Your NFL career made it pretty easy."

"Anyway, Mr. Rankin, I'm sorry to report that your mother is in the final stages of lung cancer. Doctors estimate that she has perhaps a week to live at best. She is on full oxygen. Her voice is extremely frail. She doesn't have the strength to call you herself. She's totally bedridden."

After a lengthy silence, Russell responded, "And where is she now?"

"It's called the Regency Health Service located just east of the UNLV campus."

"She asked to see me?"

"Yes, sir, that's correct – you and your sister."

"Ms. Docherty…"

"Doherty."

"I'm sorry. Ms. Doherty, this comes as a complete shock out of nowhere. My sister and I haven't had any contact with our mother for over twenty years." Russell took a deep breath and a lengthy pause. "I'm a high school teacher and a class of mine starts in less than ten minutes, so there is no way I can give you a definitive answer, not right now. Plus, I need to run this by my wife and sister."

"I understand."

After taking down needed contact information, Russell expressed gratitude for the call. This was one of the infrequent times when he would lean on high school administration to find a sub for his final class of the day.

On arriving home, Russell found Sandra absent, most likely running errands.

Russell found the phone number for Guardian Travel in Sexton and placed a call to Ruth Ellen Heck, a travel agent with whom he had worked since moving to North Carolina.

"Ruth Ellen, this is Russell Rankin"

"Oh, hello, Russell. How've you been? It's been awhile."

"Well, it could be better. I have a family emergency in Las Vegas, and I need you to work on two tickets to Las Vegas for tomorrow morning."

"I'm sorry to hear that, Russell. What about a return date?"

"That's got to be open-ended since we don't know how long we'll be there."

"Greensboro or Charlotte?"

"Doesn't matter. Just not super early."

"What about a rental car and hotel?"

"I'll work on that later tonight. I just need to know my options on the flights."

"OK, I'll get right on this. I'll call you later today when I have some flights and prices."

"Sure thing. Thanks, Ruth Ellen. I should be home and easy to catch when you call back."

Russell grabbed a ginger ale from the refrigerator and plopped down in his favorite lounge chair in the family room. He closed his eyes, clasped his hands behind his head, and attempted to make sense of the unsettling news from Las Vegas.

It had been almost twenty-four years since his last contact with Loretta.

There had been vague rumors that she was living in Las Vegas or Reno, but neither Russell nor Rachel attempted any follow-up. Loretta never had any interest in sports so she might not even know of Russell's accomplishments within professional football. She may have actually hidden her relationship to Russell for fear that the abandonment of her children would become an issue.

Despite her abrupt forsaking of her children in 1982, Russell felt no hesitation; he would leave for Las Vegas the next day. And while Sandra and he needed private time to process the news, her nature would likely be to accompany him on the trip.

Russell knew Rachel would react far differently. Out of obligation, he phoned her at her home in Hawaii and left a message.

On hanging up the phone, he heard the garage door open, signaling Sandra's arrival. Her hurried steps up the basement stairs suggested she was concerned about Russell's presence in the home at this time of day.

Sandra arrived in the kitchen, carrying two bags of groceries, and she noticed Russell slumped in his lounge chair. "Honey, why are you home so early? Is everything OK? Anything wrong?"

Turning from his chair to look at her, Russell responded, "It's about my mother. She's in hospice care in Las Vegas with only a few days to live. I got a call at school after lunch. I'm leaving in the morning. You're free to come along if we can get things covered for the kids."

Sandra joined her husband in the family room, and he rose to hug her. She said softly "I'm so sorry, honey. This is such a shock. I'll do whatever you want."

"I'd never force this on you. This is my ordeal to deal with."

"My only issue is how long we might be there," Sandra said. "Plus, we need to line up Aunt Helen or someone else if she can't help out. Let me call her right now. I want to go, or I should say, I need to go."

Sandra shook her head slowly in continued disbelief. "Does Rachel know?"

"No, not yet. I need to call her."

The couple hugged again, and Russell whispered in Sandra's ear, "Thank you, darlin'. I'm so lucky to have you."

* * *

Russell called Rachel late in the evening North Carolina time. After the short greetings, he got straight to the point.

"Rach, I got a call this afternoon from a hospice center in Las Vegas. Loretta has a few days to live. She's dying from lung cancer."

Rachel didn't respond for several seconds. When she did, as too often was her style, it was with cruel insensitivity. "So what do you want me to do?

Get all choked up? Drop everything and fly to Vegas to watch the woman who abandoned us die? Is that what you're asking for, Russell, huh?"

Showing characteristic composure, Russell gently answered, "Rach, I'm simply letting you know, that's all. I'm not asking for anything. I'm just giving you the news. You know what I know."

Rachel continued her harsh retort. "And I suppose you're dumb enough to fly to Vegas and hold her hand while the woman dies. Am I right? Oh, I know I'm right because that's your style, Russell."

Before Russell could answer, she added, "How'd you find out anyway? How'd they track you down?"

"Some hospice employee, but Loretta wanted us to know, that's what the nurse said."

"*Loretta wanted us to know.*" Oh, I'll bet she does. Now, after abandoning two kids over twenty years ago, just up and leaving, she's reaching out. Oh, this is just beautiful. This is just stellar. Just so perfect. Russell, you're so predictable, and I know you're dumb enough to fly out there. All I have to say to our darling mother is that I know. That's all. Be sure to let her know that I know."

"I'm flying out in the morning. Rach. I'll call you when I get back."

Knowing that any further conversation would be pointless, he ended the phone call.

Sandra entered the room just as Russell hung up the phone.

"How'd it go?"

"The way we know it would. And she thinks *I'm* predictable."

★ ★ ★

Aunt Helen came through as usual and agreed to care for the children. Uncle George would help out as well, which was an added plus.

Sue Ellen had suggested an 11:35 a.m. departing flight the next day out of Greensboro, and after a short layover in Dallas, Russell and Sandra boarded their connecting flight to Las Vegas. By 4:15 p.m., they were in a rental car on the way to the hospice facility.

On entering the bland, one-story building, Russell and Sandra met with a nurse, who had been briefed on the couple's pending arrival.

"Mr. and Mrs. Rankin, I'm Lorraine Phyllis. I hope your traveling went well under the circumstances. It's good that you got here when you did since your mother doesn't have much time left. She's been fading the past forty-eight hours. She may not be conscious when you visit her. Poor thing is likely under ninety pounds by now. Plus, she's on oxygen and morphine. You need to prepare yourselves because her appearance is probably not like anything you might remember or expect."

Nurse Phyllis escorted them to Loretta's small single room. Despite supposed readiness to meet her, Russell and Sandra were aghast at Loretta's appearance. In response, Sandra grabbed Russell's arm and quietly gasped. "Oh, Russell, she looks so pathetic. This just breaks my heart." Sandra began to sob.

To reassure Sandra, he tapped her hand as they sat down by the bed. The woman, laboring to breathe, held little resemblance to Russell's mother. She wore a frayed pink nightgown that seemed sizes too large. Her salt-and-pepper hair was unruly and badly in need of a beautician's attention. Her face was thin and drawn with protruding cheekbones. Dark circles underscored her eyes, her lips were dry and peeling, and she had purple blotches on her thin arms. Her hands were bony, the veins raised and purplish.

Russell cupped Loretta's hand in his, and gently said, "Momma, it's me, Russell." There was no response.

"I don't know if you can hear me or not, Momma, but it's me, Russell." Again, there was no response.

Russell continued to hold her unresponsive hand, and in the process, he was surprised that his thoughts of his near sixteen years with his mother turned warm and positive. The negative recollections, the poor decisions, even her unthinkable desertion started to wane. Russell saw through Loretta's pale wrinkled skin and frail body to recall the beautiful woman she had been during his childhood.

Memories locked away for decades tumbled forth—"remnant" dough-nuts from the Scandia bakery, dollar matinee movies at the Gem Theater, free summer concerts at DeMooy Park, the countless bus rides across Lancaster, the Stavros Brothers' Restaurant and Otis, Lancaster's Fourth of July parade, Loretta's love of Fruit Loops and nonpareil candy. The more Russell thought, the more fond memories returned.

Another nurse interrupted his thoughts to check Loretta's vital signs, and he noticed Sandra's absence from the room. He assumed she was visiting a restroom.

"You must be Russell." The nurse smiled. Russell stood and shook her hand.

"Yes, ma'am."

"Even though she may not be able to show it, I'm sure your mother is thankful for your presence.

"How is she?"

"The hospice nurse is the real expert here, and she'll be back tomorrow morning, but to answer your question, your mother is fading quickly. She's a fighter, though. There's still some kick in that frail, little body of hers. Her vital signs are poor. You can see from her sporadic breathing that she's strug-gling. The best we can do is limit the pain and discomfort as much as possible. That's why your presence here is so important."

Sandra returned to the room and gently massaged Russell's neck and shoulders.

"Thank you, and your name is?" Russell said to the nurse. "Andrea."

"Andrea, this is my wife, Sandra."

"My pleasure to meet you." Andrea turned to leave the room. "Likewise, thank you for taking such good care of Loretta."

Loretta issued a weak groan, interrupting the conversation. For the first time, her eyes opened, and she stared straight ahead, seemingly unaware of anyone in her company.

"Hey, Momma, it's Russell." He grasped her hand a little tighter.

Loretta remained unresponsive, staring directly at the gray wall before her. "It's good to see you, Momma, after all these years. It really is."

She slowly lost her grip on Russell's hand, and he motioned for Sandra to join him bedside.

"This is Sandra, my wife."

Ten minutes of light chatter followed, Loretta oblivious to words and movement. Sandra left the room again to call Aunt Helen and check on the children. In returning, she reassured, "Everything's under control. Aunt Helen said Anna was a little whiney this morning, but the kids are both doing fine."

"That's good. Listen, here's what I'm thinkin'. Maybe around six, why don't we drive over to the motel and check in? I'll come back here to stay for the night, but I'll return in the morning to shower and eat breakfast. That way, you can get a decent night's sleep."

"But what about you?"

"That chair in the corner reclines. You know me. Just like Esther, I can sleep anywhere."

The couple agreed to the plan, and in short order, Russell delivered Sandra to the Holiday Inn, then returned to his mother's side. The scene had not changed.

He took his same bedside position and again clasped Loretta's unresponsive hand in his. He began a ramble of additional childhood memories that took no real order or form. Throughout his monologue, Loretta remained quiet and still.

During his discourse, he lost eye contact with her, focusing on their entwined hands instead. To Russell's astonishment, Loretta had slowly shifted

293

her head toward him, opened her eyes, and attempted a feeble smile from her dry, trembling lips.

Russell smiled back. "Hey, Momma—it's Russell." Loretta's hold on his hand tightened slightly.

The visual connection lasted less than a minute. She soon closed her eyes and softened her grip. Russell rose, kissed Loretta on the forehead, and exited the room to take a needed break.

Russell realized he had not had any dinner and remembered a twenty-four-hour diner across the street. He informed Nurse Andrea of his destination, returning shortly with a disappointing takeout order.

Russell dozed intermittently in a recliner as Loretta experienced a restless night. With her condition unchanged in the morning, Russell kissed Loretta on the cheek and hurried off to the Holiday Inn as planned for a quick shave and shower. He returned with Sandra to continue their visit with Loretta around 9:10 a.m.

The nurse on duty intercepted them and informed that Loretta had passed at 8:20 a.m., only a few minutes after Russell had left the building.

The attending physician was currently in an office signing the death certificate of a woman who left no will, no possessions, and no trace of history since 1982. The cause of death on the death certificate read: lung cancer, cardiac arrest.

42

AUGUST 1, 2009
COLBY, NC

———

RUSSELL sat contentedly with his cup of freshly brewed coffee on one of the four white rocking chairs that graced the wraparound front porch of the family's farmhouse. One of Sandra's requests in the decision to relocate and raise their family in Pratt County was the design of a home similar to the one in which she was raised in Wisconsin.

The home had taken almost a year to build with the property situated contiguous to Grandma Esther's land. The home provided a marvelous view of the Blue Ridge to the north. It also included a tennis court and a swimming pool, which were heavily used by the family. On this pleasant July morning, Russell thought his current seat as peaceful a spot as could be found anywhere.

Sandra and the children had flown to Wisconsin the day before for a long week with her family. Roger and Anna favored these excursions for the playtime with cousins and the lavish attention doted on them by their only set of living grandparents.

Russell was up early as was his nature. He had at least an hour until he intended to visit the Farmer's Market at the county fairgrounds and decided to spend some time at The Point. Last spring, he had cut a crude path through the woods connecting the family properties, which while still traversable, had become overgrown.

Even though passage on the rarely used trail would wet his shoes and trousers and expose him to an abundance of glistening spider webs, Russell, with a freshened coffee mug in hand, grabbed a worn towel from the kitchen to begin his short hike to The Point.

Upon his arrival, Russell, found the ancient Adirondacks coated in dew. He dried off a chair and coated himself with sunscreen as a wise caution to the summer sun.

History was repeating itself, thought Russell. On these same chairs, his grandfather and grandmother had sat and carefully reviewed life's events while forging major family decisions.

On these same chairs, Russell had shared conversations with Grandma Esther, Aunt Helen, Rachel, and even his former high school girlfriend, April McNaughton. For Russell, this vantage was part classroom, part counseling office, and part cathedral, with the view always soothing and reassuring. As was Grandma Esther's practice, Russell began an unhurried review of family members and events.

Esther was now eighty-eight years old. Despite having suffered a mild stroke three years ago, she remained alert, healthy, and active. She still drove, did most of her own shopping, and attempted to complete a daily crossword puzzle. She remained active with her church despite relinquishing her music responsibilities when her second husband, Judge Harlan Ballard, died from pancreatic cancer.

Esther's sister, Libbie, eighty-six, lived in an assisted living retirement facility north of Charlotte. Relocating to live with Esther in Colby was considered, but Libbie rejected the option, to Esther's understanding for medical reasons. Like her older sister, with whom she talked daily by phone, she remained active and independent with an array of loyal friends. When transportation could be arranged within the family, Libbie visited the Homestead for extended weekends.

Even on Harlan's passing in 2001, Esther continued to live at home, rejecting all suggestions of any alternate living arrangements. She adamantly declared, "This will always be home to me. As long as I can still fend for myself, bathe, dress, make my meals, why would I reckon to leave?"

Phone calls from Esther's children were frequent. Russell, Sandra, Andrew, and Helen visited routinely to assist with errands and home maintenance.

With weather permitting and with Helen's assistance, Esther visited her husbands' gravesites at the Methodist Church cemetery on a regular basis. She would take a folding wooden chair, borrowed from the church basement, to the grave sites and sit and hold what she called "conversations" with her departed partners, ending each visit with a prayer and a finger kiss to the gravestones.

She visited Peter's grave as well. These conversations were more painful. Even decades later, she remained riddled with guilt acknowledging that she and the family should have kept better connected with Peter over the years.

Russell never lost recognition that his relocation to North Carolina had been Rachel's as well. Her middle school and high school years were less accomplished than Russell's. Her high school years proved difficult, and her disagreements with Esther during this rough stretch nearly prompted her moving in with Aunt Helen. On many occasions during Russell's years at McClendon, Rachel had called him, upset and angry. Lengthy conversations were held to hear her grievances and suggest coping strategies between Rachel and Esther.

The majority of Rachel's wrongdoing during her high school years was school-related. She had occasional run-ins with teachers and counselors due to her flip attitude, obstinate behavior, and conflicts with female peers. Rachel made average to below-average grades in high school. During her senior year, the focus of school personnel was simply to nurture Rachel's academics to ensure graduation.

To the surprise of many, including most family members, Rachel decided to enlist in the U.S. Navy upon graduating from high school. Recognizing her lack of drive and direction, she sought military service by design for the structure and discipline that she lacked. Russell was as surprised as anyone with his sister's decision.

On a March Saturday during Rachel's senior year, Aunt Helen escorted Rachel to a naval recruitment station in Winston-Salem to begin the enlistment process. Rachel passed all initial requirements, and by mid-summer, she entered the U.S. Navy, completing her eight weeks of boot camp with high ratings.

Rachel built a successful twenty-two-year naval career as a meteorologist, or aerographer as recognized in Navy terms, that included balanced exposures to fleet and shore duty. Her shore assignments included Norfolk, Jacksonville, Memphis, Pensacola, and most recently Honolulu. Her fleet assignments were to aircraft carriers and guided missile cruisers.

During her navy years, Rachel earned bachelor and master degrees in meteorology and became a naval instructor in meteorology and atmospheric science. Never married, she resided with a retired disabled navy veteran, Ray Esslinger, in a house that they jointly purchased in Honolulu.

Russell, Sandra, Roger, and Anna made annual visits to Hawaii to visit Aunt Rachel and Uncle Ray, while Rachel returned every fall to visit family in Pratt County.

Despite her physical distance from North Carolina, Rachel remained loyal to Grandma Esther and Aunt Helen; however, her relationship with Russell had suffered over the years. Some family members had speculated that Russell's NFL success was the wedge between brother and sister. Regardless, sister and brother had grown closer in recent years since Loretta's death.

Aunt Helen continued to work as the county librarian, although at age sixty-nine, she was nearing and accepting of retirement. She and George still lived in Rex. Their married daughters, Charlotte and Grace, lived out of county, raising three grandsons between them.

Uncle Daniel had filed for divorce in 1997 due to Aunt Janice's ongoing affair with a divorced Charlotte investor. On a positive note, Daniel received a handsome advancement when he took a regional manager's job with Food

Lion that same year. He now lived in a Charlotte suburb in close proximity to his Aunt Libbie.

Uncle Andrew continued to reside locally with his wife, Christa. He had embraced the role of stepfather and most recently grandfather. His auto-repair business remained prosperous. Since 2007, he operated a renewed venture, a successful airport shuttle agency servicing Charlotte and Greensboro airports from a three-county area.

Esther kept a current ledger of birthdays and anniversaries and remained current with cards and phone calls in recognizing family milestones. Lester and Esther had produced four children, eight grandchildren, and at last count, thirteen great-grandchildren. She also maintained contact with Judge Ballard's son, Ethan, and his family.

To Russell's delight, Sandra grew to love her adopted home in the Blue Ridge. With ease, she embraced the history and culture of the region, but it was the people who were the real allure. She was well received by locals because of her unpretentious demeanor and sincere interest in others, winning ready acceptance and loyal friends. She was an active member at Colby United Methodist Church and now taught Sunday school, a development that delighted Esther.

Sandra also found fulfillment and success in writing and producing the Nancy Cutter documentary, capturing a prestigious national award for a first-time documentarian. She was well on her way toward writing the story of Nancy Cutter's life, which included the raising of eight children in a four-room mountain cabin.

Roger Rankin, now six, more physically resembled the Rankin side of the family. Roger was a capable student, who loved the outdoors and camping out on the family property. Even at this early age, Roger was enthralled by science, a trait uncommon to both of his parents. His prime interest was biology, and on his own, he collected and identified insects and leaves from the home property's fields and forests. Frequently accompanied by the family's two golden labs, Roger enjoyed exploring local creeks in his quest for fish, frogs, turtles, salamanders, and snakes, a practice that continued to unsettle Sandra.

Outside of his scientific orientation, Roger was active in Cub Scouts, a Carlsen family tradition, and youth soccer, seemingly displaying little interest in football, an indifference that left Russell unfazed.

Anna, born in 2005, was an active and strikingly beautiful four-year-old, who was tightly attached to Sandra. Sandra referred to Anna as her "little shadow," because she wished to do nearly everything in Sandra's company. Renewing some Rankin family history, Anna began taking piano lessons, practicing on an aged upright oak piano. Great-grandmother Esther found particular joy in Anna's musical focus, providing enthusiastic mentoring to her great-granddaughter during regular visits to The Homestead.

In concluding the review, Russell did something unnatural. He considered his own personal status with his chosen vocation. He was now completing his fifth year of teaching high school American History, and in the process, had fallen in love with the job.

Teaching was not a necessity since Russell's NFL earnings had been wisely invested over the years. He was now part owner of two golf courses in North Carolina and a small airport in southern Virginia. He had also partnered with a former Eagle teammate in the startup of barbeque restaurants in Lenoir and Boone.

To the surprise of very few, he was also coaching high school football, the first two years as an offensive assistant to Mo Wilkes, who stepped down in 2006 after almost three decades as the Ridge Runners' head coach. Russell's decision to accept the head coaching position was predicated upon Coach Mo remaining on staff as defensive coordinator.

Russell's won–loss record after three years was unremarkable. Regardless, during those three seasons, there was a marked increase in students signing up for high school football, primarily because Coach Rankin did everything possible to secure game time for all players. While demanding of his players, he made practices fun, keeping the season fresh into late October. Coach Rankin also became known for trick plays, at least one a game, which further endeared him to his players and fans.

Russell realized that the Blue Ridge was heating up on this summer Saturday. He patted his perspiring face and neck with the old towel. He adjusted his baseball cap and checked his watch; it was time to head to the Farmer's Market. On the return walk to the house, he smiled in anticipation of a houseguest who was scheduled to arrive next week for a brief visit.

On the return walk to the house, he smiled in anticipation of a houseguest who was scheduled to arrive next week for a brief visit.

Russell had not seen this old friend since a summer football camp held in 2000. Sandra and Coach Mo Wilkes were equally excited in meeting this influential force during Russell's adolescence. Now retired and relocating to live with his daughter's family in Mississippi, Brad Terrell, was scheduled to arrive late Friday afternoon after an all-day drive from Illinois.

4 3

AUGUST 1, 2009
COLBY, NC

———

IN his family's absence, Russell had no excuse not to visit the Farmer's Market held Saturday mornings at the county fairgrounds. This visit was only his third of the summer.

Sweet corn was on the shopping list as well as a plump, ripe mountain-grown watermelon. The ride back home would include a necessary stop at the Colby Volunteer Fire Department's barbeque pit for a whole barbequed chicken that would last Russell through the weekend.

The short drive to the fairgrounds was uneventful, and within ten minutes of visiting the Farmer's Market, he was welcomed by a lost, yet familiar voice.

"Russell, Russell, damn, is that you?"

Instantly recognizing the voice, he turned to see April McNaughton, who he had last seen at their fifteenth high school reunion in 1999.

April ran to hug a blushing Russell, the tight embrace lingering longer than was custom.

Breaking away, she said, "Oh, it's so good to see you, Russell. You're looking fabulous. What a treat running into you, of all places, at the Farmer's Market?"

Puzzled by his standoffishness, April probed, "Well, aren't you the least bit pleased to see your former high school sweetheart?"

April's surprise presence disarmed Russell and muddled his thoughts and emotions.

After gaining composure, Russell spoke from the heart. "April you look wonderful, just marvelous. Life must be treating you well. I'm just so surprised running into you like this."

April was clearly appreciative of Russell's attention.

Russell could have said much more. He had not seen April in a decade, and during that hiatus, her physique had remained thin and well-toned. Her green eyes were still striking, but the freckles that she had despised as a teenager had softened. Her blond hair, still long, was fixed in a simple ponytail. April had matured into a very attractive forty-three-year old woman.

Taking control, April grasped Russell's hand, walking him to a nearby covered seating area where they soon sat opposite to one another at an aluminum picnic table.

They eagerly caught up on family news, but April was noticeably guarded about her private life. She was back home for an extended weekend visiting her parents, who were still living at their home near Waverly. April continued to reside in Atlanta, working as a pediatric surgeon.

In discussing his immediate family, Russell carelessly revealed that his wife and children were away visiting relatives in Wisconsin. Seizing the opportunity, April suggested they grab some burgers at Slappy's for old times' sake and continue their meeting at a favorite old haunt, Mount. Wilcox State Park.

In less than a half hour, with all thoughts of shopping at the Farmer's Market suspended, Russell and April were finishing off their Slappy's order under aged oaks and sycamores in a nearly deserted picnic area adjacent to the Dunn Falls trailhead.

April grew pensive, stating that she needed to share something that Russell must keep confidential.

Impacted by her serious tone, he agreed as he consumed a final French fry.

Avoiding eye contact, April stared at the shelter's concrete floor and quietly revealed, "Matt and I are getting a divorce; it's mutual. I signed the divorce papers last week before driving up here. At least the legal trauma is over. It should all be over by Labor Day."

Russell was stunned, completely unprepared for the announcement. He was speechless and unable to offer any worthwhile follow-up. An uneasy silence developed.

"It's one thing getting a divorce, but it's the circumstances that're so hard to accept."

Their eyes met, and April took firm grasp of his hand resting on the table. Her eyes were now moistening, her voice shaken and weak, "Matt left me for another doctor."

Russell's response was genuine and from the heart as he shook his head. "Oh, no, April. I'm so sorry. I really am."

April released her grip. Her voice rose then weakened. "Can you believe it, Russell, a dermatologist? His name is William Farrell. That's right, Russell. My husband left me, after fourteen years of marriage and two daughters, for a man, and I never saw it coming."

Russell sighed, searching for any supportive response.

The couple's silence was broken by the annoying sound of a private plane that was casually patrolling the park at low altitude.

April dabbed her eyes with a Slappy's napkin and rose to cross the table to sit next to Russell.

Taking a presumptuous lead, April took refuge in Russell's arms as her sobbing continued in short, jerky waves, at times almost causing April to lose her breath. Growing more uncomfortable, Russell gazed into the woods for words of support.

After a brief lull, April regained her composure. "How am I supposed to accept this and move on? How do I make any fuckin' sense of this, Russell?

How?' emphasized April. "No one can. It's been over seven months now, seven fuckin' months, and everything is still so overwhelming. I still can't get a handle on this. It's nuts, just nuts."

Russell remained silent but jittery due to the couple's physical closeness.

April broke abruptly from Russell's embrace and sat up staring intently into Russell's eyes. Growing reminiscent, she said in a quivering voice, "Do you remember, back in high school sophomore year, soon after you'd moved down here, you told me that you felt your life was like a snow globe that Rachel had, that your life, like the snow in the toy, was swirling around and around out of control with no end in sight. Remember that, Russell?"

Russell nodded.

"I never told you this, but when I was in medical school, I bought a snow globe pretty much like the one that Rachel had. She showed it to me once when you invited me to Sunday dinner. I had it up until a few weeks ago. I couldn't stand lookin' at it any more. I threw the fuckin' thing away last week in the trash."

A car entering the parking briefly suspended April's recollection. Soon their eyes reconnected. April retook Russell's hand. She whimpered, "Well now, I guess it's my turn."

Still troubled by her announcement, Russell's words of support were clumsy and unremarkable. "April, I just don't know what to say. I really don't. I can only imagine how awful this has been for you and your daughters."

"It's OK, Russell. You're not alone. No one knows what to say about this, including me. My parents are as confused as anyone."

April continued gazing into Russell's eyes. "I hate being so fuckin' weak and vulnerable right now." Her voice raised. "I hate it. I just hate it!"

A minute passed. April regained a degree of composure. She again took refuge in Russell's arms. "How am I supposed to regroup and go on from this? Russell, tell me? My confidence is totally shot. My life is such a fuckin' mess because this is common knowledge at the hospital. I'm a laughing stock, Russell, a laughing stock, four years of med school, a five-year residency, a successful practice, and I'm known as much for being the female doctor who lost her husband to another man."

April waved away an annoying fly.

"How are your daughters handling all of this?"

April hesitated, growing more reflective, continuing to take refuge in Russell's presence.

"That's probably the hardest part of all. A colleague referred me to a psychologist who specializes in families going through divorce. The girls and I have been seeing a therapist for a few months now. It's helped me on a number of levels, but our oldest daughter, Taylor, is really struggling. Poor Abby is just confused, but the impact on Taylor is deeper. She's angry and withdrawn. Her grades are dropping, plus, she wants nothing to do with Matt, absolutely nothing."

Time passed, and the couple grew eerily silent. April abruptly sat up, changing the subject as she released herself from Russell's arms.

"Remember that Dolly Parton song that Esther used to sing in the kitchen, *Do I Ever Cross Your Mind?*"

A forgotten memory had been unlocked.

"I wonder now and then if I ever cross your mind?" Russell smiled but did not answer.

"Well, I think of you more than you might imagine. How our lives went in different directions."

April briefly turned her attention to an approaching car on the park's access road. She smiled and recalled another distant recollection.

"I saw you play against the Falcons in Atlanta when I was in medical school at Emory. You guys beat the Falcons by a point. I didn't pay much attention to the game except when you were on the field. I just kept staring at you on the sidelines, number four, wondering if I should be so bold as to contact you. And look where we are now."

April sat up and grew somber. She turned and rested her hands on Russell's shoulders begging with wet eyes, pleading with an unsteady voice,

"I need you so much right now, Russell. Just this, just this one time, would you?"

Russell shot up, instantly removing her grasp, his strong hands steadying on her shoulders. He had grown angry from her advance. He looked intently into her eyes and said firmly as he pressured her shoulders with his hands, "April, that's not going to happen. Not now or ever. This thing's gone too far already. You understand? Never."

April hesitated. She then sheepishly nodded her head, slowly accepting Russell's rejection as he moved to the opposite side of the table.

Silence followed, but this void was different. A page had been turned.

Now more melancholy, April said in rambling fashion, "Another brilliant fuckin' decision on my end was leaving you. I knew I would regret it. I knew it even back then at school."

The annoying private plane returned for another pass.

With his anger now checked and, in an attempt to provide some form of closure to their meeting, Russell said, "I know I haven't been any help today, but you've always been tough and resilient. That's your nature. It'll take time, but you'll take command of this and bounce back. You will. You and I both know you will."

April responded sarcastically, "Phenomenal words of consolation, Russell. Really great. That the best you can offer? Really?"

Ignoring her tone, Russell continued in a confident tone, "This is not going to defeat you or define you. It won't. You're too smart for that to happen."

Russell hesitated. It was now his turn. "There's something I never told you face to face, but." He shook his head. "Oh, I don't know. The timing's probably all wrong."

"No, you can tell me. You better fuckin' tell me with a buildup like that." April's interest was piqued as she dabbed a lingering tear with a used napkin.

Russell paused and then confessed. "I never really thanked you enough."

"Thanked me for what?"

He had April's full attention and continued in thoughtful delivery. "When I moved here, I was completely alone. I never felt more lost and alone in my life. Everything was new and different. Everything. Momma had run off. Daddy was sicker than any of us knew, and within weeks of bein' down here, he was dead. Grandma Esther and Aunt Helen couldn't have been nicer, but I barely knew them. I had no anchor, no grounding. Life just had to get better."

"Russell, where are you going with this?"

He looked at her across the picnic table with utmost sincerity. "Life got better because of you."

April was engrossed by the revelation but stunned. She remained motionless and attentive. Her eyes glistened once more.

"I don't know how everything would have worked out if you hadn't been there. I think it started at the market during our breaks together, but you helped me more with everything than anyone, just by bein' there, showin' up by yourself at Daddy's funeral, givin' a damn, listening. So, for all of that, thank you, twenty-some years later."

A short interlude passed with April trying to maintain her composure.

Avoiding eye contact, she toyed with a rubber band abandoned on the picnic table. "My mom and Esther had a talk someplace a couple years ago. I think it was something to do with the library. I don't recall who brought it up, but they both agreed and always figured we'd get married."

She gazed teary-eyed at Russell and said with an unsteady voice, "Funny, huh?"

Russell chose to inquire about April's family, a change in subject that served to relax them both.

"Daddy's fine. He's still daddy, fixin' to retire in a year or two, says his knees can't take much more hoppin' on and off the truck. He'll have more than thirty years in with UPS when he retires. Momma's still doin' her craft thing, mainly quilts, samplers, organic gardening, stuff like that."

"How 'bout Autumn?"

"Married right out of Appalachian. She teaches middle school in Wilmington where her husband runs a marina. Two boys, Jeremy and Joshua. The girls and I see them several times a year"

After another clumsy lull, April said, "I don't know, Russell," as she shook her head. "Maybe we tied up some loose ends today. I know I haven't made much sense to you about any of this. I've been all over the fuckin' place, but our time here may actually have given me some hope, even a little confidence, maybe because I'm drawing on your strength. I don't know, but today, in a strange way, might just help me move on." April paused. "I'll just have to wait and see."

April continued her play with the rubber band as she added, "When we talked at the reunion, it was so safe and superficial. Any talk between us then was so guarded with classmates millin' around, people checking us out. All I really wanted was to grab you and sit alone undisturbed at some distant table. No one else even mattered."

What strikes me the most from today is how little you've changed. You would think with your NFL success that you would be different, with a big head and everything, that you 'got above your raisin' as my Granddaddy McNaughton would say, but you haven't. That's refreshing to see, but I shouldn't be surprised, I guess."

April took a deliberate pause. "In many ways you're no different than that shy boy back in high school, the boy who became my first real love."

Their eyes locked again. April announced, "Russell, you are now who you were back then."

The couple sat silently transfixed in the intensity of the moment until Russell felt confident in April's emotional stability to drive. After April dabbed her eyes one more time, Russell rose and slowly led his one and only high school girlfriend, hand in hand, to their parked cars.

Their parting hug lingered and was accented by one gentle kiss.

April's final words were soft and poignant as she stood by her car, "You were the first, Russell, you know?" Her voice trembled. Her eyes glistened one final time. "How was I supposed to know back then that you'd be the best, the unforgettable one? How was I ever to know that?"

The former high school lovers both recognized the finality to the parting, one more accepting than the other.

Russell responded with a kind glance, and then stood quietly as April took her seat and started her car. In backing out of her parking space, she offered a light smile and weak wave. Then, she slowly proceeded down the park's access road to begin the drive to her parents' home.

Still shaken, Russell walked back to the picnic table in an attempt to make sense of all that had transpired. Seated at the table, he found the same rubber band with which April had played. He smiled and took up the band, examined it for a few seconds, and then initiated a slow, therapeutic threading of the band between his fingers.

After the third stretch, the band unexpectedly snapped and broke. Russell smiled and sat in quiet reflection for several minutes. He then left the picnic area to begin the return drive home, forgetting to make the intended stop for barbeque.

The trailhead picnic shelter to Dunn Falls would never seem the same for him. Today, it had taken on a whole new meaning.

Later that afternoon, Russell phoned Sandra in Wisconsin, and to an understanding and supportive spouse, he offered a full disclosure of the day's events with April at the Farmer's Market and Mount Wilcox State Park.

EPILOGUE

THE Pratt County High School class of 1984 held its twenty-fifth class reunion on Saturday evening, October 9, 2009, at the recently opened Pratt County Pavilion. Russell and Sandra Rankin were among the seventy-one classmates and guests in attendance.

Russell's celebrity status made him a popular draw with former classmates.

Sandra wowed the crowd, demonstrating her ease and skill in meeting and winning over complete strangers.

Drinks were downed, a forgettable buffet dinner was served, and old recollections were told, some more truthful than others. Class president Dale Troutman read announcements and emceed a trivia contest after dinner.

Later in the night, a disc jockey spun hits from the late seventies and eighties as the socializing continued. Russell tipped the disc jockey and requested the playing of Chicago's hit, *You're the Inspiration*, the tune that Russell and Sandra had adopted as their song during their courtship. No one danced that evening more than Russell and Sandra, the couple seeming oblivious to those around them.